THE PEN
FOUNDER EDIT
Editor

PIERRE CORNEILLE, t
in 1606 in Rouen, where
and worked for a time as Crown Counsel. His first
resounding success came in 1636 with *Le Cid*, which
made his reputation as a master of serious drama
and represents the first great French classical tragedy.
During the next forty years he produced over twenty-
five plays. He died in 1684.

JOHN CAIRNCROSS was educated at Glasgow
University, at the Sorbonne, and at Trinity College,
Cambridge. After a period in the British Civil Service
he settled in Rome (where he still spends much of
his time). Later, he worked for the United Nations in
Bangkok, and was for a time Head of the Depart-
ment of Romance Languages, Western Reserve
University, Cleveland. He has translated a previous
volume of three Corneille plays (*The Cid, Cinna* and
The Theatrical Illusion) and six of Racine's tragedies
(in two volumes, *Phaedra and Other Plays* and *Andro-
mache and Other Plays*), all for the Penguin Classics.
He is the author of *Molière bourgeois et libertin, New
Light on Molière,* and *After Polygamy Was Made a Sin.*

Pierre Corneille

POLYEUCTUS
THE LIAR
NICOMEDES

Translated and introduced by
JOHN CAIRNCROSS

PENGUIN BOOKS

Penguin Books Ltd, Harmondsworth, Middlesex, England
Penguin Books, 625 Madison Avenue, New York, New York 10022, U.S.A.
Penguin Books Australia Ltd, Ringwood, Victoria, Australia
Penguin Books Canada Ltd, 2801 John Street, Markham, Ontario, Canada L3R 1
Penguin Books (N.Z.) Ltd, 182–190 Wairau Road, Auckland 10, New Zealand

—

First published 1980

—

—

Made and printed in Great Britain
by Richard Clay (The Chaucer Press) Ltd,
Bungay, Suffolk
Set in Monotype Garamond

To BILLIE AND LESTER – *the perfect friends*

CONTENTS

TRANSLATOR'S FOREWORD

The present volume – the second of the Penguin Corneille – rounds off the list of the great French playwright's better-known works. In fact, the six plays coincide with those in the handy Hachette anthology except that the early comedy, *The Theatrical Illusion* (in volume one in my translation*), replaces *Horatius*, the sombre tragedy of Corneille's great creative period. This selection should make reference to the French original fairly easy, though all six plays have been extensively – and ably – edited in separate volumes.

Both *Polyeuctus* and *Nicomedes* are Roman plays, but approach Rome from the rather unusual angle of respectively Christianity on the eve of victory and the independent kingdoms in Asia Minor opposing territorial expansion. In both cases, the clash heightens the dramatic excitement of the play. *Polyeuctus* belongs, like *The Cid* and *Cinna*, to the central period of Corneille's well-known masterpieces, while *Nicomedes* is the sole of his later works to have been deemed worthy of ranking as a classic. Although, in the translator's opinion, neither work is in Corneille's very first flight, they are both outstanding, and their study is essential for a comprehension of Corneille's genius. *The Liar*, a comedy of prodigious verve, ends the central phase of his work, and makes one regret that he did not devote more of his seemingly endless energy to such effervescent efforts. I have deliberately tried to transpose the style into a modern key, since, apart from certain romanesque and contemporary fixtures, the comedy has a timeless gaiety and verve, and lends itself easily to performance in any age or language.

JOHN CAIRNCROSS

* *Pierre Corneille: The Cid/Cinna/The Theatrical Illusion*, translated by John Cairncross, Penguin Classics, 1975.

PIERRE CORNEILLE

FATE has dealt unkindly with the great seventeenth-century French dramatist, Pierre Corneille, even in his native land. 'As a result of an over-simple and restrictive tradition,' writes Raymond Picard in his admirable analysis of the writer,[1]

it has long been contended that, of all Corneille's plays, only a handful of tragedies such as *Le Cid, Horace, Cinna*, or *Pompée* (1637–43) deserve to survive. By disregarding all the rest, critics have had no trouble in reducing Corneille's genius to a few dramatic devices, some psychological stances and a certain lofty tone, and thus, by an obvious over-simplification, they have frozen the founder of the classical theatre in a pose of exaggerated sublimity.

But in fact

his thirty-two plays show a prodigious range of talent. Far from having worked to a formula, Corneille again and again struck out in original directions, renewing his strength and genius over forty long years of writing. His work pulsates with an extraordinary creative vitality. A tragedy follows a comedy or a tragicomedy; a tragedy-ballet comes after a heroic comedy; and within the same genre there are profound differences between the plays.

His first plays are poles apart from the stereotype of the bombastic tragedies he is represented as having written. 'With such works as *Mélite, La Galerie du Palais* and *La Place Royale* (1629–34), he created an original type of five-act comedy in verse.' They are remarkable for 'the naturalness, the freshness and the grace of the young people [portrayed], the badinage and the wit, the truth to life of the attitudes, the penetrating observation of the manners of the age – all in a simple colloquial style'. As Corneille himself pointed out (in 1634), 'My vein . . .

1. *Two Centuries of French Literature*, pp. 66–82.

often combines the lofty buskin with the comic sock, and ... pleases the audience by striking contrasting notes.'

But, at about the same time as Corneille wrote these three 'contemporary' comedies, he produced in *Clitandre* an Elizabethan play in which fantasy runs wild. The stage changes from a wood to a prison, and then to a cave. Before the spectator's eyes, Pymantes tries to rape Dorisa who in her turn puts out one of his eyes. Frenzied, utterly impossible actions are enacted in an entirely fanciful world.

The Theatrical Illusion (*L'Illusion Comique*), dated 1636, also takes place in this world of fantasy; the irrepressible Corneille even parodies the martial sentiments of *The Cid* before that play was written.

What is more, though he

appealed much more to the mind than to the eye in four or five of the finest tragedies of the seventeenth century ... he continued to delight and astonish visually ... 'My main aim,' he wrote of the musical play of *Andromède*, 'has been to satisfy the visual sense by the gorgeousness and the variety of the scenery and not to appeal to the intellect by cogent arguments or to touch the heart by delicate representations of the passion.'

The second obstacle to Corneille's demummification is the old but tenacious fallacy that his plays represent a school-book conflict, especially in *The Cid*, between

love which is alleged to be a passion replete with weaknesses and honour which dictates duty. The carefully pondered love, which one feels for and claims from someone whom one deems worthy of it, is also a duty. Rodrigo goes so far as to affirm in a lyrical meditation at the end of the first act

> Duty's not only to my mistress. It
> Is also to my father.

Moreover, the two types of duty do not really conflict. If he does not avenge the insult done to his father, Rodrigo will draw down on himself the contempt of Ximena and will thereby forfeit her love for him, for that love implies esteem and even admiration. Paradoxically it is his love for her, as well as his honour, that forces him to kill his sweetheart's father and thus to raise an obstacle between the two lovers which might to some appear insurmountable. As soon as Rodrigo has transcended the basic option between cowardice which would have involved the loss of everything – honour and love – and heroism, which is his vocation, he has no alternative but to fulfil his destiny as a hero. In this as in other tragedies, what is *cornélien* is the intolerable and sometimes agonizing situation in which the character is trapped and from which he can free himself only by shouldering his responsibility as a hero.

Now, as it happens, Corneille's characters are nothing if not heroes. Rodrigo, Horace, Augustus and Nicomedes are of more than human stature. Endowed with extraordinary moral strength, they possess to the utmost degree the virtue of *générosité* (nobility of soul); they are ready to devote all their inner resources to the task of incarnating their sublime image of themselves. Will-power, self-control, courage and judgement, all these enhance man's powers and his greatness. In the humanist world in which they live, it would seem that nothing – misfortune, suffering or catastrophe – can undermine their overweening integrity. Fortified by their energy and stoicism, they have nothing to fear at the hands of Destiny. They will parry its blows, or bear them uncomplainingly. Fate may dog their steps. For them, it is nothing but a congeries of external accidents and mishaps, and it is powerless to force an entry into their hearts and alter their resolve. Man is entirely free and fully responsible. He has no grounds for dreading the gods. When treating the most sombre theme in Greek tragedy, Corneille in his *Oedipe* (1659) radically transforms the spirit of the legend and does not shrink from writing

> The heavens, fair in reward and punishment,
> To give to deeds their penalty or meed
> Must offer us their aid, then let us act.

This concept of free will is clearly borrowed from the Jesuits and the humanist tradition. The tragic element in Corneille, then, is not to be sought in the pathetic helplessness of the characters but in the harrowing circumstances in which a wicked fate has placed them. What we have, in a way, is a tragedy of circumstances, over which the hero must rise superior, relying on his own forces.

But he does so only after exacting and grievous efforts. Corneille's characters are no cardboard supermen. For them, heroism is not a second nature to which they need merely abandon themselves. They are not sublime automata. They know what suffering is, and they sometimes vent their feelings in lyrical stanzas and in monologues. They are tugged this way and that. They are rent by inner conflicts, and they admit as much. Ximena confesses that Rodrigo 'tears [her] heart to pieces'; but she adds, it is 'without dividing [her] soul' (III, 3); Pauline also, in *Polyeucte*, recognizes that her duty 'tears her soul' although it 'does not alter its resolve' (II, 2). There is no doubt that we must jettison the half-baked concept of the swashbuckling Cornelian hero, always sure of himself and unhesitatingly sublime, whose greatness is manifested primarily in a swaggering boastfulness. Even Augustus (in *Cinna*) complains of having 'a wavering heart' (IV, 3). It is only at the end of the play when he proves victorious over himself that he exclaims (and this is more wishful thinking than actual fact):

I'm master of myself as of the world. (V, 3)

There is a quivering sensitivity at loggerheads with itself, a three-dimensional reality, in these characters who are too readily described as being all of a piece. Heroism is not something already conferred on them. It is conquered stage by stage as the action unfolds. The hero takes shape before the spectator's eyes. People are not born heroes, they become heroes. Corneille's Theatre is, in the literal sense of the phrase, 'a school of moral greatness'.

This greatness is not always synonymous with goodness and virtue. A great crime is also a great deed. Moral power and energy are important in their own right and not only because of the enterprises on which they are brought to bear. Thus, Cleopatra's crimes in *Rodogune* (1644) 'are accompanied by a moral greatness which has something so grandiose about it,' notes Corneille, 'that, at the same time as we detest her actions, we admire the source from which they spring' (*First Discourse*). What one has to do is to arouse in the spectators' hearts a feeling of astonishment, indeed a transport, whether of horror or admiration, at the deeds of which man is capable at the summit of his powers. Now in Corneille the hero arrives at this paroxysm only when the society in which he lives and his place in it are challenged, when his *gloire* – that is, his dignity, his reputation, his honour – are at stake, as well as the safety of the state. Political interests are regarded as providing the hero with the best opportunity and means for their fulfilment. Hence their important role in this theatre. Love, as against this, remains in the background, for tragedy 'calls for some great issue of state ... and seeks to arouse fears for setbacks which are more serious than the loss of one's mistress'. In *Sertorius* (1662), one character asks

> When plans of such importance are conceived,
> Can one put in the balance thoughts of love? (I, 3)

And in the same play, another character gives the following advice:

> Let us, my lord, let's leave for petty souls
> This lowly give and take of amorous sighs. (I, 3)

Love, which is convincingly portrayed in many guises in such a host of characters, may prove their downfall. It cannot shape their destiny.

It could be added that the particular type of heroism analysed by Picard is not to be found in the early works. It is only in *The Royal Square* (1634) that we find the first traces of the conviction which was to pervade all his later plays – that the hero must retain his inner, moral independence, especially in love. The dominant note until then is 'a joyous lust for life, a certain cruelty, a pronounced taste for women in their simplest and most sensual aspects, a love for sword play and adventure'. There is no trace, for example, of his subsequent ideals in *The Theatrical Illusion*, which has the same freshness and fantasy as some of Shakespeare's comedies. In the same way, Corneille was uninhibited by the famous three unities which demanded that the central subject be closely knit, the scene unchanging, and the action confined to the space of twenty-four hours.

In *The Cid*, on the contrary, the new heroic ideal is the driving force in the minds and acts of the main characters, as Picard has so lucidly shown. But in that play there is such a powerful charge of youthful passion and excitement and such a balance between richness of episode and tautness of construction that the work is free from pompousness, unreal heroism or contrivance.

However, *The Cid*, though universally popular and the first masterpiece of the classical French stage, came under heavy fire from the playwright's rivals and was later submitted (in 1637) by Cardinal Richelieu to the newly founded French Academy (the literary establishment of the day) which was to act as an arbiter between the opposing factions. The Academy, though it tried hard to be fair, was in the main composed of 'the learned' who, while able to see the formal weaknesses of the work, were blind to its elemental greatness. Their findings praised Corneille warmly, but agreed with the critics that he had not observed the rules. Corneille was deeply hurt by the verdict, and his friend, Chapelain, found him two years later still obsessed by this issue and working out arguments to refute the Academy's strictures. Even in 1660, he was still trying in his critical writings to win a retrospective battle on this debate.

And hence, when he emerged from a three-year silence and produced *Horatius* and *Cinna* (in 1640), his craftsmanship, his choice of subject and his views had suffered a sea-change. True, he was always to maintain that he accepted the rules only to the extent that they suited him (but, as a modern writer has put it neatly, only once he had established what the rules were), but all his life, as far as he possibly could, he tried to stick to them, and often with the most disturbing results. For his innate tendency was to cram his five acts with the most varied action, whereas the three unities are suited to the spare psychological tragedy where external action is reduced to the absolute minimum (as in Racine's works).

The same switch in emphasis is reflected in his subjects. Whereas both *The Cid* and *The Theatrical Illusion* are Spanish by inspiration and source, *Horatius* and *Cinna* (for the first time in Corneille's theatre) take place in ancient Rome. Of course, the change was not an absolute one, for Corneille by no means abandoned Spain as a quarry for dramatic themes. But that he veered in a different direction is clear.

And lastly, there is a difference in the political values

underlying his work. In *The Cid*, even if we make the fullest allowances for the fact that the action takes place at the height of the Middle Ages in Spain when kings were by no means absolute, there is a distinct contrast between the image of the monarch in, say, *The Cid* and in *Cinna*. In the former play, the king is still very much *primus inter pares*. He is dependent on, and is defied by, his general (the Count) to a far greater degree than any other prince in Corneille's theatre, and certainly than Augustus. What is more, the spotlight in *The Cid* is focused on a mere knight – and a twenty-year-old stripling at that. On the other hand, the men who challenge the limitless power of Caesar (Cinna, Maximus and the rest) would be ignominiously swept into the discard of history were they not rescued by the equally limitless nobility of soul of the emperor. Here again, of course, it is not a question of a complete volte-face. Corneille retains his belief in the superiority of the concept of the king as a Christian knight, firm but merciful, as against that of the centralized monarchy and its Machiavellian ethos which was being sponsored by Richelieu. And the heroism which, from *The Cid* on, is a constant of his work is not only based on grandeur of soul, but is placed at the service of the romanesque ideal of honour.

'Romanesque', as the form of the word indicates, stands for the type of literature and ethos derived from the medieval romance, and hence impregnated with its spirit. The romanesque thus meant the far-fetched, the unusual, the adventurous, the ideal, often with a touch of the supernatural. The typical subjects were the exploits of knights errant – single combats and abductions. The guiding principle was that of honour and a romantic devotion to the beloved, and the ending was always a happy one. Much of the material for romanesque novels or plays was taken from Spain. (There was, it has been noted, a large Spanish colony in Corneille's native Rouen.) In this largely feudal world, nobility of soul and nobility of rank are broadly identical. If abstraction is made of this equation, however, the romanesque ethos of the early seventeenth century is disconcertingly similar to that of the cinema. There are also close analogies with the works of Shakespeare, and it is perhaps in this perspective that Corneille can best be appreciated by an Anglo-Saxon public. In fact, in the rare cases where the language barrier has been surmounted, the reaction of English and American readers is usually one of incredulous delight at finding a French classical dramatist in whose plays events actually happen and which do not consist simply of endless discussions.

Of Corneille the man, only the briefest account is called for. He was born of sound bourgeois stock in 1606 in the Norman town of Rouen, and, after studies with the Jesuits (who at the time had most of pre-University education in their hands), he entered the legal profession and practised till 1662 when he moved to Paris with his brother and fellow writer, Thomas. He was a model father to his seven children, though perhaps somewhat over-keen in soliciting pensions and favours, for example by obsequious dedications. He was also the first dramatist to treat his works as an important source of income, which shocked many of his contemporaries. He was awkward in speech and manner, but was always attracted, though within respectable limits, by women. He was justifiably proud of his works and fiercely aggressive in defending them against criticism. As Adam puts it, he had an unfortunate way of proving that he was right. He resented competition and used the 'Norman clan' (his brother and Donneau de Visé, who controlled much of the press at the time) to suppress his competitors such as the up-and-coming Racine, who referred to him waspishly as 'an ill-intentioned old playwright'. Corneille had small cause for such defensiveness, for he was the uncontested master of the dramatic scene. In 1663, a collected edition of his plays was published in two folio volumes – an honour usually reserved for the classics such as Virgil. He lived modestly, but there is no truth in the assertion that he died in poverty (1684, at the age of seventy-eight).

There is no obvious link between Corneille's life and theatre, unless we regard the latter as an escape from his relatively modest social position in an aristocratic world. He was a typical representative of his age in his attitudes, but he was highly untypical in his literary craftsmanship. To his inventive and inexhaustible dramatic genius must be added an infinite capacity for going over his works again and again, usually but not always, with felicitous results, which, however, improved the clarity and impact of the lines rather than the music. If he lacks the harmony of Racine, he has a power and sonority which often, in the original, remind the listener of the finer flights of Elizabethan tragedy.

A fuller understanding of Corneille can be achieved only through a study of his works. In the Prefaces to the three plays that follow, the reader will find an elaboration of most of the ideas set out in the present Introduction.

BIBLIOGRAPHY

The best introduction to Corneille in English is the section on the dramatist by Raymond Picard in his *Two Centuries of French Literature* (English translation, London, Weidenfeld & Nicolson, 1970), where the emphasis is on Corneille's wide variety and irrepressible originality. In French, readers should consult Georges Couton's works, and, to start with, his *Corneille*, revised edition, 1969. The chapters devoted to Corneille by Antoine Adam in his monumental *Histoire de la Littérature Française au XVIIe Siècle,* especially in Volume I (1948), are admirable. Other studies worth consulting are:

Paul Bénichou, *Morales du grand Siècle* (1948).

Louis Herland, *Corneille par lui-même* (1968). The title is misleading and the study somewhat garrulous, but stimulating and well illustrated.

Octave Nadal, *Le Sentiment de l' Amour dans l' Oeuvre de Pierre Corneille* (1948).

On a less academic level:

Robert Brasillach, *Corneille* (1938). An enthusiastic panegyric of the writer.

Jean Schlumberger, *Plaisir à Corneille* (1936). A delightful annotated anthology.

The Bordas, Larousse and Blackwell editions of *Polyeuctus* are useful in varying degrees, but all approach the play in a spirit close to veneration. Bordas is the most balanced of the three. That publisher has also produced excellent presentations of the other two plays in the present volume.

POLYEUCTUS

PREFACE

For the last forty years, critics have placed *Polyeuctus* (? 1642) on a pinnacle. The wave of enthusiasm can be traced back to Péguy's famous essay, *Victor-Marie, comte Hugo* (1910). But the groundswell of enthusiasm starts, significantly, just before the Second World War with Brasillach's *Corneille* (1938), where he defines the work as the greatest sacred drama of France, 'the one in which all virtues, human or divine, are blended. Truly, the whole of Christianity is here.' Monseigneur Calvet, whose commentary on the play comes four years later, is unremittingly dithyrambic. In 1949, a certain Francis Ambrière has no hesitation in assuring his readers that it is 'the greatest religious play *in the world*'. The last three words are even written in English, possibly to make sure that the implications do not escape Anglo-Saxon readers. Since then, apart from a few dissenting voices such as Schlumberger (a Protestant) and Adam (who can be roughly defined as anti-clerical), there has been almost complete unanimity on the subject. Pierre Michel, in his edition of the play (1972), lays it down that, in the current age, *Polyeuctus* is regarded 'not only as the summit of Corneille's art, but as his most living play'.

Yet, strangely enough, until about 1935, critics were at one in showing considerable reservations about the work. As Petit de Julleville notes in the Hachette edition (p. 32), 'No illustrious voice was raised among the contemporaries to praise this tragedy highly.' Boileau, the uncrowned king of literary circles, never mentions it, nor does Racine allude to it when welcoming the playwright's younger brother to the French Academy. The 'learned' were unanimous in condemning it. Such success as it did achieve was among the groundlings, and was attributable to the touching idyll between Paulina (before her conversion) and her pagan suitor, Severus. The 'Christian' section, on the contrary, was condemned on all hands. We are told that, in the opinion of the influential Hôtel de Rambouillet, 'the Christian element in particular had jarred very badly' – for reasons which will be dealt with below. This dichotomy in the play was stressed by almost all critics at the time.

Thus, the prince de Conti, a former patron of Molière and later a vigorous campaigner for purer morals, asks: 'Is there anything dryer and more unattractive than the sacred half of the play? Is there anyone who is not a thousand times more deeply touched by the grief of Severus when he finds that Paulina is married than by the martyrdom of Polyeuctus?' Saint Evremond, a freethinker, is of much the same opinion. 'What would have made a fine sermon would make a wretched tragedy were it not that the dialogue between Paulina and Severus, animated by other feelings and passions, saved the author's reputation which the Christian virtues of our martyrs would have deprived him of.' According to Voltaire, the classical scholar, Dacier, at a slightly later date, also attributed the success of the play to the scene between the former sweethearts. And Voltaire goes on to say: 'This opinion is fairly general.'

Voltaire's own view, apart from its frequently irreverent tone, is very much in line with these reactions. He admits that there are many fine traits in *Polyeuctus* and that it needed a great genius to handle such a difficult subject. But his main contention is that the hero-martyr and his pious verse would long ago have been forgotten but for his wife's attraction to the handsome pagan. In the same spirit, he notes that 'the undying success of the play is due to the extreme beauty of Severus' role and to the *piquant* situation of Paulina'.

Even in the nineteenth century, attitudes changed little. Talma, the famous actor, would have none of the martyr's role, but plumped unhesitatingly for that of Severus whom he regarded as the main character. Sainte-Beuve is of much the same opinion. Petit de Julleville, as usual, sums up the position neatly when he says: 'For two hundred years, everyone seems to have sided against Polyeuctus; he is the obstacle in the way of the happiness of Paulina and Severus; he is the disastrous accident which brings out the nobility of Severus and the virtuousness of Paulina' (op. cit., p. 35). Such an interpretation, the critic continues, is completely wrong. In other words, the public has consistently misunderstood the playwright's intentions, and it is only through the superior insight of modern critics that we can get the play into perspective.

This is surely a somewhat naive approach and confuses intentions with effectiveness. No doubt Corneille *meant* Polyeuctus to be the central figure in the drama, but one cannot simply excuse the writer for failing to translate his plans into effect by putting all the blame on the perversity of the audience who applauds at the wrong points.

In fact, there is a much simpler explanation. This is that the public were perfectly right in their preference – on literary and to some extent also on 'ideological' grounds; it usually *is* in the right. Both the ethos and aesthetics of Corneille's other dramas correspond exactly to the aristocratic and this-worldly code set out in the pagan romance in *Polyeuctus*. But this code is utterly at odds with the values of asceticism and contempt for the things of the world defended by the martyr. Corneille is thus operating on alien ground in the latter episodes. Moreover, the other-worldly precepts preached by the hero never really took deep roots in France, even at the height of the Counter-Reformation. And the two halves simply do not blend.

What is perhaps more serious is that, in an age when absolute subservience to the state was current, Corneille had to represent his main character as a hot-headed and fanatical rebel, and at the same time contend that the Christians were faithful soldiers of the Emperor in order to justify the final triumph of Christianity. Then, persecution would give way (under the same monarch) to tolerance going as far as the appointment of a Christian provincial governor. Such a reassuring *dénouement* was inevitable in a play dealing with martyrdom, or indeed in baroque 'tragicomedies' in general. Lastly, the attempt to cram such a rich tale into the tight framework of the classical tragedy was bound to fail, especially in the exposition, the more so as Corneille observed the three unities more scrupulously in this work than in *The Cid* and even than in *Cinna*.

On the success of Corneille's stagecraft, characterization and verse in the Severus–Paulina idyll there is no need to dwell. Critics of the most varying schools are in agreement on this point, while sometimes deploring its beauty and power. Adam is surely right when he describes the meeting of the two former sweethearts as 'one of the summits of the literature of all time'.

Similarly, Severus' moral grandeur, which makes him cousin to so many others of Corneille's heroes, provides another example of that nobility of soul so vigorously applauded in his plays.

But, when we turn to Polyeuctus, the picture changes. In the exposition, the problem is largely a technical one. Even the most resourceful genius could hardly develop a subject which presupposes the marriage and conversion and covers the baptism of the hero in the space of twenty-four hours (or less). The subject – a baroque one if there ever was – imposed an impossible strain on the classical framework. The perceptive Schlumberger rightly defines the tragedy as 'the most hazardous undertaking on which Corneille had ever ventured'.

Yet, in chalking out his plan, Corneille started with the substantial advantage of having invented almost all the details. No other tragedy of his owes so little to his sources. But such freedom availed him little. The setting out of the facts is both inadequate and unenlightening. All we can glean from the play is that the hero has been married for two weeks, but the courtship seems to have lasted a somewhat longer period. Presumably, the conversion came after the marriage. It can hardly be supposed that Polyeuctus, who seems to have plunged into action against paganism without worrying about the complications for his wife, married her without telling her of the momentous change in his faith. Moreover, he never appears to have posed the question of being remarried by a Christian rite, and defines his marriage as realizing 'a just and holy love' (51).

The essential point is that he is a young man deeply in love, and the whole tone of the first few scenes vis-à-vis his wife is one of *galanterie* and high comedy (especially when he takes flight in order to be baptized). He puts the fear of offending his wife (in the case of 'men like me') above fear of death. And his amorous attitude extends (though not always very tactfully) up to the point immediately preceding his conversion (621–6). So much so, that Michel (op. cit., p. 59, n. 6) asks: 'How could one ever suspect that grace is about to take possession of [the hero] and make him give up the woman he loves?' How indeed?

The contrast between Nearchus' severity and Polyeuctus' light-hearted approach clearly emerges. To the bachelor mentor, he replies that his marriage justifies a little delay, and that, if he is called upon to face torture, God will give him strength. One has the impression, notes Schlumberger, that the change of faith for the hero is a somewhat superficial affair. He 'does not seem to suspect that conversion means a reversal of all feelings and that a man does not hasten to baptism between two rounds of billing and cooing during his honeymoon' (*Plaisir à Corneille*, p. 90).

Ideally what was needed was a much wider time horizon, in which we would have been shown Polyeuctus revelling in his married bliss, *then* the conversion, and gradually the realization of what such a profound change entails and of the fearful conflict which it may raise (or *will*, in Nearchus' view) between earthly and heavenly love.

As it is, the evolution is such as to leave the spectator unconvinced, and nowhere as much as when the hero experiences the inrush of grace. Up till line 636, as has often been pointed out, Polyeuctus has behaved perfectly 'normally'. When he takes leave of Paulina to attend the pagan ceremony, he promises her that he will be correct towards Severus.

> We two will only vie in courtesy.

But four lines later we guess and, three lines after that, we know, that he means to commit an outrage on the established faith. This is the crucial development in the play, since it paves the way for his baptism.

The switch from day-to-day behaviour to religious fervour is so abrupt as to be inexplicable. Naturally, we know that the change is to be attributed to grace. And the new-found ardour can be explained theologically, and faithfully reflects the doctrines – especially those on grace – which Corneille imbibed from his Jesuit mentors. But *Polyeuctus* is a play, and not an exposition of doctrine. In all the rest of Corneille's dramatic works, sudden changes (such as those of Augustus and Emily in *Cinna*) have been carefully led up to – as is essential if the spectator's assent is to be won. This particular episode is totally at odds with Corneille's usual stagecraft, or, we might add, with that of any other accomplished playwright.

The problem raised by the hero's conduct after his conversion is of much the same nature. It is that of a clash between the ethos of martyrdom and the values which he consistently expounded in his other plays. In short, when trying to cast some of his material in a Counter-Reformation mould, he was imposing a serious constraint on his creative genius.

The values which he was propounding in the Christian part of *Polyeuctus* are explicitly formulated. A convert must, we learn,

> For [God] neglect wife, property and rank,

a precept at the antipodes of a code which glorifies rank, and the corresponding ambition and privileges.

The maxim in the line just quoted is, as the Bordas edition observes, in line with the teaching of the Gospels. But it is not usually practised. And it required no great skill on Molière's part to hold this attitude up to ridicule in *Tartuffe* when he makes Orgon confess:

> And I would see wife, mother, children, all,
> Perish without my feeling ev'n a qualm.

Little wonder that, ever since the première, the audience's sympathies have usually been all with Paulina who is sacrificed, 'without a qualm', on the altar of the convert's convictions. What is more, when she urges him desperately to allow himself to be saved from execution, she finds her devotion contemptuously rejected as a 'shameful attachment of the flesh and world' (1107) and as 'diabolic wiles' (1653).

Polyeuctus' conduct has been defended by an English editor who writes: 'In an age of tranquillity, it is easy to dismiss his actions as fanatical and inhuman. Recent events have shown us that anyone may find himself face to face with similar problems.' But the fact is that Polyeuctus does not 'find himself' in a debacle. He plunges into it, committing in the process 'both treason and sacrilege' (925). He is not, like anti-Nazis or Soviet dissidents, willing to risk death or imprisonment for his beliefs. He is heaven-bent on martyrdom, regardless of the consequences (for his wife, among others). He sees his friend, Nearchus, go to death 'with envious eyes' (958). Earlier in the play, when the same Nearchus tries to dissuade Polyeuctus from committing his rash gesture of overthrowing the idols, he replies that he knows he is risking his life, but that he will be certain of salvation.

> My crimes, if I live on, may rob me of
> The prize. Why hazard then what death ensures?
> When it unlocks the heav'ns, can death be harsh? (664–6)

In fact, the totalitarian spirit in the play is represented by the martyr, and not by the tolerant Roman pagan régime.

Similarly, he has a masochistic desire for suffering.

> Tortures [to Christians] are what pleasures are

[for pagans] (951), says Paulina. And her husband amply confirms this view.

> In suffering lies true Christian happiness.
> The fiercest torments are rewards for them.
> God, who repays good deeds a hundredfold,
> Adds persecutions as a crowning bliss. (1535–8)

Lines 89–90 express the same concept.

If we look for a true parallel with such a delight in the morbid, we have not far to seek. *The Martyrdom of Saint Bartholomew* by Ribera, in the Prado, echoes the mood to perfection. Ribera, it may be recalled, was a Spanish artist who spent a great part of his life in Naples (then the capital of the Spanish dominions in Italy), and used his Caravaggesque technique to emphasize the harrowing mental and physical sufferings of martyred saints and penitents. The picture is generally dated 1639, or just before *Polyeuctus* was first performed.

The clash between the martyr's profession of faith and the ethos prevailing in France at that time is particularly visible in the relation of the Christians in the play to established authority. We have already seen the negative reaction of the Hôtel de Rambouillet to the work because of the Christian element. The nature of this opposition is spelt out in an account by Voltaire. According to this writer, the whole of the Hôtel de Rambouillet, and particularly Godeau, the Bishop of Vence, was loud in its denunciation of the hero's iconoclastic zeal. 'People said that this [gesture] was imprudent, that several bishops and synods [of the early church] had expressly forbidden the attacks on law and order; and that Christians were even refused communion if, by such foolhardy attacks, they exposed the church to persecution.'

The all-powerful Cardinal de Richelieu also frowned on the play, allegedly on the grounds that nobody was put up to refute the slanders on the early Christians put into the mouth of Stratonice (780–83). This is not impossible, but it overlooks the fact that the main charge against the Christians was that they were rebels, and that Polyeuctus behaves as a rebel in the play. It seems much more probable that the prince of the church who, like most of the men of his age, glorified 'la raison d'état' was more concerned with a Christian defying the state and revelling in his defiance. It should be remembered that France had just emerged from bloody wars of religion and that most Frenchmen were profoundly disturbed at any threat to the new-found equilibrium and order. The hero's reckless attack on the official cult and his unbridled militancy filled the average Frenchman with horror.

The probability of such an interpretation being correct is borne out by a similar view, expressed by Madame de Maintenon, the power behind Louis XIV at the time of the Revocation of the Edict of Nantes (which had guaranteed tolerance to French Protestants). Writing in 1688 (three years after the Revocation), she said: 'One ought above all to forbid performances which convey the idea of martyrdom, nothing being more dangerous for the New Catholics [as the forcible converts were called] and for the old ones.'

It need only be added that the average theatre-goer of the time was much better read in ecclesiastical history than his modern equivalent, and was well aware of the ban on the provocation of the authorities by the early church – a point which is skated over gracefully by many modern writers.

In the play, the Christians are constantly stamped (by the pagans) as rebels. And Polyeuctus, by his gesture, amply justifies this charge. It will be remembered that, in ancient Rome, civic and religious rites were inextricably interwoven. Even such a liberal emperor as Marcus Aurelius was determined, notes Michel (op. cit., p. 36, n. 7), to stamp out Christianity as representing a threat to social order.

The subversiveness of Polyeuctus' outrage is, if anything, underlined by him in subsequent declarations. He denounces Decius, the Emperor, as 'pitiless ... rav'ning tiger, fiend' (1125), an anti-Christ who has destroyed God's saints and who will soon be called upon to pay for his sins. (He was in fact killed the following year.)

In the face of these statements, it is difficult to take very seriously his announcement that

> I owe my life to people and to king. (1211)

It is a strange way of serving his king to profane a ceremony of which the king was an integral part.

Nor does he show the slightest sign of retracting or of

apologizing for his deeds. On the contrary. He would repeat the gesture

> Were Felix or Severus looking on,
> Or ev'n the Senate and the Emperor. (1672-3)

Given such defiance, it is hardly to be wondered at that Decius is represented as taking a firm line with the new religion.

The conversion of Paulina suffers from the same flaws as that of her husband – and for the same reasons. Partly it takes place with such speed and lack of motivation that the spectator is left unconvinced, and partly it is manifestly inserted in the play in order to show the blood of the martyr working wonders from on high and preparing the final triumph of the church. Both aesthetics and substance combine to weaken this episode.

Throughout Act IV and most of Act V she is rejected by her husband, and his lack of response to her devotion has certainly not endeared him to her. Thus, in line 1580, she cries to Felix and Polyeuctus:

> . . . Which of you is now my murderer?

Five lines later on, she addresses her husband as 'Fiend', and urges him to

> Kill me at least without insulting me.

Just before she is led off to die, she exclaims:

> Drive not a heart who loves you to despair. (1607)

In the spirit of conjugal fidelity, she swears that she will follow him to the grave (1681). When she next appears on the stage (1719), she tells us that

> My husband, dying, has enlightened me. (1724)

And she cries,

> I see. I know, believe, am undeceived. (1727)

It is not clear what she sees, and the only psychological explanation of her sudden change is that she has decided to adopt Polyeuctus' faith in order to preserve her links with him. The real answer is that the *dénouement* called for her conversion.

Another line of approach is that Paulina has all the virtues needed for conversion and has been consistently sympathetic to her husband's new creed. Neither contention will hold water. Many of Corneille's pagan heroines are similarly virtuous, but it has never been suggested that they should turn Christian. Paulina is in fact typical of the playwright's 'generous' (or noble-hearted) ethos, as is the whole of the pagan section of the play. And her comments on the Christians are consistently hostile. Her first reference is unambiguous. 'An impious band of Christians' (234). When Paulina tells her attendant to stop talking about the sectarians (265), it is not because she dislikes the girl's strictures, but because she does not want the delicate subject to be discussed in her father's hearing (especially after the nightmare, with its various threats and its mention of the impious sect).

Her later statements are on the same lines. In line 254, she refers to 'the Christians' plots and spells'. When Polyeuctus' outrage is denounced, she agrees that the Christians have all the defects and vices. They are 'wicked, rebellious, impious and false' (780–84).

Again, when she stresses the Christians' resistance to torture (934–6), she is not defending them, but persuading Felix that it is useless to expect his son-in-law to recant under pressure. In the key scene between husband and wife, Paulina sweeps aside Polyeuctus' arguments in defence of his conduct with the withering comment:

> These are your Christians' crazy fantasies;
> Their lies have cast a spell upon your mind. (1199–1200)

When, a little later, Polyeuctus urges her to adopt his creed, she is profoundly shocked:

> What! wretch. You dare to wish for *that*? (1273)

And, in a final plea to her father, she admits that the prisoner's crimes 'can hardly be excused' (1615) and terms

33

the offender 'mad'. In short, she is always and unvaryingly hostile to Christianity.

The conversion of Felix is even more astonishing. If we are to adopt virtue as the explanation of conversion, what are we to say in this case? Again, the real reason for his sudden and unforeseeable switch is to pave the way for the *Laus dei* at the end.

But it is not only his unmotivated illumination that mars this part of the play. It is also the sharp contradiction between his role of villain (heavily underscored by Corneille) and his clarity as regards the happenings in the tragedy. True, he is hardly a lovable character, especially when he daydreams that, once Polyeuctus is out of the way, Severus, the Emperor's favourite, will be free to marry his daughter. He is utterly mistaken, too, when, with his cheap Machiavellianism, he imagines that Severus is merely trying to trap him by pleading in favour of the prisoner's life.

However, the constant attacks on his decision to execute his son-in-law are completely unjustified (1747–50). Felix rightly emphasizes that Polyeuctus' crime is treason, and he has gone to great lengths in trying to save the offender. He should by rights, and in observance of the Emperor's instructions, have dispatched him at once. In such circumstances,

> No kin, no friendship, can be privileged. (926)

When Felix's confidant, Albinus, joins the pressure group to have Polyeuctus pardoned, Felix replies coolly that such an act would mean forfeiting his own post and probably his life. Severus may indulge in the belief that he is strong enough at court to sway the Emperor, but Felix, with every show of reason, replies that

> Better than he I know how Decius feels. (1484)

In short, the idea that Felix is merely being hard-hearted in sticking to the law is a carefully fostered *trompe-l'oeil*. Corneille needed to generate sympathy for Polyeuctus and hate for Felix. But, as the Governor constantly repeats,

34

if Polyeuctus goes to his death, this is because he is determined on it and refuses to grasp any of the lifebuoys offered him.

Neither Severus' pleas for mercy (misinterpreted) nor the curious rising (1067–72) of the mob (which had at first been horrified (833) at the attack on its idols) affects the main issue. They may have hastened the prisoner's death (1752 and 1080). They have not influenced what was, short of a miracle, an inevitable execution. Like Felix's manoeuvre, they create suspense and also the illusion that Polyeuctus *might* have escaped.

Lastly, there is the question of the *dénouement*. Petit de Julleville suggested (op. cit., p. 178, n. 4) that the play could with advantage have ended on line 1762, that is, before Felix's conversion. But such a course, though more dramatically satisfying, would have deprived the playwright of the very effects which were essential for him. Nevertheless, that critic was right in feeling that there was an odd incongruity between the play and its end. It is not just that Felix's change of heart strikes one as bizarre, especially when he refers to the previous events (including the chopping off of his son-in-law's head) as the 'happy adventure' (1811). It is rather that the *dénouement* and the premises of the play do not correspond.

The contradictions are particularly patent in the words and deeds of Severus. The evolution of this character is worth following. Up to line 1394 (i.e. almost to the end of Act IV), he is the great-hearted pagan gentleman who is deeply in love with Paulina and ready to intervene at her request in favour of Polyeuctus. His confidant warns him that this is an impossible venture, since Decius regards the Christians as rebels and traitors. The favourite will therefore run the risk of forfeiting his standing at court should he persist in his quixotic gesture of trying to rescue a sectarian accused of a serious crime against the state. Nevertheless, Severus goes so far as to threaten Felix with disgrace unless he pardons the offender. Here we are in an unreal world, for it is unthinkable that Decius should remove or downgrade a trusted functionary merely because he has faithfully carried out orders (as indeed Felix had done in the past) (256).

But this curious conduct (with its underlying misunderstandings or illusions) is simply the forerunner of a curious transmogrification of Severus' role. All of a sudden, the Roman Knight launches out into a lengthy tirade which reveals him as a sympathizer with the new creed (1411–43). A kind of Christian fellow-traveller, he affirms that he is unaware of the reasons for their persecution (1413). But all the other pagan characters in the play could, and in some cases do, enlighten him on this matter. And he has seen for himself Polyeuctus' 'treasonable' act in toppling the idols.

Leaving aside the positive reasons for his sympathy with them (such as their blameless morals), we may concentrate on the two heads of accusation stressed in the play. One is that they are sorcerers. Severus does not deal very convincingly with this charge, but sidesteps it deftly, and comments that other religions 'have secrets just like them' (1420). Hence, he suggests, discrimination against them on that score is unjustified.

But the crux of the problem is elsewhere. It lies in the charge of disloyalty to the Emperor and his cult. Severus delivers a certificate of good conduct to them on the field of battle (1439–42). But, as Couton points out (*Corneille*, p. 79), the Christians cannot possibly render unto Caesar what is Caesar's if that involves bowing the knee to what they regard as false gods. Which it does. Hence, Severus is simply being naive or disingenuous, or both, when he puts serving God and the Emperor on the same plane and in the same line (1804) – unless of course he is deceiving himself into thinking that the new religion has already become the established one.

In fact, Severus' acts imply that the new régime is already here, or at least is imminent. He not only confirms the Christian convert, Felix, in his office as Governor of the province, but also promises an end to persecution – both of which are utterly improbable in the circumstances. (In fact, the change came over fifty years later.) His optimism is based on his naive conviction that he can win round the Christian-eater, Decius. He comments somewhat airily that the Emperor and he see eye to eye on everything except on this one point (the persecution of the Christians), on which the official policy seems unjust (1414), much as if this were a minor detail which need merely be brought to the Emperor's attention for it to be immediately corrected.

These illusions are only explicable by the fact that he, too, is virtually a convert who pities the Christians 'and will defend their cause' (1443).

This change of heart and the illusory hopes which it inspires (illusory not just in terms of history, but of the dramatic presuppositions of the action) are needed to complete the picture of harmony and of the triumph of the faith – a kind of baroque 'glory', suffusing the end of the play in a rich reassuring glow.

The ending thus devised is miraculous. As Polyeuctus points out:

> ... these are secrets hard to understand;
> God makes them clear to his elect alone. (1539–40)

Such a form of art is poles apart from the Jansenist approach exemplified in Racine's *Athaliah* or *Phaedra* where miracles are portrayed as being plausible, and hence distinguishable as such only to the elect (as was the case of the ageing queen's tenderness for the youthful Joash). The gain to verisimilitude in art in such a conception is clear. This probably explains why most critics, regardless of belief, are agreed in regarding *Athaliah* as the supreme religious tragedy in French literature.

Polyeuctus, however, is a masterpiece, too, though a flawed one, and for slightly different reasons than those usually advanced. Hence, if readers do not pitch their expectations too high, they can only derive pleasure from such an unusual and remarkable play.

POLYEUCTUS: SUMMARY

ACT ONE

POLYEUCTUS, a leading Armenian nobleman, has just married Paulina, the daughter of Felix, the Roman Governor of that province, and has also been secretly converted to Christianity by his friend, Nearchus. Paulina has had a nightmare in which she sees her husband killed, and begs him not to leave his palace. However, Polyeuctus wishes to receive baptism, and, without explanations, hurries out with his friend. Paulina explains to her confidante one reason why the dream has upset her so badly. She was formerly (before leaving Rome for Armenia) in love with a Roman knight called Severus, whose addresses, however, were not approved by Felix because of his modest situation. She had thought that Severus met his death in battle. But, in the dream, he appears triumphant, and announces the imminent death of Polyeuctus. In fact, it is Felix, her own father, who seems to have killed him in the dream. Immediately after, Felix comes in and declares that Severus is not dead, but, on the contrary, is high in the Emperor's favour. Felix fears that Severus will take revenge for the rejection of his courtship in Rome, and appeals to Paulina to use her influence with Severus in his (Felix's) favour. This Paulina agrees reluctantly to do.

ACT TWO

SEVERUS learns that Paulina is married. He is in despair, but decides all the same to see her. In a moving encounter, she begs Severus not to disturb her married happiness and to avoid any further meeting. Severus agrees. Polyeuctus goes off to a sacrifice to be held at the temple in celebration of a recent victory of the Emperor at which Severus (who played a key part in the battle) will of course be present. Paulina therefore decides not to attend it. Polyeuctus pro-

ises that he will merely vie with Severus in courtesy.
Nearchus tries to prevent Polyeuctus from going to the
pagan temple, but Polyeuctus suddenly announces that
he means to topple the idols. Nearchus objects, but is
finally won round to taking part in the enterprise.

ACT THREE

PAULINA'S confidante reports how the two converts
carried out their plans and openly derided the idols.
Felix condemns Nearchus to death at once, and forces
Polyeuctus to look on as an incentive to recanting. Paulina
pleads with her father to free Polyeuctus, but in vain.
Polyeuctus sees his friend executed 'with envious eye'.
Felix appeals to Paulina to try and make Polyeuctus change
his unbending attitude. The Governor then explains to his
confidant how difficult his position is. The Emperor has
given strict instructions to suppress the new heresy, and,
even if Felix were to try and postpone punishing Polyeuctus, Severus, now the Emperor's right-hand man, is there
to make sure (Felix thinks) that the official policy is carried
out and no undue leniency shown. However, Felix also
has the unworthy thought that, if Polyeuctus is put to death,
Severus will be free to sue for Paulina's hand, and such a
marriage would enhance Felix's position, as well as re-
moving any grudge Severus might have against him. He
orders the prisoner to be brought into the palace, where
Paulina will seek to make him see reason and avoid execution.

ACT FOUR

IN a lyrical monologue, Polyeuctus expresses his ardent
thirst for martyrdom. Paulina is shown in. She urges him to
recant. He refuses brusquely. He is bent on dying for his
new-found religion. She reproaches him with not loving
her, but he merely insists on the blessings of his faith and
begs God that Paulina, too, will see the light. Severus (who
has been sent for by Polyeuctus) comes on the scene. The

prisoner urges Severus to marry Paulina after the execution. She declares that such a proposal is out of the question since Severus, unwittingly, will be responsible for her husband's death, and she appeals to him to show greatness of soul and save Polyeuctus' life. After an initial burst of astonishment, he intercedes, partly because of his sympathy for the Christians.

ACT FIVE

FELIX, who thinks that Severus' intervention on Polyeuctus' behalf is a trap (since any leniency on his part would be used to ruin him at court), decides to talk to Polyeuctus himself together with Paulina, and, if the son-in-law persists in his fanatical attitude, there will be no other course open but to have him executed. Felix launches his appeal. He even pretends to be converted to Christianity. He fails in his attempt. Paulina makes a second effort, but with no more success than before. Polyeuctus urges her to live with Severus or to die with *him*. The prisoner is led away to death, and Paulina swears to follow him. On witnessing the execution, Paulina embraces Christianity. Felix follows her example. Severus (originally angry at Felix's Machiavellian approach to the request to pardon Polyeuctus) orders Felix to remain Governor, and expresses confidence that he can persuade the Emperor to end the persecutions. A new age of tolerance and evangelism opens up. Felix and Paulina hope that Severus too will eventually see the light, and they go off to give the martyrs decent burial.

TO THE QUEEN REGENT[1]

MADAM,

Whatever knowledge I may have of my weakness, how-ever deep the profound respect which Your Majesty imprints in the souls of those approaching you, I confess that I throw myself at your feet without mistrust or bashfulness, and that I feel assured of pleasing you because I am assured of speaking to you of what you most like. This is only a play which I submit to you, but it will speak to you of God, and the dignity of the subject is such that the incompetence of the workman cannot lower its level; and your royal soul takes so much pleasure in this debate to be offended at the defects of a work in which you will find what delights your heart. It is on that score that I hope to obtain from Your Majesty the pardon for all the time I have waited to render you this kind of homage. Whenever I have put on the stage moral or political virtues, I have always thought the tableaux too unworthy of appearing before you, when I considered that, with however much care I chose them in history and whatever ornaments might enrich them, you could behold greater examples within yourself. To ensure a proper relation of proportion, I had to go the highest level and not undertake to offer anything of this nature to a most Christian queen, who is even more so by her actions than by her title, except by offering you a portrait of the Christian virtues of which the love and the glory of God formed the finest traits, and which made the pleasure which you might take in them as suitable for exercising your piety as for refreshing your mind. It is to this extraordinary and admirable piety, Madam, that France owes the blessings which she sees bestowed on the first battles of the King. The happy outcomes thereof are the visible

---

1. Anne of Austria, Louis XIII's widow, assumed the regency in 1643 during the minority of Louis XIV. She was noted, in later life, for her devotion.

retributions and divine interventions which shed abundantly over the whole kingdom the rewards and favours which Your Majesty has deserved. Our ruin seemed assured after the death of our great monarch. The whole of Europe was already pitying us, imagining that we were about to be cast into utter chaos because we were all extremely depressed. However, the prudence and concern of Your Majesty, the good counsels which you have taken, the great figures which you have chosen to carry them out, have had such a powerful effect on all the needs of the State that this first year of Your Regency has not only equalled the most glorious ones of the other reign, but has even, by the recapture of Thionville,[1] effaced the memory of the setback before its walls which interrupted such a long series of victories. Allow me to abandon myself to my delight at this thought and to utter the following thoughts in my transports:

> How you give birth, great Queen, to miracles!
> Brussels, Madrid, are both abashed by them;
> And, if Apollo had predicted them,
> I would have doubted such great oracles.

> At your command men storm the obstacles,
> Strike terror ev'n into the boldest hearts,
> And, by your earliest battles, offer us
> Of hostile flags illustrious spectacles.

> Vict'ry itself, hast'ning to greet the King,
> Gives him Thionville and Rocroi[2] as spoils,
> Proclaims this verse on the banks of the Seine.

> France may expect from this triumphant start
> Everything, since the orders of the Queen
> Make of an infant's[3] arms a thunderbolt.

1. Thionville was retaken in 1643 in the war in the Low Countries against Spain. It had been captured in 1639 from the French by the Imperial troops.

2. Rocroi was the battle (in 1643) by which the army, fighting under the Prince of Condé, saved the country from a Spanish invasion.

3. Louis XIV was then only five.

There can be no doubt that such a marvellous start will be followed by still more astounding progress. God does not leave his works imperfect. He will complete them, Madam, and will make not only Her Majesty's regency but also your whole life a constant chain of prosperity. These are the prayers of the whole of France and those offered with the greatest zeal.

> Madam,
> by Your Majesty's humble, obedient and
> most faithful servant and subject,
>   CORNEILLE

CAST

FELIX, *Roman senator, Governor of Armenia*
POLYEUCTUS, *Armenian lord, son-in-law of Felix*
SEVERUS, *Roman knight, favourite of the Emperor Decius*
NEARCHUS, *Roman lord, friend of Polyeuctus*
PAULINA, *daughter of Felix and wife of Polyeuctus*
STRATONICE, *confidante of Paulina*
ALBINUS, *confidant of Felix*
FABIAN, *a member of Severus' suite*
CLEON, *a member of Felix's suite*
Three guards

The scene is at Melitene, capital of Armenia, in Felix's palace.

POLYEUCTUS

ACT ONE
Scene One

POLYEUCTUS, NEARCHUS

NEARCHUS

What, you're unsettled at a woman's dream!　　　　1
Such trifles can unnerve a heart like yours!
A woman's dream-born peril can alarm
Your bravery, tried in so many wars!

POLYEUCTUS

I know what dreams are worth and that a man　　　5
Should set small store by such absurdities,
Which, from the hazy vapours of the night,
Form empty images effaced at dawn;
You do not know the power of women or
The boundless claims they have upon our heart,　　10
When, after long subjection to their spell,
We see at last the wedding torches blaze.
Paulina, plunged in an unreasoned grief,
Fears and believes my dream-predicted death;
She pits her tears against my plans, and, when　　15
I seek to leave the palace, bars my way.
I scorn her fear, but, when she weeps, I yield.
I pity her, but I am not alarmed;
And so my heart, receptive but not cowed,
Dares not, by love possessed, displease her. Is　　20
The urgency, Nearchus, such that I
Must steel my heart against her loving pleas?
Let us accord some respite to her fears
And do at leisure what disturbs today.

45

NEARCHUS

25 But meanwhile are you fully satisfied
That life and perseverance will suffice?
Does God, who in His hand holds life and soul,
Promise that you can act tomorrow? He
Is always good and just, but yet His grace
30 Does not with equal force always descend;
If our delays let certain times go by,
Grace can no longer penetrate our souls.
Hardened, our hearts repulse it and deflect
What then's dispensed to us more sparingly;
35 That holy ardour, meant to work our good,
More rarely falls and operates no more.
The zeal which urged you on to be baptized
Already falters, is not what it was,
And, for a few sighs which assail your ears,
40 The bright flame flickers and will peter out.

POLYEUCTUS

You know me not. My zeal is still the same;
Desire increases when the deed's delayed.
These tears I look at with a husband's eye
Leave me as Christian in my heart as you;
45 But, to receive its sacred character,
Which in the font washes away our crimes
And which, purging our soul, unseals our eyes,
Restores to us our pristine right to heav'n,
Though I prefer it to an empire's sway
50 As the one goal to which I now aspire,
To satisfy a just and holy love,
I think I can delay it for one day.

NEARCHUS

Thus you're deceived by man's archenemy.
What can't be done by force, he tries by guile.
55 He seeks to weaken good intentions, and,
When he can't thwart them, engineers delay.
Yours[1] will be foiled by streams of obstacles,

1. Good intentions.

Today by tears, tomorrow by fresh wiles;
Paulina's dream and sombre visions are
His first manoeuvre in illuding you. 60
He brings on everything – entreaties, threats;
Always on the attack, he never tires;
He thinks that final victory is sure,
And what's postponed is half prevented. So,
Prevent these moves and let Paulina cry. 65
God does not want an overworldly heart;
Which, backward-looking, doubtful how to choose,
When called by God, harks to another voice.

POLYEUCTUS

But to be His must one love nobody?

NEARCHUS

He lets us, nay, bids us love everyone. 70
But, to be quite sincere, this lord of lords
Demands the highest honour, deepest love.
His grandeur is supreme. We must then love
Nothing but after Him and in Himself,
For Him neglect wife, property and rank, 75
And for His glory risk and suffer all.
But you're still far from this consuming zeal
Which you so need and which I augur you!
I can but speak to you with tear-drenched eyes.
When the world hates us and when all believe 80
By persecuting us they serve the State,
When fiercest tortures are the Christians' lot,
How can you rise above your trials if
You are unable to resist ev'n tears?

POLYEUCTUS

You move me not. The pity which I feel 85
Is not unmanly. Brave men feel it too.
On men like me fair eyes exert their power.
Some fear to thwart it who do not fear death;
If cruel torments are in store for me,

90 If I must joy, nay, revel in them, then
Your God, whom I as yet dare not call mine,
Will, making me a Christian, give me strength.

NEARCHUS

Haste then to baptism.

POLYEUCTUS

          Yes. I cannot wait.
I burn to bear its glorious imprint. But
95 This dream affrights and grieves Paulina so,
She will not hear of letting me go out.

NEARCHUS

She'll be the more entranced by your return.
At latest in an hour you'll dry her tears;
And seeing you again will seem more sweet,
100 The more she's wept for her beloved spouse.
Come. We are waited for.

POLYEUCTUS

          Allay her fears
And calm the sorrow which now weighs on her.
She comes.

NEARCHUS

    Then flee.

POLYEUCTUS

I cannot.

NEARCHUS

          But you must.
Flee from a foe who knows your weakest link,
105 Who finds it easily, whose eyes deal wounds.
Whose fatal blow pleases you when it slays.

Scene Two

POLYEUCTUS, NEARCHUS, PAULINA, STRATONICE

POLYEUCTUS

Flee, since I must. Paulina, fare you well.
At latest in an hour I shall return.

PAULINA

What urgent matter summons you from here?
Say. Is your honour, is your life at stake?   110

POLYEUCTUS

Much more than that.

PAULINA

     What is the secret, then?

POLYEUCTUS

One day you'll know. I'm loath to leave you, but
I must.

PAULINA

  You love me?

POLYEUCTUS

      Yes, I love you, dear,
Heaven knows, a hundred times more than myself;
But . . .   115

PAULINA

  But my desolateness moves you not!
You have your secrets which are barred to me!
What a great proof of love! Husband, I beg,
Devote to my affection this one day.

POLYEUCTUS

A dream affrights you?

PAULINA

          It presages naught,
120 I know; but after all I love you, and
I fear.

POLYEUCTUS

Fear not an absence of an hour.
Farewell. Your tears are far too powerful;
Only by flight can I withstand their sway.

Scene Three

PAULINA, STRATONICE

PAULINA

125 Go, spurn my tears. Go, run and haste to meet
The death predicted by the gods to me.
Follow this agent[1] of your evil fate
Who may deliver you to murderous hands.
You see how, Stratonice, the times are;
130 This is the power we wield over men's minds;
This is what's left to us, the usual end
Of the love offered, the vows made to us.
While they're still courting us, we're sovereigns,
And, till they've won us, we are queens for them;
135 But after marriage, it is *they* who reign.

STRATONICE

No. Polyeuctus is not out of love.
If he does not show total confidence,
If he goes off despite your tears, he's wise;
Sorrow not at it, but like me assume
140 It's better if he does not tell you why;
There must be reasons for behaving so.
A husband should keep something from us, and
Sometimes he should be free, and should not stoop
Always to give account of every move.

    1. Nearchus.

You two have but one heart which feels the same   145
Reverses, but which functions differently,
And hymen's law, by which you two are joined,
Does not bid *him* to tremble when *you* do.
What affrights *us* cannot disquiet *him*.
He is Armenian. *You* were born in Rome.   150
And our two nations, as you doubtless know,
Do not see eye to eye on such affairs.
To *us* a dream appears ridiculous;
It causes us no scruple, hope or fear;
But it is firmly held, in Rome, to be   155
The faithful mirror of our destiny.

PAULINA

However little you may credit it,
I feel that your dismay would equal mine
If such grim horrors had assailed your mind,
Ev'n if I just recounted them to you.   160

STRATONICE

To tell one's troubles often brings relief.

PAULINA

Listen; but I must tell you something more;
If you're to understand a woeful tale,
Know then my weakness and my earlier love.
A virtuous woman can without a blush   165
Confess the senses' force which reason quells.
Only in these attacks does virtue shine,
And hearts are suspect if they've never fought.
In Rome where I was born these ill-starred eyes
Entranced the heart of a brave Roman knight.[1]   170
Severus he was called. Forgive my sighs,
Torn from me by a name I still hold dear.

1. In the Roman Empire, the knights constituted the minor aristocracy.

STRATONICE

Is he the man who, laying down his life,
Saved from his foes Emperor Decius,[1] who
175 Then, dying, wrested vict'ry from them, and
From Persia turned the tide of victory?
Among the many victims of his sword
He was not found, at least not recognized;
And did not Decius for such great exploits
180 Erect imposing, empty monuments?

PAULINA

Alas! 'twas he, and never did our Rome
Produce a greater soul or finer man.
You know him. So I need not speak of him.
I loved him, and he well deserved my love;
185 But what avail deserts when one is poor?
His qualities were great, his fortunes mean.
An obstacle invincible, and one
Fathers rarely forgive in suitors.

STRATONICE

What
A fine occasion for long constancy!

PAULINA

190 Say rather for resistance base and mad.
Whatever fruit a girl can reap from it,
It's but a virtue for a rebel heart.
Immersed in passion for Severus, I
Waited until my father would select
195 A husband for me. Never did my will
Avow th' endearing treason of my eyes.
He ruled my heart, my thoughts and my desires;
I did not hide all that I felt from him.
We sighed together and bemoaned our woes;
200 Instead of hope, tears were his only mead;
And so, despite these sweet and favouring sighs,
My father and my duty won the day.

1. Decius was emperor from A.D. 244 to 251.

I left this perfect lover, left my Rome,
Following my father here as governor.
He in despair went off to seek renown   205
By dying in the wars a glorious death.
The rest you know. On my arrival here,
I met my Polyeuctus, won his heart.
And, as he's head of the nobility,
My father was delighted at the match,   210
Imagining that the connection would
Swell his prestige and his authority.
The courtship was approved; the marriage planned,
And, since thus Polyeuctus had
My hand, I gave him out of duty all   215
The other had been giv'n from tenderness.
If you can doubt it, judge by the alarm
With which, on this grim day, my soul's oppressed.

STRATONICE

Clearly enough it shows your love for him.
But what's this dream which now affrights you so?   220

PAULINA

Last night I saw ill-starred Severus, with
Avenging sword in hand, inflamed with wrath.
He was not clad in those depressing rags
Which sorrow-laden shades bring from the tomb.
He was not pierced by glorious wounds which gave   225
Renown undying, cutting short his days.
He seemed triumphant, as when Caesar rides
On his victorious chariot into Rome.
After the fear which this grim sight inspired,
'Give whom you will the favour due to me,   230
Ingrate,' he said to me. 'When this day ends,
At leisure mourn *him* you preferred to me.'
I shuddered at these words aghast. And then
An impious band of Christians, to advance
The execution of this fateful doom,   235
Cast Polyeuctus at his rival's feet.
I called my father to his help at once.

Alas! This is what drives me to complete despair.
My very father, then, dagger in hand,
240 Entered with arm upraised to pierce his breast.
My overwhelming sorrow blurred the scene;
My husband's blood sated their furious rage.
I know not when or how they killed him, but
I know that all of them have worked his death.
245 *That* was my dream.

STRATONICE
            Truly, most ominous;
But you must grapple firmly with these fears.
The vision in itself may horrify,
But should not cause you terror. Can
A dead man or a father frighten you?
250 He likes your husband, is revered by him.
And he himself chose you this husband as
A sure and solid anchor for his power.

PAULINA
He's said as much and laughs at my alarms.
But still I fear the Christians' plots and spells.
255 They're mustering to take revenge upon
My husband for the blood my father's shed.

STRATONICE
Their sect is impious, sacrilegious, mad,
And uses witchcraft in its sacrifice;
But it destroys our altars, nothing more.
260 Its hate is for the gods, and not for man.
However brutally they are repressed,
They suffer uncomplaining, die with joy,
And, since they first were classed as traitors, they
Have never been accused of murder.

PAULINA
                    Hush!
265 Here is my father.

54

Scene Four

FELIX, ALBINUS, PAULINA, STRATONICE

FELIX
Into what strange fears
Your dream has plunged us both! And how I dread
Its grim fulfilment as it seems to near.

PAULINA
What makes you feel thus suddenly alarmed!

FELIX
Severus is not dead.

PAULINA
And what of that?

FELIX
He is the Emperor Decius' favourite.   270

PAULINA
When he has saved him from his enemies,
He well may hope for such distinction. For
Fate, often cruel to nobility,
Sometimes resolves to do it justice.

FELIX
                           He's
Expected here.   275

PAULINA
He is?

FELIX
You'll see him.

PAULINA
                    That
Would be the end. But whence derives this news?

FELIX

Albinus met him as he neared the town.
The courtiers crowd around him on his way,
And clearly show his rank and his prestige.

[*To* ALBINUS]

280 Repeat to her his retinue's account.

ALBINUS

You know about that memorable day
Which by his death gained us the victory.
The Emperor taken captive, freed by him,
Rallied Rome's forces which were losing heart.
285 He was by weight of numbers overpowered.
You know the honours that were done to him
When he could not be found among the dead.
In fact, the Persian king had borne him off.
Witnessing his exploits and valiancy,
290 That monarch wished to see the hero. He,
Placed in the royal tent, riddled with blows,
Seemed dead, but all were envious of him. There,
He soon displayed signs of recovery.
The noble-hearted prince was overjoyed,
295 And so, despite his latest setback, he[1]
Honoured the gallantry which led to it.
He[1] had him tended well, but secretly,
And in a month the patient was restored.
He[1] offered dignities, alliance,[2] gold
300 To win Severus over – all in vain.
And, having lavished praise on this rebuff,
Proposed to Decius plans for an exchange.
At once the Emperor offered to return
The king's own brother, any hundred chiefs.
305 Thus was Severus handed back to camp
Where he received his valiancy's reward.
The Emperor's favour was the fitting prize.
Fighting resumed, and we were caught off guard.
But this misfortune merely swelled his fame.

1. The Persian king.
2. Alliance by marriage.

He alone saved the day, reaped victory 310
So full, so sweeping, with such fine exploits,
That we were offered tribute and made peace.
The Emperor, with unbounded love for him,
Dispatched him to Armenia after this.
He comes to bring us news of this success, 315
And sacrifice in homage to the gods.

FELIX

O heav'n! how low my fortunes are reduced.

ALBINUS

That's what I learned, Sir, from the retinue,
And I have rushed to bear the news to you.

FELIX

Without a doubt, he comes to marry you. 320
This sacrifice is but a trifle and
A pretext. It is love that brings him here.

PAULINA

That might well be. He loved me tenderly.

FELIX

What will he not, in his resentment, do?
How far will his revenge be carried by 325
His righteous wrath and all his influence?
He'll ruin us.

PAULINA

    He's much too chivalrous
For that.

FELIX

   In vain you reassure me. He
Will ruin us. How bitterly I rue
Not to have loved his virtue unadorned. 330
You have obeyed me, daughter, all too well.
Duty betrayed you and your sentiments.
How your rebellion would have aided me!

You would have saved me from my wretched plight.
335 If still some hope remains, it lies alone
In the full power he gave you over him.
Exploit for me his love for you. Extract
From my misfortune's source a remedy.

PAULINA

What! *I'm* to see again the man I loved,
340 Expose myself to eyes which pierce my heart?
I am a woman, know my weaknesses.
I feel my heart already beat for him.
It will no doubt, despite my troth, express
A sigh unworthy of both you and me.
345 I will not see him.

FELIX

Show your self-control.

PAULINA

He still attracts me. I'm a woman still.
Given the power his eyes had over me,
I dare not vouch for my resistance. Hence,
I will not see him.

FELIX

Daughter, but you must,
350 Or you'll betray your father and your kin.

PAULINA

It is for me t' obey, since you command.
But what grave perils you involve me in.

FELIX

I know your virtue.

PAULINA

Doubtless it will win.
It's not the outcome which my soul redoubts,
355 I fear this combat and these violent storms
Which the rebellious senses rouse within.

But, since I have to fight a foe I love,
Let me now steel myself against my heart,
And have some leisure to prepare for him.

FELIX
I'll go and welcome him beyond the walls;   360
Meantime muster your strength in disarray.
Remember, in your hands you hold our fate.

PAULINA
I shall subdue my feelings once again,
And be a victim of your stern commands.

ACT TWO

Scene One

SEVERUS, FABIAN

SEVERUS

365 While Felix now settles the sacrifice,
Let's seize a chance propitious for my love.
Let's see Paulina, and let's pay to her
The sovereign homage we shall pay the gods.
I've not concealed from you what brought me here;
370 The rest's a pretext to relieve my heart;
I come to sacrifice, but it's for *her*
I lay upon the altar my desires.

FABIAN

You'll see her, Sir.

SEVERUS

       I will, O crowning joy!
My darling will agree to meeting me.
375 But do I still mean anything to her?
Can one espy some vestiges of love?
Does my arrival move, transport her heart?
Can all my hopes thereafter be fulfilled?
For I would rather perish than misuse
380 The letters writ to help me marry her,
Which are for Felix, not to force her hand.
My heart was always ruled by her desires;
If *hers* was by my ill-starred fortune changed,
I'd overcome my feelings and desist.

FABIAN

385 You'll see her, Sir. That's all that I can say.

SEVERUS

Whence comes it that you shudder deep and sigh?
Does she not love me any longer? Speak.

FABIAN

If I may urge you, see her not again.
Bear your addresses to a higher rank;
You'll find others enough to court in Rome;   390
And, giv'n your present power and prestige,
Ev'n the most eminent will smile upon
Your love.

SEVERUS

      My soul will never sink so low.
Should I regard her as beneath me now?
She acted better. I should copy her.   395
My good luck serves only to merit her.
Let's see her. I dislike this talk. Let's go
And place my glorious fortune at her feet.
I met with it in th' auspicious wars,
Seeking a death worthy of my beloved.   400
My rank is, therefore, and my favour hers.
In short, there's naught I do not owe to her.

FABIAN

No, yet again I say, don't see her, Sir.

SEVERUS

Come, you exaggerate. Explain yourself.
Was her reply to my request so cool?   405

FABIAN

I tremble to inform you. She's ...

SEVERUS

        What?

FABIAN

          Wed.

SEVERUS

Ah! lend me your support. I'm thunderstruck,
All the more so, since taken by surprise.

FABIAN

Where is your old nobility of heart?

SEVERUS

410 Constancy's difficult in such a pass;
Great hearts are overwhelmed by thunderbolts,
And the most resolute are all unmanned.
For, when a soul's by such a love possessed,
It's stunned by death less than by sudden blows.
415 The world turns ashen when I hear such news.
Paulina married!

FABIAN

Fifteen days ago.
And Polyeuctus, an Armenian lord,
One of the highest, revels in this joy.

SEVERUS

At least I cannot blame her for her choice.
420 He is renowned and is of royal blood.
Weak solace for an ill past remedy!
Paulina, someone else has won your hand!
You who, despite me, brought me back to life,
O destiny, who gave my love new hope,
425 Take back the favour which you lent to me,
And give me back the death you robbed me of.
Let's see her, though, and, in this dismal spot,
Let's die for good, saying farewell to her.
So, bearing off her image to the dead,
430 My heart, with its last sigh, will worship her.

FABIAN

My lord, consider . . .

SEVERUS

I've considered all.
What is there a despairing heart can fear?
She has agreed to see me.

FABIAN
But . . .

SEVERUS
                    What then?

FABIAN
This heartache will be ev'n more harrowing.

SEVERUS
It's not an ill I would be cured of. All   435
I want's to see her, long for her and die.

FABIAN
When she appears, your self-control will snap.
A suitor, losing all, does not forgive.
He lets his passion carry him away,
And vents his spite in curses and abuse.   440

SEVERUS
Judge me not so. For I respect her still.
Ev'n in my deep despair I worship her.
And what can I reproach her with? What can
I charge her with who gave no pledge to me?
There is no breach of faith or fickleness.   445
Her duty, my mishaps, her father – all
Betrayed me, but duty and father were
Right, and my mishaps were alone to blame.
A little less good fortune earlier
Would have resolved the rest, secured her hand.   450
Too lucky but too late, I win her not.
Let me then see her, long for her and die.

FABIAN
Yes, I'll assure her that, in this extreme,
You're strong enough to keep your heart in check.
Like me, she feared these first reactions which   455
A sudden loss causes a lover and
Whose violence causes such disarray
Without the loved one's presence heightening them.

SEVERUS

I see her coming.

FABIAN

Sir, remember that ...

SEVERUS

460 Alas! she loves another and is his.

Scene Two

SEVERUS, PAULINA, STRATONICE, FABIAN

PAULINA

Yes, Sir, I love him and make no excuse.
Let anyone but I delude your heart.
I am straightforward and without reserve.
Your rumoured death's not what defeated you;
465 If heav'n in my own hands had placed my choice,
To you alone I would have giv'n my hand,
And all the rigour of your earlier fate
Against your merit would have fought in vain.
In you I found virtues outstanding, which
470 Would rank you higher than the greatest kings;
But, since I had to bow to other laws,
Whichever man my father chose for me
(Ev'n had you joined the lustre of a crown
To all the power your valiancy confers),
475 If I had met you and had hated him,
I would have sighed, but I would have obeyed,
And reason, sov'reign of my passions' moods,
Would have reproved my sighs, dispelled my hate.

SEVERUS

How fortunate you are! A sigh or two
480 Can remedy all your unhappiness!
Thus, always perfect, queen of your desires,
The greatest changes find you resolute;

From the most ardent love your spirits move
To mere indifference, perhaps contempt,
And how your firmness changes, effortless,   485
Your favour to disdain, your love to hate.
How even a tithe of all your moral strength
Would ease the sufferings of my prostrate heart!
A sigh, a tear's regret would have, by now,
Cured me completely of my loss of you;   490
My reason could have crushed a waning love,
Made me indifferent, made me ev'n forget,
And, modelling myself on you thenceforth,
I would be happy in another's arms.
Lovable lady who entranced me so,   495
If this is love, were you in love with me?

PAULINA

I've shown you all too well I really was.
If I could stifle the remains of love
What rig'rous torments, gods, I would avoid!
My reason, true, subdues my sentiments,   500
But yet, whatever its authority,
It does not rule; it acts the tyrant. Thus,
Although I'm outwardly impassive, I
Am inwardly all uproar and revolt.
I'm drawn to you by some mysterious spell.   505
My reason's strong, but all your qualities
Are still as when they set my heart on fire,
All the more powerful because they shine
Enhanced by power and glory's brilliancy,
Draw victory unfailing in your train,   510
They have a clearer value and have not
Deceived the glorious hopes I placed in them.
But that same virtue triumphing in Rome,
Which here subjects me to a husband's rule,
Repulses still the onslaught of these charms.   515
It rends my heart, but does not weaken it.
It's that same virtue, cruel to us both,
Which *then* you praised, while cursing its effects.
Complain of it again, but praise its strength,
Which triumphs over both my heart and yours;   520

A wavering, less sincere integrity
Would not have merited Severus' love.

SEVERUS

Ah! pardon one who, blinded by his grief,
Sees nothing else but grief unlimited.
525 I called inconstancy, and thought a crime,
This effort of sublime integrity.
I beg you, show my grieving senses not
The greatness of my loss and of your worth.
Hide out of pity this self-mastery,
530 Which swells my love, ev'n when it severs us.
Show me some defects able, in their turn,
To dull my heartache and my love.

PAULINA

Alas!

Self-mastery, though it's invincible,
Shows but too well too sensitive a soul.
535 These tears are witness, and these craven sighs
At cruel memories of days gone by –
This meeting's searing outcome against which
My duty offers only slight defence!
But, if you value this integrity,
540 Leave me its glory; cease from seeing me.
Spare me these tears which flow but to my shame;
Spare me a passion I can scarce control;
Lastly, spare me these woeful meetings which
Can only add to both our torments.

SEVERUS

What!

545 Give up the one delight that's left to me?

PAULINA

Save yourself from what must destroy us both.

SEVERUS

Is this my labours' and my love's reward?

66

PAULINA

Yes, the one remedy for all our ills.

SEVERUS

I'll die of mine. Cherish their memory.

PAULINA

I'll vanquish mine. They'd sully my renown.　　　550

SEVERUS

Ah! since your honour passes sentence on
My woe, I yield to its authority.
There's naught this honour can't obtain from me.
It gives me back desire to tend my own.
Farewell. I go to seek amidst the wars　　　555
The fame undying of a glorious death,
And, by a memorable end, fulfil
The expectations of my first exploits,
Provided that, after this fatal blow,
I yet have life enough to search for death.　　　560

PAULINA

And I, whose suffering grows with seeing you,
Will shun you even at the sacrifice;
And, closeted with my regrets, I shall
Offer the gods my secret prayers for you.

SEVERUS

May the just heav'ns, pleased with my ruin, heap　　　565
Good luck, long life, upon your spouse and you.

PAULINA

May you, after so many mishaps, find
Happiness worthy of your qualities.

SEVERUS

But I found that in *you*.

PAULINA

　　　My father's will . . .

SEVERUS

570 O duty! how you fill me with despair.
Farewell, my virtuous and entrancing love.

PAULINA

Suitor, too perfect and ill-starred, farewell.

Scene Three

PAULINA, STRATONICE

STRATONICE

I've pitied both of you and weep for you;
But now your mind is free from its alarms.
575 It's clear to me your dream is meaningless.
Severus does not come with sword in hand.

PAULINA

Give me some respite if you've pitied me;
At my grief's zenith you revive my fear.
Give my disturbed spirit some relief,
580 And do not crush me under mounting ills.

STRATONICE

What! are you still afraid?

PAULINA

I tremble still,
And, though on slender ground, I'm terrified;
This groundless terror ceaselessly brings back
The nightmare pictures I beheld last night.

STRATONICE

585 Severus has a noble heart.

PAULINA

And yet
My husband, dripping blood, still harrows me.

STRATONICE

This rival, though, wishes him happiness.[1]

PAULINA

In case of need, he would support him, but
Whether my view is false or accurate,
His presence here must always weigh on me.   590
Though his intentions may be chivalrous,
He's powerful, he loves me, and he comes
To marry me.

Scene Four

POLYEUCTUS, NEARCHUS, PAULINA, STRATONICE

POLYEUCTUS

It's time you dried your tears.
Come, end your grief, and let your fears be calmed.
Despite your gods' misleading warnings, I   595
Am still alive. You see me back again.

PAULINA

The day is far from done. What chills me most,
Already half the warnings have come true.
I thought Severus dead, and now he's here.

POLYEUCTUS

I know. But still that does not worry me.   600
Whoe'er Severus be, your father rules
In Melitene and I'm much esteemed.
I greatly doubt that there is cause to fear
Treason from such a noble heart as his.
I was assured that he had called on you.   605
I came to honour him as he deserves.

PAULINA

He's just gone off, saddened and much dismayed,
But I've prevailed on him to keep away.

1. See lines 567-8.

POLYEUCTUS

You think already I am jealous.

PAULINA

If
610 I did, I would insult all three of us.
I shield my peace of mind which he disturbs.
The staunchest virtue does not challenge fate.
Who bares himself to peril courts defeat;
If I may speak with an unfeigning soul,
615 Since I responded to his qualities,
Present, he still can exercise his spell.
One blushes, too, when taken unawares;
One suffers having to defend oneself,
And, although virtue triumphs in the end,
620 The fight is shameful, vict'ry dearly bought.

POLYEUCTUS

O perfect virtue and integrity!
How much Severus must regret his loss!
How happy am I at your sacrifice;
What balm you spread over my loving heart!
625 The more I see my defects, your deserts,
The more I marvel . . .

Scene Five

POLYEUCTUS, PAULINA, NEARCHUS, STRATONICE,
CLEON

CLEON

Felix summons you.
The victim's chosen, and the people kneel,
And they await you for the sacrifice.

POLYEUCTUS

Go, we will follow.

[To PAULINA]
Are you coming too?

PAULINA

Severus' love on seeing me revives.   630
I'll keep my word to him and stay away.
Farewell. You'll see him there. Think of his power.
Recall again his boundless influence.

POLYEUCTUS

In his high standing there is naught to fear;
And, as I know how chivalrous he is,   635
We two will only vie in courtesy.

Scene Six

POLYEUCTUS, NEARCHUS

NEARCHUS

Whither away?

POLYEUCTUS
I'm for the temple bound.

NEARCHUS

What! mingle with a band of infidels?
Do you forget you are a Christian?

POLYEUCTUS
You,
Who made me one, do you remember?   640

NEARCHUS
All
The false gods I abhor.

POLYEUCTUS
No more than I.

NEARCHUS

Their cult is impious.

POLYEUCTUS

And baneful too.

NEARCHUS

Then flee their altars.

POLYEUCTUS

I will tear them down,
And in their temple die or stamp them out.
645 Come, dear Nearchus, come, let's openly
Defy idolatry, profess our faith.
This, heaven expects. We must fulfil its hopes.
I have just sworn it, and will keep my word.
I thank the God whom you revealed to me
650 For this prompt opportunity in which
His charity, ready to crown me, deigns
To put my new found credo to the test.

NEARCHUS

Your zeal's too ardent. You must let it cool.

POLYEUCTUS

One cannot have too much of it for God.

NEARCHUS

655 You'll meet your death.

POLYEUCTUS

I seek to die for Him.

NEARCHUS

And if the heart should flinch?

POLYEUCTUS

He'll be my stay.

NEARCHUS

God does not bid you hasten to your death.

POLYEUCTUS

The more it's willed, the more the merit earned.

NEARCHUS

One need but wait for it, not seek it out.

POLYEUCTUS

One suffers when one dares not offer up   660
Oneself.

NEARCHUS

    Death's certain in the temple.

POLYEUCTUS

                But
Already up in heav'n a crown's prepared.

NEARCHUS

One must deserve it by a holy life.

POLYEUCTUS

My crimes, if I live on, may rob me of
The prize. Why hazard then what death ensures?   665
When it unlocks the heav'ns, can death be harsh?
I am a Christian and completely so.
I long to show by deeds my new found faith.
Who flees is craven, and his faith is dead.

NEARCHUS

Husband your life. It's vital ev'n for God.   670
Live to protect the Christians here.

POLYEUCTUS

              My death
Will spur them on and fortify them more.

NEARCHUS

And so you wish to die.

POLYEUCTUS

And you to live?

NEARCHUS

Frankly, I find it hard to follow you.
675 I fear I would succumb upon the rack.

POLYEUCTUS

Who walks with confidence need fear no fall.
God will, if asked, impart his boundless strength.
He who fears to deny Him inwardly
Already does so, doubting of his faith.

NEARCHUS

680 Who nothing fears is overconfident.

POLYEUCTUS

I count not on my weakness, but His grace.
Far from you urging *me*, *I* urge you on!
Whence comes this coldness?

NEARCHUS

Even God feared death.[1]

POLYEUCTUS

He offered Himself, though. Let's follow Him;
685 On mountains of demolished idols, raise
Altars. Let us (I still recall your words)
For Him neglect wife, property and rank
And for His glory risk and suffer all.[2]
What have you done with this abounding love
690 You augured me and which I wish for you?
Are you not jealous, if you feel it still,
That, barely Christian, I have more of it?

1. Jesus on the Mount of Olives.
2. See lines 75–6.

NEARCHUS

You come straight from your baptism. You're inspired
By God's own grace, not weakened yet by crime.
As it is still entire, so is its power,   695
And, to its ardour, all seems possible
But that same grace, in me diminishèd,
And by a thousand sins whittled away,
Acts in great crises so halfheartedly,
Its flabbiness thinks all impossible.   700
These craven pretexts, this base spinelessness
Are punishments for one's transgressions, but
God, in whom always one must place one's trust,
Has given me your help to buoy me up.
Let's go, dear Polyeuctus, openly   705
To brave idolatry, profess our faith.
May I show *you* how to bear suffering,
As you've shown *me* to offer yourself up!

POLYEUCTUS

In this elation heav'n inspires in you,
I recognize Nearchus, weep for joy.   710
Let's waste no time. The sacrifice will start.
Let's go and to the true God testify.
Let's trample on this pseudo-thunderbolt
With which they arm a bit of rotten wood,
And bring some light where darkness reigned before;   715
Let's break these gods of metal and of stone,
Give up our lives to this celestial urge,
And make God triumph. Leave the rest to Him.

NEARCHUS

Come, let us blazon forth His glorious might,
And die for Him as He has died for us.[1]   720

---

1. This line is taken from the 1643 edition, as the final version
(adopted for this translation) is flat.

ACT THREE

Scene One

PAULINA

How many worries, cloudy, vague and blurred,
Evoke swift changing images within!
Sweet peace of mind for which I dared to hope,
How slow you are to shed your light on them!
725 A thousand impulses, born of my fears,
Destroy each other in my storm-tossed heart.
No hope wells up which I dare count upon,
No terror reigns in which I dare believe.
My mind, embracing its imaginings,
730 Sees now my ruin, now my happiness,
And, tantalized by their elusive shapes,
Cannot indulge in either hope or fear.
Severus clouds my vision ceaselessly.
I hope in his nobility, but fear
735 His jealousy. With an indifferent eye,
My husband cannot see his rival here.
As, between rivals, hate is natural,
Meeting, perhaps they'll come to blows. *One* sees
The *other* hold what he thinks should be his;
740 The *other*, one who in despair will stop
At naught. Whatever wisdom guides their souls,
One takes offence; the *other's* envious.
The shame of an affront which each one thinks
Received (or just about to be received),
745 Exhausting all their patience from the start,
Gives rise to anger and mistrust, and thus,
Possessing both of them despite themselves,
Gives them both up to their resentment. But
Into what curious fantasies I stray,
750 And how unfair to these two men I am!
As if these glorious rivals' chivalry
Could never rise about these sordid flaws!

The soul of each is master of itself,
And is too lofty for such baseness. They
Meet at the sacrifice as gentlemen.   755
But woe is me! They'll meet. That's fatal. What
Avails my husband Melitene if
Severus brings to bear the might of Rome,
If Felix rules and fears this favourite,
And now regrets his choice of husband? Hence   760
My slender hope burns only fitfully.
It straight miscarries and gives way to fear;
What ought to strengthen it dispels it quite.
Gods! May my fears prove baseless in the end.

Scene Two

PAULINA, STRATONICE

PAULINA

But tell us, Stratonice, what occurred.   765
How ended this imposing sacrifice?
These rivals, then, met at the temple?

STRATONICE
                              Ah!
Paulina!

PAULINA
          Were my wishes, then, deceived?
I see your visage clouded over. Say,
Did they fall out?   770

STRATONICE
           Nearchus, Polyeuctus,
The Christians ...

PAULINA
          Speak. The Christians ...

77

STRATONICE

I am dumb.

PAULINA

What strange forebodings now assail my soul.

STRATONICE

You could not have a juster cause for them.

PAULINA

Say, have they murdered him?

STRATONICE

That would be naught.
775 Your dream's all true. Your husband is no more . . .

PAULINA

He's dead?

STRATONICE

No, he still lives, but, useless tears!
This godlike and high-hearted figure is
Not worthy of Paulina or to live.
Gone is that husband who entranced you so.
780 He is an enemy of State and gods,
Wicked, rebellious, infamous and false,
A villain, scoundrel, coward, criminal,
To all right-thinking men a loathsome scourge,
An impious knave; in short, a Christian.

PAULINA

That
785 Would have sufficed. You could have spared th' abuse.

STRATONICE

Are all these names, applied to Christians, wrong?

PAULINA

He's what you say if he's embraced their faith,
But he's my husband, and you speak to *me*.

STRATONICE

Consider but the God whom he adores.

PAULINA

I loved him out of duty. That endures.   790

STRATONICE

He gives you reason now for hate. If false
To all our gods, he would be false to you.

PAULINA

I still would love him were he false to me.
And, if at so much love you're stupefied,
My duty does not turn on *his*. He may   795
Fail in it if he will. *I* must do *mine*.
What if he loved another? Would I then
Follow his libertine example? No.
Be he a Christian, I'll not shrink from him.
I cherish him. I hate his misbeliefs.   800
But is my father angry at this change?

STRATONICE

He's furious inwardly, bursting with rage,
And yet some vestiges of friendship still
For Polyeuctus show some pity. He
Will not allow justice to take its course   805
Until your husband's seen Nearchus die.

PAULINA

He's in it too?

STRATONICE

                    Nearchus is to blame.
This is the fruit of their old friendship. Yes,
Despite his friend's resistance, this false knave,
Wresting him from you, dragged him baptismwards.   810
That is the great, mysterious secret which
Your prying love could not extract from him.

PAULINA

You blamed me for insisting overmuch.

STRATONICE

Such a disaster could not be foreseen.

PAULINA

815 Before abandoning myself to grief,
I must assay the power of my tears.
As daughter and as wife I hope my pleas
Will win a husband over and will move
A father. If in either case they fail,
820 I will take counsel only of despair.
What did they do, though, at the temple? Speak.

STRATONICE

It's an unparalleled impiety.
I cannot without shuddering think of it,
And fear I err merely in telling you.
825 Learn in a word their brutish insolence.
The priest had scarcely hushed the gathered throng
And turned his visage to the eastern sky
Than both of them displayed their disrespect.
At every turn in all our rites, they vied
830 In flaunting their destructive madness. They
Openly mocked the sacred mysteries
And scorned the gods the gath'ring called upon.
The people murmured. Felix was dismayed.
But both stepped up their gross irreverence.
835 'What!' Polyeuctus said, raising his voice,
'Do you adore idols of wood or stone?'
Dispense me from repeating blasphemies
Which they both vomited at Jove himself.
Adult'ry, incest, were the least of them.
840 'Hear,' he then said, 'Hear, people all. The God
Of Polyeuctus and Nearchus is
Of heav'n and earth the ruler absolute,
Being supreme, and lord of destiny,
Eternal principle and sovereign end.

It is the Christians' God we here should thank   845
For vict'ries giv'n to Decius Emperor.
He's the sole arbiter of battle. He
Can grant success but can abase as well.
His kindness, pow'r and justice are immense.
He alone punishes, alone rewards.   850
In vain you worship monsters powerless.'
They on the wine and incense throw themselves,
Scatt'ring the holy vessels to the ground,
Fearing not Felix nor the thunderbolt,
The two fanatics storm the altar. Heav'n!   855
Was ever such a sacrilegious sight?
We see the statue of great Jove himself,
By impious hands o'erturned, come crashing down.
The temple is profaned, the rites disturbed,
The flight and clamour of a mob distraught   860
Which fears the wrath of heav'n will fall on it.
Felix . . . But here he is. He'll tell you all.

PAULINA

How sombre, overwrought he looks, and how
Despair and rage are painted on his face.

Scene Three

FELIX, PAULINA, STRATONICE

FELIX

To dare to manifest such insolence!   865
In public! In my sight! He'll die for it.

PAULINA

Suffer your daughter to embrace your knees.

FELIX

I mean Nearchus, not your husband. He,
Howe'er unworthy as a son-in-law,
Still has some claim to my affection. No.   870

His heinous crime and my unbounded woe
Have not wiped out the love which chose him.[1]

PAULINA

This
I had expected from a father's heart.

FELIX

I could have sacrificed him to my wrath.
875 You doubtless know to what appalling lengths
The fury of his impious daring went.
You must at least have heard reports from her.
[*Pointing to* STRATONICE.]

PAULINA

I know he'll see Nearchus put to death.

FELIX

He will be clearer what he ought to do
880 On seeing slain the man who led him on.
At that grim fate which re-enacts his own,
The fear of death and the desire to live
Will unreservedly win back his soul.
The sight of death cancels the wish for it.
885 Examples are of more effect than threats.
Misguided ardour soon will turn to ice,
And soon his heart, disquieted, will ask
Remission for his grave impiety.

PAULINA

You hope that he will change his feelings?

FELIX

Yes.
890 Nearchus' death will make him see the light.

PAULINA

It ought to. But what hopes have I, alas?
What grievous dangers does my husband run

1. As his son-in-law.

82

If I must hope from his inconstancy
The boon I hoped for from a father's heart?

FELIX

I'm too indulgent letting him avoid   895
Sentence of death if he will but repent.
The same crimes carry the same penalties.
Discriminating,[1] I have sacrificed
The course of justice to a father's love.
For him I've made myself a criminal,   900
And I expected from you, 'midst your fears,
More gratitude and somewhat less complaints.

PAULINA

Why should I thank a man who gave me naught?
I know a Christian's temper and resolve.
He's obdurate until the end. To ask   905
For his repentance is to will his death.

FELIX

His pardon's in his hands. It's up to him.

PAULINA

Make it complete.

FELIX

He can do that himself.

PAULINA

Do not abandon him to his wild sect.

FELIX

I to the laws abandon him which I   910
Respect.

PAULINA

And thus you treat a son-in-law?

1. Between Polyeuctus and Nearchus.

FELIX

Let him do for himself as much as I
For him.

PAULINA

He's blinded.

FELIX

Which he wants to be.
One will not recognize one's error, loving it.

PAULINA

915 Father, in the gods' name . . .

FELIX

Call not upon
These gods, defence of whom demands his death.

PAULINA

They listen to our prayers.

FELIX

Well, let him pray.

PAULINA

Then in the Emperor's name whose place you hold . . .

FELIX

His power is in my hand. He gave it me
920 Only to use against his enemies.

PAULINA

Is Polyeuctus one?

FELIX

All Christians are.

PAULINA

Forget these cruel maxims in his case.
By wedding me, he has become your kin.

FELIX

His grievous fault obliterates his rank.
When treason is combined with sacrilege,   925
No kin, no friendship, can be privileged.

PAULINA

Your verdict's harsh.

FELIX
                    Less so than is his crime.

PAULINA

Alas! my hideous nightmare has come true.
You wreak your daughter's downfall just like his.

FELIX

The gods and Caesar come before my kin.   930

PAULINA

What! our joint downfall cannot stay your hand?

FELIX

I have the gods and Decius both to dread.
But we've still nothing serious to fear.
Think you he will continue to be blind?
If he seemed bent on racing to his doom,   935
That is the convert's first fine rapture.

PAULINA
                    If
You still are fond of him, give up this hope
That twice in one short day he'll change his creed.
Christians are fashioned of much sterner stuff,
And can't be lightly swayed as you expect.   940
It's not an error he was suckled on,
Which, without analysing, he's embraced.
If he's turned Christian, he was bent on it,
And wrecked the temple with determined mind.
You must assume he's like the rest of them.   945

For *them*, death's neither shameful nor the end.
They covet glory, scorn the gods on high;
Blind to the earth, they set their heart on heav'n;
Believing death opens the door to it,
950 Tormented, rent in twain, no matter what,
Tortures to them are what our pleasures are,
And lead to their desires' accomplishment.
The vilest death they christen martyrdom.

FELIX

Then Polyeuctus will be satisfied!
955 Enough of this.

FELIX

    Father . . .

Scene Four

FELIX, ALBINUS, PAULINA, STRATONICE

FELIX

    Is justice done?

ALBINUS

Nearchus, Sir, has paid the penalty.

FELIX

Our Polyeuctus saw the man dispatched?

ALBINUS

He saw it, but, alas! with envious eyes.
He burns to die instead of pulling back;
960 Instead of flinching, he is more resolved.

PAULINA

I told you so, my father. Once again,
If ever I have shown respect for you,
If you've esteemed him, if you've cherished him . . .

86

FELIX

You love a shameful husband far too much.

PAULINA

My love is guiltless, since you gave him me,   965
Chosen by you as most illustrious;
And I, accepting him, have crushed my love
For one who most deserved to win my heart.
In view of this obedience, prompt and blind,
Which I have always shown my father, if   970
Over my heart your power has been complete,
Let me in turn wield power over you.
By your much-to-be-feared authority,
By all my feelings I've been forced to curb,
Do not withdraw your gifts from me. For they   975
Have cost so dear that now I value them.

FELIX

You press me hard. Although my heart is soft,
I pity only when I want to. Put
Your sad affliction to a better use.
To work on me is losing time and tears;   980
I want my pity under my control,
And disavow it when extorted. Hence,
Prepare to see this wretched Christian, and
Exert your pressure when I've finished mine.
Go. Irk no more a loving father. Try   985
To make your husband gain his liberty.
I'll have him presently escorted here.
Meantime, withdraw. I wish to talk to him.
                    [*Pointing to* ALBINUS.]

PAULINA

I beg you. Let . . .

FELIX

                    Leave us alone, I say.
Your grief offends me, though it saddens me.   990

To win your husband over, spare no pains.
The less you say, the more you'll win my ear.

Scene Five

FELIX, ALBINUS

FELIX

How did he die? Speak.

ALBINUS

      As an impious brute,
995 Without regret, cry or astonishment,
Clinging to error, obdurate; in short,
He died a Christian, full of blasphemy.

FELIX

And his accomplice?

ALBINUS

      Nothing touches him.
Far from unmanning him, this heartens him;
1000 We had to drag him from the scaffold, Sir.
He's in the prison where I had him led;
You still are far from having worn him down.

FELIX

Unhappy I!

ALBINUS

Everyone pities you.

FELIX

One does not know the ills which rack my heart.
1005 By countless thoughts my soul is buffeted;
By countless cares it is disquieted.
I am possessed and torn by love and hate,
By fear and hope, by sorrow and by joy.

Feelings incredible come over me,
Some of them violent, some pitiful,   1010
Some generous I dare not act upon,
And some despicable which make me blush.
I love this wretch I chose as son-in-law;
I hate his sudden blind fanaticism;
I mourn his downfall and would rescue him.   1015
I must uphold the honour of the gods;
I dread their wrath and Decius' thunderbolt.
My office and my life are both at stake;
Now I expose myself to death for him,
And now I doom him, not to doom myself.   1020

ALBINUS

Decius will pardon your indulgence for
A son-in-law of noble family.

FELIX

His[1] anti-Christian orders are severe.
Prominent examples are more dangerous.
Public offences must be all repressed,   1025
And, when one hushes up a family crime,
By what authority can one condemn
In others what one tolerates in friends?

ALBINUS

If you can not make this exception, write
To Decius, asking him to settle it.   1030

FELIX

Severus, if I acted thus, would strike.
My greatest worry is his hate and power.
If I delayed to punish such a crime,
Although he's noble and magnanimous,
He is a man, and I've rejected him;   1035
Indignant, wounded at so much contempt,
Driv'n by Paulina's marriage to despair,
Through Decius' anger he would ruin me.

1. *His* refers to Decius.

89

All is permitted to avenge affronts,
1040 And openings tempt ev'n the most temperate.
Perhaps – this is a plausible surmise –
He harbours in his heart a newfound hope,
And, thinking Polyeuctus will be slain,
Revives a passion which he had suppressed.
1045 Judge if his wrath, implacable, would hold
Me guiltless if I saved the guilty. And
If he would spare me, seeing once again
His plans miscarry by my clemency.
Shall I reveal to you my shameful thoughts?
1050 I crush them. They beguile and anger me;
Ambition dangles them before my eyes,
And I can only spew them out. Though here
My family has Polyeuctus' backing, if
He died, the other[1] could then wed my daughter.
1055 Thereby I would have stronger backers who
Would raise me far, far higher than I am.
My heart unwillingly delights therein;
But rather let the heavens strike me down
Than that I should consent to such base thoughts
1060 Or that my honour to itself be false!

ALBINUS

You're too kind-hearted and too noble, but
Are you resolved to punish this offence?

FELIX

I'm going to his prison to attempt
To win him round by playing on his fear
1065 Of death. After, we'll let Paulina try.

ALBINUS

What will you do if he's still obdurate?

FELIX

Refrain from pressing me. I do not know,
In my affliction, what I should resolve.

1. *The other* is Severus.

ALBINUS

But I must warn you in all loyalty
That, in his favour, all the town rebels,   1070
And will not suffer that the laws condemn
The scion of its kings, its last fond hope.
I gather ev'n his prison is not safe.
I left the guards there all demoralized.
I fear it may be stormed.   1075

FELIX
                          We'll take him out
And bring him here, thus making sure of him.

ALBINUS

Do so, and hold out prospects of release.
Appease the fury of a raging mob.

FELIX

Come. If he still persists in his new creed,
We'll make arrangements unbeknown to them.   1080

ACT FOUR

Scene One

POLYEUCTUS, CLEON, THREE OTHER GUARDS

POLYEUCTUS

What is it, guards?

CLEON

Paulina asks for you.

POLYEUCTUS

O presence, combat, O my greatest fear!
Felix, I've triumphed over you in gaol.
I've mocked your threats and seen you, undisturbed.
1085 You, to revenge yourself, choose stronger arms;
I feared your hangmen much more than her tears.
Lord, who behold the perils I incur,
In this grave need, increase your aid to me.
And you, Nearchus, fresh from victory,
1090 Who see my trials from your glorious stance,
Lend from on high a helping hand to me
To vanquish such a pow'rful enemy.
              [To the guards]
Guards, would you venture to oblige me? Not
To save myself from execution. I
1095 Do not intend to compass my escape.
Three are enough to keep a watch on me;
The fourth should bring Severus here to me.
I think that you can safely grant my wish.
If I could tell him secrets of import,
1100 *He* would live happier. *I* would die content.

CLEON

If you command me, I shall use dispatch.

POLYEUCTUS

Severus will reward you if not I.
Go, waste no time, and come back speedily.

CLEON

I shall, my lord, be back within the hour.

Scene Two

POLYEUCTUS
[*The guards withdraw to the corners of the stage.*]
Source of delight, fertile in misery,   1105
What do you want of me, deceiving joys?
Shameful attachments of the flesh and world,
Why leave you not *me*, when I have left *you*?
Go, honours, pleasures who make war on me.
      All your felicity   1110
      Is fraught with instability.
      All mortal glories pass,
      And, as they gleam like glass,
      They have, too, its fragility.

Thus, hope not that I hanker after you.   1115
In vain you flaunt your powerless delights;
In vain you show, throughout this realm's expanse,
God's enemies in grandeur flourishing.
He in his turn displays deserved defeats
      By which the mighty are cast down;   1120
      And the swords He suspended holds
      Over the guilty, whatsoe'er their rank,
      Are all the surer to descend,
      The less expected are their blows.

Pitiless Decius, rav'ning tiger, fiend,   1125
Too long has God let you destroy His saints;
Behold the fearful sequel of your fame.
Scythia will take revenge for Persia, and
The Christians. Wait a while, your hour has come.
      Nothing can shelter you from it.   1130

The thunderbolt which soon will strike,
Ready to penetrate the clouds,
Can be no more suspended by
The hope that you will now repent.

1135 Let Felix sacrifice me to your wrath;
Let a more powerful rival dazzle him;
Give him your daughter's hand once I am dead,
And, as a slave, let him here rule supreme.
I'll meet my downfall, nay, aspire to it.
1140   World, you are nothing to me now.
        I bear in a most Christian heart
        A flame that's utterly divine:
        And I regard Paulina as
        Only an obstacle to me.

1145 O holy sweets of heav'n, fair images,
You fill a heart which can receive your grace.
The souls by your divine delights possessed
Conceive naught else by which they can be moved.
You promise much, and you bestow far more.
1150   Your treasures never rust.
        The blessèd death which I await
        Is for you only a gentle change
        To introduce us to the lot
        Which makes us ever satisfied.

1155 Through you, O fire divine which nothing quells,
I'll see Paulina without fearing her.
She's here; my heart, inflamed with holy zeal,
Feels not the fascination once I did.
My eyes, enlightened by celestial grace,
1160 No longer find the old enchantment there.

Scene Three

POLYEUCTUS, PAULINA, GUARDS

POLYEUCTUS

What plan has made you ask to visit me?
Is it to combat or to back me up?

This noble effort of your perfect love,
Comes it to aid me or to vanquish me?
Do you bring hate or friendship with you here,   1165
As loving wife or as an enemy?

PAULINA

You have no enemy but you yourself.
You hate yourself alone when loved by all.
Alone you execute what I have dreamed.
Do not desire your downfall, and you're saved.   1170
To whatsoever lengths your crime may go,
You're innocent if you will spare yourself.
Consider now the race from which you spring,
Your valiant deeds and your rare qualities;
Cherished by everyone, esteemed at court,   1175
And the provincial ruler's son-in-law,
That you're my husband, too, I count as naught.
It's my good fortune, but it's hardly yours.
But, after your exploits, after your birth,
After your power, we place great hopes in you.   1180
And do not let the executioner
Destroy a splendid, promising career.

POLYEUCTUS

I shall consider more. I know my strength
And the high expectations placed in me.
My friends aspire only to fleeting joys   1185
Which danger follows and which cares disturb.
Death takes them from us. Fortune mocks at them.
Now on a throne, tomorrow in the mire;
Their brightest glory makes such malcontents,
Few of our Caesars have enjoyed them long.   1190
I have ambitions, but they're nobler far.
This greatness fades. I want one which will be
Immortal, happiness, boundless, assured,
High above envy, above destiny.
Is a poor wretched life too dear a price   1195
Which in a moment can be snatched from me,

Which gives me but an instant to enjoy,
And which can not ensure the life to come?

PAULINA

These are your Christians' crazy fantasies;
1200 Their lies have cast a spell upon your mind.
Your blood's a modest price for such sweet bliss;
But is this blood yours to dispose of? No.
Your life's not giv'n you as a legacy;
The day you're born, your life's already pledged
1205 Both to the King, the public and the State.

POLYEUCTUS

I'd gladly lose it for them in the wars;
I know the glory gained by serving them.
The mem'ry of Decius' ancestors [1]
Is vaunted, and his name, still dear to Rome,
1210 Has giv'n it power after six hundred years.
I owe my life to people and to king,
But even more to God who gives it me.
If dying for one's king is glorious,
How much more still when dying for one's God.

PAULINA

1215 What God?

POLYEUCTUS

Paulina, stop. He hears our words.
He's not one of your trifling images,
Devoid of feeling, deaf and impotent,
Or marble, gold or wood as you prefer.
He is the Christians' God. He's mine. He's yours,
1220 And heav'n and earth know of no other one.

PAULINA

Worship him inwardly, not to the world.

POLYEUCTUS

What! be both Christian and idolater?

1. An allusion to the devotion of the two Decii who, as consuls,
in the fourth and fifth centuries B.C. respectively, offered their lives
in order to ensure victory for Rome.

PAULINA

Feign but a moment till Severus leaves,
And leave my father's kindness free to act.

POLYEUCTUS

God's loving kindnesses are far more vast.   1225
He saves me from the risks besetting me,
And, making sure there is no turning back,
His favour crowns me entering the lists.
With the first breeze, he guides me into port,
And, fresh from baptism, sends me to my death.   1230
If you could grasp the paltriness of life
And all the sweetness following that death!
But why speak of these hidden treasures to
Spirits which have not yet been touched by God?

PAULINA

Cruel one! (for it's time to voice my grief,   1235
And heap reproaches on an ingrate soul)
Is this your boundless love, are these your vows?
Do you display the slightest care for me?
I did not stress the lamentable plight
In which your death would leave me. For I thought   1240
Your love would speak to you enough of that,
And did not want forced sentiments from you.
But the so well deserved affection which
You promised me, which I have had for you,
When you would leave me and would make me die,   1245
Can it extract a sigh, a tear, from you?
You leave me, ingrate, leave me, nay, with joy.
You hide it not. You flaunt it in my face,
And, scorning my unhappy charms, your heart,
Aims at a happiness I cannot share.   1250
Is that, then, the disgust which marriage brings?
You loathe me now after possessing me!

POLYEUCTUS

Alas!

PAULINA

You find it hard to speak that word!
If ev'n it was a prelude to regret,
1255 Forced as it was, how I would welcome it!
But, courage, he is moved; I see tears fall.

POLYEUCTUS

Yes, would to God that, just by shedding them,
Your hardened heart could finally be pierced!
The sorry state in which I leave you now
1260 Is worthy of my passion's tears for you.
And if, in heaven, one can still feel grief,
I'll weep for the excess of your mishaps.
But still, if in that glorious, bright abode,
The just and kindly God will hear my prayers,
1265 If there he listens to a husband's love,
He'll change your blindness into clarity.
I must obtain her of Your kindness, Lord,
She has too many virtues not to be
A Christian. You created her too good
1270 For her to lack knowledge and love of You,
To live enslaved to the grim powers of hell
And perish in their yoke as she was born.

PAULINA

What! wretch. You dare to wish for that?

POLYEUCTUS

A wish for what I'd purchase with my blood.

PAULINA

1275 Rather let me . . .

POLYEUCTUS

Defence is vain. This God
Touches our hearts when least we think of it.
This happy moment has not yet arrived.
It will. But *when* is not yet known to me.

PAULINA

eave these wild ravings. Love me.

POLYEUCTUS

                   But I do,

Iuch less than God, but far more than myself.   1280

PAULINA

ı that love's name, do not abandon me.

POLYEUCTUS

ı that love's name, I beg you, follow me.

PAULINA

You leave me and would lead me far astray.

POLYEUCTUS

Going to heav'n, I want to take you there.

PAULINA

Empty imaginings!   1285

POLYEUCTUS

Celestial truths!

PAULINA

Curious blindness!

POLYEUCTUS

Nay, eternal light!

PAULINA

You put death higher than Paulina's love.

POLYEUCTUS

You put the world above God's kindness.

PAULINA

                         Go.

Go, cruel one. You never loved me. Die.

POLYEUCTUS

1290 Live happy in the world. Leave me in peace.

PAULINA

Yes. I shall leave. You need have no concern.
I go . . .

Scene Four

POLYEUCTUS, PAULINA, SEVERUS, FABIAN, GUARD

PAULINA

Severus! But what brings you here?
Would one have thought so generous a heart
Could come so far to gloat upon a wretch?

POLYEUCTUS

1295 You are, Paulina, most unjust to him.
He pays this call at my request alone.
I've done you a discourtesy, my lord,
Which, as a captive, you must pardon me.
I own a treasure I'm not worthy of.
1300 Let me resign it to you ere I die,
And leave the finest, rarest character
A woman ever was vouchsafed by heav'n
To the most valiant gallant gentleman
Rome has engendered and the earth adored.
1305 You're worthy of her, as she is of you.
Do not refuse her from a husband's hand.
In death he'll join what he did once disjoin.
My going should not damp your former love.
Give back your heart to her. Receive her troth.
1310 Live happily together. Die like me.
This is what I desire for both of you.
Lead me to death. I've nothing more to say.
Come, guards. This is the end.

Scene Five

SEVERUS, PAULINA, FABIAN

SEVERUS

        I'm thunderstruck.
His blindness leaves me utterly dismayed.
And his decision's so unheard of that   1315
I scarcely can believe the words I've heard.
A heart which loves you (but what heart so base
Could ever know you and not cherish you?),
A man you love wins you, and suddenly
Leaves you without regrets, nay, yields you up,   1320
As if your ardour were a fatal gift.
He himself gives it to his rival. Sure
Either the Christians have strange madnesses,
Or their felicities are infinite,
Since, to aspire to them, they even reject   1325
What the whole empire's power could never buy.
For me, if destiny had favoured me,
And with your hand honoured my courtship, I
Would not have just adored your shining eyes,
But made of them my kings, indeed my gods,   1330
And would have gladly been reduced to ash,
Rather . . .

PAULINA

      Enough. I fear to hear too much.
This ardour of your love from former times
May lead us both into unworthy paths.
Severus. Know my full integrity.   1335
My Polyeuctus nears his final hour;
He has but one brief moment yet to live.
You are the cause, although unwittingly.
I know not if, listening to your desires,
You dared conceive some hope based on his death.   1340
But know there are no deaths so horrible
Which with composure I would not embrace,

There are no horrors I would not endure
Rather than sully my unblemished name,
1345 Or marry one after this dreadful death,
Who in a way must bear the blame for it.
And, if you think me so unsound of heart,
The love I had for you would turn to hate.
You're chivalrous. Remain so till the end.
1350 My father can accord you everything.
He fears you. And, if he decrees that death,
It is to you that he will sacrifice
My husband. Save him. Use your influence.
Constrain yourself to intervene for him.
1355 It's no slight favour that I ask of you.
But greater effort offers great renown.
Preserve this rival you are jealous of.
Such selflessness can come from you alone,
And, if renown is not enough for that,
1360 Think that a woman once so deeply loved,
And who perhaps tugs at your heartstrings still,
Will owe your chivalry what's dear to her.
Remember lastly, you're Severus. Now
Farewell. Resolve alone on what to do.
1365 If you are not such as I hope you are,
I'll still esteem you by ignoring it.

Scene Six

SEVERUS, FABIAN

SEVERUS

What is this, Fabian? What new thunderbolt
Falls on my happiness and crushes it?
All's lost just when I think it's won. The more
1370 I think it's near, the further it recedes.
And always fortune, bent on harming me,
Cuts short my hope as soon as it is born.
Before I even woo, I am refused.
Always depressed, embarrassed and perplexed

That hope should basely raise its head again,   1375
That ev'n more basely it has dared emerge,
And that a woman, when disaster looms,
Should give me lessons in highheartedness.
Your soul's as great as it's unfortunate,
Paulina, but it's harsh if noble. And   1380
Your grief lords it with ruthless cruelty
Over my utterly devoted heart.
I must not only lose but give you to
A rival helped when he abandons you,
And by a fearful, noble act of will,   1385
To hand him back to you, wrest him from death.

FABIAN

Leave to its fate this ingrate family.
Let it join father, daughter, husband, wife,
Felix and Polyeuctus, all of them.
From such a fearful effort what's your gain?   1390

SEVERUS

The moral pride of showing her myself
As equal to and worthy of her heart,
Proving that she was due to me and that,
Denying her to me, fate did me wrong.

FABIAN

Without denouncing heaven as unjust,   1395
Beware the danger following such an act;
You hazard much, my lord; think carefully.
You undertake to save a Christian! What!
Can you be unaware how Decius hates –
Always has hated – this ungodly sect?   1400
It's such a capital offence towards him
That ev'n *your* favour might be wrecked by it.

SEVERUS

This warning is for ordinary souls.
If he controls my fortune and my life,

1405 I'm still Severus. All this show of pow'r
Can not affect my honour or my name.
These are decisive. They dictate my course;
If, after, fate proves kindly or adverse,
Since by its nature it's inconstant, I,
1410 In dying gloriously, will die content.
I will go further still. In confidence,
The Christians' sect is not what people think.
They're hated. Why, I know not. Decius seems,
On this one point alone, to me unjust.
1415 I wanted to find out about the sect.
They're classed as diabolic sorcerers.
On this assumption, we condemn to death
For mysteries we do not understand;
But other gods – Ceres, Cybele – have
1420 Their secrets just like them in Rome and Greece.
Yet there exist, unpunished everywhere,
Except for theirs, all sorts and types of gods.
Monsters from Egypt are endured in Rome;
Our forebears' whim made of a man a god;
1425 And, since these fallacies were handed down,
We fill the heav'ns with all our emperors;
But frankly the reality of these
Metamorphoses leaves me sceptical.
The Christians have one God alone, the lord
1430 Of all, whose will unaided does what he
Resolves. But, if I dare to speak my mind,
Our gods are often ill-assorted, and,
Ev'n were their wrath to strike me down at once,
There are too many to be real gods.[1]

1. From 1656 on, the following four lines were suppressed:

It may be, after all, these State beliefs
Are the invention of wise statesmen who
Would keep the mob in check or stir it up
And, through its weakness, fortify their power.

This attitude reflects the free-thinking and, more specifically, Machiavellian conception of religion, which is probably why Corneille
suppressed these lines.

Lastly, the Christians' morals, too, are pure,   1435
Vices detested, virtues flourishing.[1]
For us who harass them, they offer prayers;
And all the time we have tormented them,
Have they been mutinous, have they rebelled?
Are there more faithful soldiers of our king?   1440
Furious in battle, they are put to death,
And, lions in the wars, they die like lambs.
I pity them, and will defend their cause.
Where's Felix? Let us free his son-in-law,
And, by a single act, thus satisfy   1445
Paulina, my compassion, my renown.

    1. A further four lines were similarly cut out here:

            Never a villain or a murderer;
            No drunkenness, theft or adultery.
            Love, charity, supreme among them reign
            They help each other out fraternally.

No doubt this passage was felt to be insisting too heavily on the
point made in lines 1435–6.

ACT FIVE

Scene One

FELIX, ALBINUS, LEON

FELIX

Albinus, did you see the cunningness
Severus showed, his hate, my wretched plight?

ALBINUS

I saw in him a rival's selflessness;
1450 In you a father's harshness, nothing more.

FELIX

How you confuse feeling and artfulness!
Felix he hates, Paulina he disdains.
If *once* he loved her, *now* he treats her as
A rival's cast-off who's beneath him. He
1455 Pleads for the prison'r, begs and threatens me
With ruin if I do not pardon him.[1]
Such tactics will, he fancies, frighten me.
The crude pretence is easily unmasked.
I know the Machiavellis of the court.
1460 I can outdo him in politicking.
In vain he storms, pretends to be enraged.
I know how he'll approach the Emperor.
He'd make a crime of what he asks me for,
Sparing his rival, I'd be victimized;
1465 If he were dealing with some blunderer,
The trap's well set; doubtless he'd ruin him.
But an old hand at court's not so naive.
He knows when he's been fooled, sees through the act,
And in the world I've been about so much
1470 That I could teach the man a thing or two.

---

1. *Him*, i.e. Polyeuctus.

ALBINUS

God! how you let mistrust torture your soul!

FELIX

That is the art how to survive at court.
When once we have incurred a person's hate,
We should assume he will betray us. We
Should deem his friendly acts all suspect. No.   1475
If Polyeuctus will give up his sect,
Whatever his protector plans for him,
I'll carry out the orders giv'n to me.

ALBINUS

Sir, spare him, spare him for Paulina's sake.

FELIX

The Emperor's pardon would not follow mine.   1480
And, far from helping him in this debacle,
My clemency would ruin both of us.

ALBINUS

Severus swears, though . . .

FELIX

                    I distrust all that.
Better than he I know how Decius feels.
If he[1] defied his wrath to plead for them,[2]   1485
His downfall would be sure as well as ours.
I shall, however, try a different tack.
Bring Polyeuctus. If I send him back,
If he's immune to this, our last démarche,
Leaving this place, let him be put to death.   1490
                    [*Exit* CLEON.]

ALBINUS

That's a harsh order.

1. Severus.
2. *Them* refers to the Christians.

FELIX

I must follow it,

If I am to prevent an uproar, for
The people have been roused on his behalf.
A moment past you told me so yourself.
1495 This zeal for him which it already shows,
How long, I wonder, can I master it?
Perhaps, tomorrow, nay, this evening, now,
Events will take a most unwelcome turn.
Severus, making haste to seek revenge,
1500 Would tax me with complicity with them.
This move would wreck me. I must parry it.

ALBINUS

To look so much ahead's a curious ill.
Everything harms, offends and ruins you;
But don't you see his death will fire the mob?
1505 The cure is not to drive it to despair.

FELIX

After his death in vain it will complain;
And, if it dares indulge in violence,
Give it its head this once, just for a day.
I've done what duty bids, whate'er betide.
1510 But here is Polyeuctus. Let us try
To save him. Soldiers, go. Guard well the door.

Scene Two

FELIX, POLYEUCTUS, ALBINUS

FELIX

Is then your hate for life so powerful,
Poor Polyeuctus? Does the Christians' law
Bid you abandon your own kith and kin?

POLYEUCTUS

I hate not life. I love it in itself,   1515
But without clinging to it like a slave,
Always prepared to give it back to God.
My reason bids me do so and my faith;
And I will show you thus a way of life
If you have but the heart to follow me.   1520

FELIX

What! into the abyss in which you'd plunge?

POLYEUCTUS

Rather to glory whither I'll ascend.

FELIX

Give me at least the time to know it, and
To make of me a Christian, act as guide.
Do not disdain to teach your faith to me,   1525
Or you will answer to your God for me.

POLYEUCTUS

Mock not, for, Felix, He will be your judge,
And in His presence nowhere can you flee.
Shepherds and kings are equal in his eyes.
He'll take revenge for all his slaughtered saints.   1530

FELIX

Whatever happens, I shall shed no more.
Men shall live freely in the Christian faith.
I shall protect them.

POLYEUCTUS

       Persecute them. Thus
You'll be the means of our felicity.
In suffering lies true Christian happiness.   1535
The fiercest torments are rewards for them.
God, who repays good deeds a hundredfold,
Adds persecutions as a crowning bliss.
But these are secrets hard to understand;
God makes them clear to his elect alone.   1540

FELIX

I am sincere and would embrace your faith.

POLYEUCTUS

What can delay such an auspicious step?

FELIX

The awkward presence . . .

POLYEUCTUS

Of Severus? Speak.

FELIX

For him alone I've feigned such fury against you.
1545 Dissimulate a moment till he leaves.

POLYEUCTUS

Is that how you define sincerity?
Bear to your pagans, to your images
The poisoned honey which your words discharge.
There's nothing that a Christian fears or hides.
1550 To the whole world he always manifests
His faith.

FELIX

Your zeal but leads you far astray,
If, rather than instruct me, you would die.

POLYEUCTUS

The time is not yet ripe to speak to you.
Faith is a gift of heav'n, not of the mind.
1555 It's there that, soon, seeing God face to face,
I'll win that grace more easily for you.

FELIX

Meanwhile your death will drive me to despair.

POLYEUCTUS

It's in your power to make up for it.
You'll lose one son-in-law. Another one

You'll gain whose rank is more in line with yours.   1560
My death can bring you but advantages.

FELIX

Speak not to me in such outrageous terms.
I've been considerate more than you deserve.
Despite my calm which grows with your abuse,
This insolence would end by riling me,   1565
And I'd avenge myself, and our gods too.

POLYEUCTUS

How quick you change your language and your mood!
Zeal for your gods reoccupies your heart!
Desire to be a Christian flees. By chance
Alone I've forced you now to drop the mask.   1570

FELIX

Come. Don't presume, whate'er I swear to you,
I swallow the impostures of your sect.
I fanned your madness just to wrest you from
The precipice you're stumbling into. Yes.
I sought to gain some time to save your life   1575
Once Decius' toady had departed, but
I've outraged all our ever mighty gods.
Offer them either incense or your blood.

POLYEUCTUS

My choice is not in doubt. But here's my wife.
Heav'ns!   1580

Scene Three

FELIX, POLYEUCTUS, PAULINA, ALBINUS

PAULINA

Which of you is now my murderer?
Is it the pair of you or each in turn?
Can I make neither love nor nature yield?
Husband or father, will they give me naught?

FELIX

Speak to your husband.

POLYEUCTUS

Take Severus.

PAULINA

                                      Fiend,
1585 Kill me at least without insulting me.

POLYEUCTUS

My love seeks, out of pity, to relieve
The boundless grief which weighs upon your soul.
Another love's the only cure for it.
Once you responded to his qualities.
1590 Hence probably it always will be so.
You loved him once. He loves you. Now his fame . . .

PAULINA

What have I done you to be treated thus?
To be reproached, despite my faithfulness,
With that deep love I overcame for you?
1595 To help you to defeat a foe so strong,
How I have had to struggle with myself,
What battles I have giv'n to give a heart
So justly won by its first conqueror;
And, if ingratitude's not dead in you,
1600 Attempt to love Paulina once again.
From *her* learn to constrain your sentiments;
Take, in your blindness, *her* as virtue's guide;
Let her obtain your life from you yourself,
To live as yours for ever and a day.
1605 If you are able to reject her pleas,
Look at her tears at least, and hear her sighs;
Drive not a heart who loves you to despair.

POLYEUCTUS

I've told you, and I tell you once again,
Live with Severus or expire with me.

I do not scorn either your tears or troth;   1610
However much our love may plead for you,
Unless a Christian, you are naught to me.
Felix, enough of this. Be firm again,
Avenge your gods and you yourself on me.

PAULINA

Father, his crime can hardly be excused;   1615
But *you* are reasonable if *he's* mad.
Nature's too strong, and its endearing traits
Run in the blood and cannot be effaced.
A father always loves his children, and
In that I see a last faint glimpse of hope.   1620
Look at your daughter with a father's eye.
My death will follow the offender's, and
The gods will find his punishment unfair
Since it will mingle crime and innocence,
And it will change, by this severity,   1625
To unjust rigour a just punishment.
Our fate, inseparable in your hands,
Must make our joint unhappiness or bliss;
And it would be unmeasured cruelty
If now you severed what you once had joined.   1630
A heart linked to another never will
Withdraw, but must be torn away from it.
But you are not unfeeling to my woes,
And with a father's eye behold my tears.

FELIX

Daughter, a father loves his children. Yes.   1635
Naught can efface that sacred character.
I have a tender heart. You've melted it.
I side with you against this lunatic.
                    [*To* POLYEUCTUS]
Are you alone unfeeling, wretch? Will you
Alone make sure no pardon will be giv'n?   1640
Can you, impassive, see so many tears?
By such affection can you not be moved?
Do you disown father-in-law and wife?

113

For *him* no friendship, and for *her* no love?
1645 To make you treat us as your kith and kin,
Must then the two of us embrace your knees?

POLYEUCTUS

I find this artifice distasteful. What!
After you twice have had recourse to threats,
Displayed Nearchus' martyred corpse to me,
1650 And tried to bring love's influence to bear,
Shown me this eagerness for baptism, now
Pitting God's int'rest against God Himself,
You band together. Diabolic wiles!
Must I, before I triumph, fight so hard?
1655 All your resolves are merely buying time.
Since I am now resolved, make up your mind.
I worship one God only, lord of all,
Who makes the heav'n, the earth and even hell
Tremble, whose love for us is infinite,
1660 Who willed to die a shameful death for us,
And who, because of this excess of love,
Is offered as a victim every day.
But why appeal to those who have no ears?
See the blind error which you dare defend.
1665 With blackest crimes you soil your pantheon.
No earthly crime but's sponsored by a god –
Whoring, adultery and incest too,
Theft, murder, all that is most loathsome, *that*
Is the example which your gods have set.
1670 I have profaned and smashed their altars, and
I'd do it, were it to be done, again
Were Felix or Severus looking on,
Or ev'n the Senate and the Emperor.

FELIX

Indulgence finally gives way to rage.
1675 Worship or die.

POLYEUCTUS

I am a Christian.

114

FELIX
Wretch!

POLYEUCTUS
am a Christian.

FELIX
Are you? Obstinate heart!
Men, carry out the order I have giv'n.

PAULINA
Where are you taking him?

FELIX
To death.

POLYEUCTUS
To glory.
My dear, preserve my memory. Farewell.   1680

PAULINA
Husband, I'll follow you and die with you.

POLYEUCTUS
Follow me not, or leave your false beliefs.

FELIX
Take him away, and do as I command,
Since he is bent on dying, let him die.

Scene Four

FELIX, ALBINUS

FELIX
I do myself, Albinus, violence.   1685
But my good nature could have ruined me.
Ev'n if the people's fury is unleashed,

And, if Severus thunders and explodes,
Having constrained myself, I am secure.
1690 But at his[1] harshness are you not surprised?
Have you seen hearts as adamant as his,
Or such detestable impieties?
At least I've satisfied my conscience, for
I've left *no* step untried to melt his heart.
1695 I've even feigned the basest artifice.
But for the horror of his blasphemies,
Which filled me sudden with affright and rage,
I scarce would have restrained my leniency.

ALBINUS

One day perhaps you'll curse this victory
1700 Which smacks a trifle of dishonour, one
Unworthy of a Roman or of you –
Shedding your kin's own blood by your own hand.

FELIX

Brutus and Manlius[2] shed their blood of old.
Their glory was enhanced, not soiled by it.
1705 When, in those days, men's kin disgraced them, they
Would gladly die to wipe away the shame.

ALBINUS

Your zeal leads you astray, but nonetheless
Once it has started to decline, and once
You see Paulina, in her deep despair,
1710 By tears and cries tug at your heartstrings ...

FELIX

                                        You

Remind me she is with that miscreant,
And the despair which she will manifest
Might complicate action on my commands.

1. Polyeuctus'.
2. The consul Brutus had his sons put to death for having plotted
against the Republic (50 B.C.), and the consul Manlius condemned to
death his son who had attacked, contrary to his orders (340 B.C.).

Haste. See to it, and find what she's about,
Prevent her grief from hampering them, and   1715
Remove her, if you can, from that grim sight.
Try to console her. Go. What holds you back?

ALBINUS
There is no need, my lord. She has returned.

Scene Five

FELIX, PAULINA, ALBINUS

PAULINA
Barbarous father; finish off your work;
This second victim's worthy of your rage;   1720
Add to your son-in-law your daughter. Strike.
Our crime or our nobility are one
As are the grounds for your barbarity.
My husband, dying, has enlightened me;
His blood, with which your hangmen spattered me,   1725
Has now unsealed my eyes and opened them.
I see, I know, believe, am undeceived.
With blessed martyr's blood I am baptized;
I am a Christian, then. Need I say more?
Keep, by my death, your rank and your prestige;   1730
Quake at Severus; dread the Emperor.
If you refuse to perish, I must die;
My Polyeuctus calls me to this death;
He and Nearchus both hold out their arms.
Lead, lead me to your gods whom I detest;   1735
They've broken only one. *I'll* break the rest.
You'll see me set at naught all that you fear –
These pow'rless thunderbolts you paint them with,
And, with the sacred banner of revolt,
For once defy your old authority.   1740
It's not my sorrow which I show thereby.
It's heaven's grace which speaks, and not despair.
Felix, I am a Christian, I repeat.

Improve your lot and mine by my decease.
1745 My deed will be of value to us both,
To *you* on earth and *me* above in heav'n.

Scene Six

FELIX, SEVERUS, PAULINA, ALBINUS, FABIAN

SEVERUS

Unnat'ral father, vicious, scheming rogue,
Ambitious slave of non-existent death,
So Polyeuctus met a cruel death,
1750 And by *your* will. You think you'll keep your power!
The backing which I offered you, instead
Of saving him, has hastened on his end.
I threatened, begged, but without moving you.
You thought me cunning or unpowerful.
1755 Well then, you'll have to learn at your expense
I never make unrealistic boasts;
And by your downfall you will see that I,
Who can destroy you, could have shielded you.
Pursue this faithful service to the gods;
1760 Show them your zeal by outrages like these.
Farewell, but, when the storm breaks over you,
Doubt not from where the rain of blows descends.

FELIX

Stop and allow yourself to be appeased;
Let me afford you easy vengeance, Sir.
1765 Reproach me not with having, by my crimes,
Tried to retain my paltry dignities.
Their tinsel glory at your feet I lay;
The ones that I desire are nobler far;
Some secret lure attracts me to them, and
1770 I yield to transports which I do not know;
By promptings which I cannot understand,
My fury's turned to Polyeuctus' zeal.
It's he, I doubt it not, whose guiltless blood

Prays God to aid his persecutor; and
His love, shed over the whole family,   1775
Draws after him daughter and father too.
I've martyred him, and he's converted me.
This is the Christians' anger and revenge.
Give me your hand, Paulina. Bring us chains;   1780
Sacrifice two new Christians to your gods.
I'm one, and so is she. Now wreak your will.

PAULINA

O joy! I and my father are at one
Again. This makes my happiness complete.   1785

FELIX

Thanks to the hand alone effecting it.

SEVERUS

Who would not melt at such a touching sight?
Such changes are the fruit of miracles.
Your Christians whom one persecutes in vain
Have something superhuman about them.   1790
They lead a life of such pure innocence
That heaven owes them gratitude. They rise
With greater strength, the more they are abased.
This, common virtues never can achieve.
I always liked them, be they so reviled.   1795
I see none die that does not make me grieve;
Perhaps one day I'll know them better. I
Meanwhile approve that each should have his gods,
Worshipping freely, with impunity.
If you're a Christian, fear no more my hate.   1800
I like them, and, as their protector, I
Will not turn persecutor harming you.
Retain your pow'r. Take back th' insignia.
Serve faithfully your God, and serve your king.
I'll lose my standing with the Emperor,   1805
Or you will see this persecution end.
This hate is wrong, and but rebounds against
Himself.

FELIX

May heaven end what it's begun,
And, to make sure you have what you deserve,
1810 Inspire you soon with all its verities!
As for the rest of us, let's bless this day.[1]
Let's give our martyrs proper burial,
Kiss their remains, inter them fittingly
And let all places with God's name resound.

END

1. The original reads: *bless this happy adventure.*

THE LIAR

PREFACE

THE LIAR (1643) is the last of the masterpieces of Corneille's vintage period which stretched from *The Cid* to *Polyeuctus* before closing with this gay and dazzling comedy. It combines a sustained verve of style and dialogue, an amusing if somewhat complicated plot, a perceptive portrayal of contemporary Parisian manners and a modest dose of dignified emotion – all fused smoothly into a unified and satisfying work. One is hardly surprised that Corneille was fond of it, and one guesses that he wrote it fairly effortlessly in a burst of splendid creative vigour. Small wonder, then, that it has consistently played to full houses ever since it was first performed. The play presents few problems of interpretation, and may, therefore, be introduced with the briefest of notes. In my comments, I have drawn heavily on the excellent commentary of the comedy in Antoine Adam's standard book on French seventeenth-century literature (*Histoire de la Littérature Française au XVIIe Siècle*, Vol. II, pp. 383–6).

The source of the play is, as so often with Corneille, a Spanish one – *La Verdad Sospechosa* by Alarcon – but comedies in the Spanish style had been in fashion since 1638. Although the French author has drawn copiously on that work, he has not, like the other *espagnolisants*, kept the scene in Madrid and stressed the exotic elements. True, there are still typically Spanish touches such as the passion born from a single glance, nocturnal adventures beneath a grilled window or a balcony, parties on the river and serenades, but the essence of the play is elsewhere. The scene has been transferred to Paris, and the action and characters have been fairly fully gallicized. The manners and psychology are French, and are much more keenly analysed than in similar French adaptations from the Spanish – as is to be expected if we recall the vivid pictures of upper-middle-class youth in the earlier works of Corneille such as *The Widow* and *The Royal Square*. As one critic notes, the hero in *The Liar* may be an expert in inventing a romantic tale, but, like the other characters in Corneille's comedies, he has his feet firmly on the ground and rapidly draws up a detailed summary (of the facts about the fair unknown lady) worthy of a competent marriage agency. The absence of any other heir to her father's estate is noted with particular care.

There is, however, no real comedy of character. We are not told why Dorante (the hero) indulges so frequently in lies. We see only in response to what situations he displays his inventive virtuosity. His mythomania seems to be due to an excess of vitality, a poetic delight in retailing a dramatic and colourful story, the need to compensate for his lack of any particular distinction or experience by inventing imaginary titles to consideration, and a gift for quick improvisation which enables him to wriggle out of a tight corner.

It has been suggested, in extenuation of his weakness, that he is himself often deceived, for example about the identity of Lucrece (the girl whom he eventually marries). But in fact Dorante needs no such pretext for lying. He is simply made that way. Nor does Corneille (unlike his Spanish original) show any marked severity in condemning Dorante, although the young man is given a vigorous scolding by his outraged father. Partly, no doubt, the absence of any kind of punishment at the end (which is anything but moral) is due to the need to preserve the light-hearted tone of the work. But mainly it would seem that Corneille, as a poet gifted with a prodigious imagination himself, had a very soft spot for his creature. As he was to write on one occasion: 'The ability to lie like this is a virtue of which fools are incapable.'

Nor, for that matter, do the feelings of any of the characters go very deep. Dorante is never really in love, but only playing with love. The essence of the play is *galanterie* – flirtation, pursuit and semi-evasion. The only exception is the father, Géronte, who strikes a note of genuine feeling. What is more, he is neither absurd nor odious. Molière almost certainly borrowed from Corneille when creating his

Don Louis in *Dom Juan*. Similar portrayals of fathers are not to be met with till the eighteenth century. Conversely, Dorante appears detestable in his disdain for his father's extraordinary forgiveness.

Cliton, the valet, is on a par with any of Molière's witty and not too scrupulous valets. And Sabine foreshadows that writer's pert serving-maids. But the two heroines are somewhat colourless.

In fact, the basic strength and charm of the play lie in the style which is rich, firm and juicy, and equally devoid of vulgarity, flatness or abstruseness. The worst that can be said of the comedy is that there are occasional verbal passages at arms composed almost exclusively of conceits which, though warmly applauded at the time, have completely lost their attraction since.

Yet Corneille, as Schlumberger observes, was one of those geniuses who never felt at ease with effortless successes. When, as a result of the play's popularity, he penned *The Sequence to the Liar,* he went to far more trouble with the style – with the result that the work is not to be compared with its predecessor. A conclusion which is more or less as encouraging for the moralist as the last four lines of the play.

THE LIAR: SUMMARY

DORANTE, a young man who has just arrived in Paris after studying law at Poitiers, is strolling in the Tuileries Gardens with his valet, Cliton. Two cousins, Clarice and Lucrece, go by. The former stumbles and almost falls. Dorante rushes to her rescue and begins to flirt with her. He retails a tall story of imaginary military prowesses and of an equally unreal pursuit of Clarice lasting over a year. Cliton tells his master that the prettiest of the pair is Lucrece, and Dorante promptly identifies that name with Clarice. Alcippe, Clarice's suitor, and Philiste come on the scene. They are old friends of Dorante's. Alcippe is worried about a report that a rival has offered his beloved a sumptuous entertainment. Dorante, who does not know of Alcippe's involvement with Clarice, tells his friends that *he* is the mysterious host, and gives a detailed description of the banquet. Dorante justifies his action to Cliton, and declares his intention of pursuing 'Lucrece'.

IN the Royal Square (Place Royale – now the Place des Vosges), Dorante's father, Géronte, sounds out Clarice about marrying Dorante, without having first talked to his son. Clarice arranges to be able to take a look at Dorante from her window, and, later, induces Lucrece to take her place and (since Alcippe might become jealous if he got wind of the matter) sends Lucrece a note asking her to fix an appointment for herself with Dorante at her window where Clarice will pretend to be Lucrece, speak to Dorante and thus size him up. Alcippe turns up, and reproaches Clarice with having spent the night at the mysterious party. Clarice is astounded, and makes fun of him. Alcippe decides to challenge Dorante to a duel. Géronte comes in with Dorante, and tells him of his decision to marry the boy to Clarice. Dorante, who thinks the girl who has fascinated him is Lucrece, feigns a sham marriage in order to escape accepting the order to marry Clarice. Géronte forgives his son the unauthorized move. Sabine, Lucrece's maid, brings Dorante the note from Lucrece for which Clarice had asked her friend. The substitution confirms him in his error of identification. Dorante is challenged to a duel by Alcippe through a note. Dorante, though puzzled, accepts.

ACT THREE

THE two men fight it out, and are separated by Philiste who happens on the scene. The latter, left alone with Alcippe, convinces his friend that Dorante has been lying and that the original report of the party is based on a misunderstanding. Alcippe decides to make it up with Clarice. The girl, having seen Dorante from her window, recognizes her unknown admirer of the Tuileries, and realizes that he has been lying about his warlike exploits. She cools off. Cliton finds out all about the real Lucrece from her servants. Clarice, speaking at the appointment as Lucrece, reproaches Dorante with his deception. Lucrece (who is standing behind Clarice) seems touched by the sincerity with which Dorante professes his feelings to 'Lucrece'. Though rebuffed by his interlocutor (Clarice), Dorante refuses to lose heart.

ACT FOUR

DORANTE tells Cliton how he has killed Alcippe in the duel. His friend thereupon comes on the scene and tells Dorante that the marriage with Clarice (which had been hanging fire for years because Alcippe's father would not come up to Paris) has at last been settled. Dorante wriggles out of his lie to Cliton. Alcippe, he says, has recovered because of a miraculous powder! Géronte asks Dorante to bring the bride to Paris, but the young man asserts that her pregnancy makes such a journey impossible. Géronte thereupon decides to write to the bride's father. Dorante greases Sabine's palm, and she agrees to accept a note from him to her mistress professing his love. Lucrece, who responds to this courtship, tells Sabine to give Dorante some hope – but not too much! Clarice, now firmly linked to Alcippe, discusses Dorante's conduct with Lucrece. The former, not without a shade of jealousy, warns the latter to be careful in her dealings with her suitor.

ACT FIVE

GÉRONTE learns from Philiste that the story about the marriage is a lie. Géronte is indignant and berates his son. Dorante pleads that he was in love with 'Lucrece' (i.e. Clarice), and induces his father to ask for the girl's hand in marriage. Dorante confesses to Cliton that he now wonders whether, after all, the real Lucrece is not prettier than the girl he thinks is Lucrece. Sabine tells Dorante of the favourable reception of his note. Dorante comes on the two girls, and at once begins apostrophizing Clarice. Halfway through the conversation, he hears Clarice address Lucrece by her name, and at last realizes his error. He pretends that, in the scene beneath Lucrece's window, he recognized that it was Clarice who was speaking, and is taking revenge for that deception. He has always, he swears, loved Lucrece alone. All ends happily. Alcippe marries Clarice and Dorante Lucrece.

DEDICATORY EPISTLE[1]

I AM submitting to you a play of such a very different style from my last one[2] that it will be difficult to believe that they are both from the same pen, and, what is more, written in the same winter. And in fact the reasons which compelled me to work at them are very different. I wrote *Pompey* to satisfy those who did not find the verse in *Polyeuctus* as powerful as that in *Cinna* and to show that I could re-create easily enough pomp and dignity when the subject lent itself to that tone. I wrote *The Liar* to satisfy the many others who, as is the wont of the French, are fond of change, and, after so many grave works with which our finest pens have enriched the stage, asked me for something lighter which would not do more than amuse them. In the former, I wanted to make a trial of what could be achieved by the majesty of reasoning and the power of verse deprived of the amenity inherent in a subject. And besides, being obliged to comedy for my first rise to fame,[3] I could not have given it up without a show of ingratitude. It is true that, as I was making ready to leave it, I did not rely on my own strength, and that, to rise to the dignity demanded by tragedy, I leant on the great Seneca from whom I borrowed all the outstanding traits which he had given his *Medea*. And so, when I decided to revert from the heroic to the natural, I did not dare come down from such heights without making sure of a guide, and let myself be led by the famous Lope de Vega[4] for fear of losing my way in the innumerable intrigues in which our Liar engages. In short, this is merely the copy of an excellent original which he produced under the title of *La Verdad Sospechosa*, and, trusting on our Horace to give freedom to dare anything to poets as well as to

1. It is not known to whom this dedication is addressed.
2. *The Death of Pompey* (1644).
3. Corneille's early success was due to such comedies as *The Widow*.
4. The Spanish original is really by Alarcon.

painters, I thought that, despite the war of the two crowns, I
would be allowed to seek my wares in Spain. If this kind of
commerce was a crime, I would long ago have offended
not only through the *Cid*, where I plundered Guilhen de
Castro, but also through *Medea* to which I have just referred, and through *Pompey* itself where, thinking to fortify
myself with the help of two Latins, I turned to two Spaniards, Seneca and Lucan, both of whom are from Cordoba.
Those who are reluctant to pardon these dealings with our
enemies will at least approve of my pillaging them. And,
whether this is regarded as a theft or a loan, I find it so
successful that I have no desire for it to be the last time I
have recourse to them. I believe that you will be of the
same opinion and that you will not esteem me any the less
for that.

I am,
Sir,
your very humble servant,

CORNEILLE

CAST

GERONTE, *Dorante's father*
DORANTE, *Géronte's son*
ALCIPPE, *Dorante's friend and Clarice's suitor*
PHILISTE, *friend of Dorante and Alcippe*
CLARICE, *courted by Alcippe*
LUCRECE, *girl friend of Clarice*
ISABELLE, *Clarice's maid*
SABINE, *Lucrece's maid*
CLITON, *Dorante's man*
LYCAS, *Alcippe's man*

THE LIAR

ACT ONE
Scene One

DORANTE, CLITON

DORANTE

Finally I've exchanged my gown against   1
A sword; what I have waited for is here.
My father's given me my head, and I
Have jettisoned this farrago of law.
But, since we've strolled into the Tuileries,   5
The world of high society, affairs,
Tell me, am I the dashing officer?
Does anything still smack of midnight oil?
It's hard, immersed in legal tomes, to learn
How to achieve a fashionable air.   10
I've cause to apprehend . . .

CLITON
                        No need to fear.
You'll soon make lots of envious rivals here.
There's nothing of the lawschool in your ways;
And that's not how we picture Bartolus.[1]
For many husbands trouble's in the air.   15
But how does Paris strike you, Sir?

DORANTE
                        I find
The air most sweet, the banishment most harsh
Imposed on me to study law elsewhere.
You know the way a good time's to be had,
Since, lucky man, you've never left the place.   20
What's the right way to handle ladies here?

1. Bartolus was a fourteenth-century jurisconsult.

133

CLITON

That is the finest sport for fine young men,
Say the fine wits. But, may I make so bold?
You're quick at working up an appetite.
25 You've only been in town since yesterday,
And fret already at your idleness.
You must be up and doing, and you want
This very day to try your hand at love!
I'm admirably placed with you to act
30 The part of one who helps you find your way.
I rate as master in this noble trade –
Purveyor of the district, if not more.

DORANTE

Now don't be shocked, for frankly all I want
Is someone I can have a laugh with, and
35 Visit and talk to and amuse myself.
You don't yet know me. You misunderstand.

CLITON

I get your point. I see you're not a rake,
And think these good-time girls beneath you who
40 Give you their favours if you jingle gold.
Nor do you want these unrelaxed coquettes
Whom every comer can at leisure woo,
But who make love in words and with their eyes.
A man the likes of you wants something more.
45 To spend your time with them's to waste it, and
The game's not worth the candle, as they say.
But what would set you dancing with delight
Are well-bred women whose behaviour's bad;
Whose virtue, when they're courted ardently,
50 Is not unmingled with a dash of vice.
You'll find them here in every sort and size.
Don't ask me how to set about it, since
Either I haven't read your face aright,
Or you are certainly no prentice hand.
55 Your law did not absorb you so much, Sir,
You always had a briefcase in your hand.

134

DORANTE

Not to dissemble, Cliton, I confess
That, at Poitiers,[1] I lived as young men do.
I dabbled there in quite a string of trades.
But Paris and Poitiers are poles apart.   60
The climate here calls for a different style.
What *there* is in is out of fashion *here*.
The differences in manners and in words
Often bring blushes to a stranger's face.
We in the provinces take what we get.   65
There, a fool passes muster faute de mieux;
But Paris needs quite other qualities.
Nobody's dazzled by an outward show.
There are such droves of gentlemen about,
That one is out unless one looks like them.   70

CLITON

You have the wrong idea of the place.
This is a city where there's good and bad;
The facts don't tally with appearances.
Here one is fooled like anywhere in France;
Amid so many fine and polished wits,   75
There are as many loafers as elsewhere.
The melting pot of this metropolis
Draws people from all places of all sorts,
And there are quite few towns in all of France
Whose dregs and whose élite are not found here.   80
As people aren't known, they try it on
And at their own face value are assessed;
Much worse than you are really in the swim.
But, coming to the point you asked about,
Are you a spender?   85

DORANTE
I'm not miserly.

1. Poitiers was an important centre for studies in law at the time.
It is pronounced here as a word of two syllables, with the accent on the
second one.

CLITON

That's a great secret for success in love,
But skill is needed putting it across.
Unskilled you show no profit, only loss.
Some men are lavish, but it doesn't work.
90 It's *how* you give, not *what* you give that counts.
Some make their present gambling it away;
Some forget gems which would have been refused.
A bumpkin's liberal, but strikes his girl
As giving alms when handing out largesse,
95 And all his actions are so badly timed
That, when he tries to please, he just offends.

DORANTE

Let's leave these blockheads you are ranting at,
And tell me if you recognize these girls.[1]

CLITON

Oh no. These goods are far too choice. They're game
100 Reserved for others, not for me. And yet
It's easy to find out about the pair;
Their coachman's sure to fill me in on them.[2]

DORANTE

He'll open up?

CLITON

Until the cows come home.
Since he's their coachman, there's no stopping him.

1. *These girls*: Clarice and Lucrece, who are coming into sight.
2. A detail taken from the Spanish original. Spanish coachmen were supposed to be specially talkative.

Scene Two

DORANTE, CLARICE, LUCRECE, ISABELLE

CLARICE
[*stumbling and seeming about to fall*]
Oh!   105

DORANTE
[*giving her his hand*]
Your misfortune favours my desires,
Since this small service is permitted me,
And it's for me a sovereign stroke of luck
To have the chance to tender you my hand.

CLARICE
Chance does not really favour you at all.
This slight good fortune's hardly to be prized.   110

DORANTE
It's true I owe it all to accident,
Not to my efforts or to your desires.
Its sweetness, mingled with this bitterness,
Means fate's not kinder than it's meant to be,
Since this good luck which I have prized so much   115
Would to my small deserts have been refused.

CLARICE
If it has lost its charm for you so soon,
I for my part feel just the opposite,
And think that one should find more happiness
Having a boon without deserving it.   120
I value more a gift than gratitude.
Who gives does more than who rewards us, and
The greater happiness, if it's deserved,
Merely gives back to us what is our due.
The favour merited is always bought;   125
The less deserved, the more the happiness.

The benefit which favour sends, unsought,
Sought after, merit would not have obtained.

DORANTE

Hence, do not think I ever shall expect
130 To win that favour by deserving it.
I know its value and my heart inflamed
The happier is, the less it merits it.[1]
It's always rightly been refused me and
If, on receiving it, this heart complains,
135 It but complains of its unhappy bliss
Which chance and not your conscious wish accords.
A lover has small reason to be pleased
At favours done him accidentally.
The value's set by the intention. Hence,
140 If that's not there, they're often linked with scorn.
Judge then what bliss my ardour can receive
From a hand given when the soul's refused.
I hold it, touch it, but I touch in vain.

CLARICE

145 This ardour comes as something new to me,
Since I have just beheld it kindle. But,
If thus your heart is in a moment fired,
Mine never could so promptly be inflamed.
But now I've been apprised of it, perhaps
150 Time will bring forth a friendlier response.
Confess, though, that unfairly you complain
Of scorn for love I did not know about.

1. Refers to the favour two lines back.

Scene Three

DORANTE, CLARICE, LUCRECE, ISABELLE, CLITON

DORANTE

That's just the awful luck that dogs my steps
Since I gave up the wars in Germany.[1]
That is to say, for a whole year at least   155
I have patrolled your quarter day and night.
I seek you everywhere – balls, promenades.
You've had from me nothing but serenades,
And I have found only this single chance
To talk to you of my affection.   160

CLARICE
                    Oh!
So you've been in the wars in Germany?

DORANTE

Four years I scattered terror there like Jove.

CLITON

God, what a tale!

DORANTE
                    And during these four years
There was no combat, no important siege,
And never did our arms win victory,   165
But this hand played a leading part in them.
Ev'n the *Gazette*[2] has often mentioned me.

CLITON
[*tugging at* DORANTE's *coat-tails*]
You're raving.

1. In the latter part of the Thirty Years War (1618–48), France
intervened, fighting on German soil.
2. The *Gazette*, an official publication, was founded by Théophraste
Renaudot some ten years earlier (in 1631).

DORANTE

Quiet!

CLITON

Dreamer!

DORANTE

Quiet! wretch.

CLITON

170 You came here from Poitiers, or I'll be damned.
You came here yesterday.

DORANTE

Be quiet, rogue.

[*To* CLARICE]

My name was in our victories to the fore,
And, not unfairly, it made quite a stir,
And I would still be nobly thus engaged
175 But that last winter here at court I caught
A sight of you and was by love detained.
Attacked by your fair eyes, I owned defeat.
I was a willing captive of your spell.
My soul surrendered to it. This proud heart
180 From the first moment gave up all for it –
To conquer in the field, command my men,
And by a thousand exploits swell my fame;
And all my noble occupations, these
Yielded at once to joy in serving you.

ISABELLE

[*whispers to* CLARICE]

185 Alcippe is coming. He'll be most upset.

CLARICE

Some day we'll hear a little more of that.
Farewell.

DORANTE
Rob me so soon of my delight!

CLARICE
We have no leisure for a longer talk,
And, welcome though this mild flirtation is,
We now must in the alley take a turn.   190

DORANTE
However, let my honourable love
Pay its addresses to such potent charms.

CLARICE
A heart that wishes and is schooled to love
Asks no permission save but of itself.

Scene Four

DORANTE, CLITON

DORANTE
Go after them.   195

CLITON
I have the gen on them.
Their coachman's tongue's been working overtime.
'My mistress is the prettiest of the two.
She lives here on the Square.[1] She's called Lucrece.'

DORANTE
What square?

CLITON
The Royal Square. The other lives there too.
He hasn't got her name, but I'll find out.   200

1. Dorante, the provincial, has to have the Parisian abbreviation
explained to him. The Place Royale (as it is in French) was an important social centre at the time, and Corneille even has an early comedy
called after it. This square has been renamed the Place des Vosges.

DORANTE

Don't bother too much to make inquiries.
The one who talked, the one I've fallen for,
Is called Lucrece. The matter's not in doubt.
Her beauty's such. And my heart tells me so.

CLITON

205 Though I must on that point defer to you,
I think the other's much the prettiest.

DORANTE

The one who was so quiet when we talked
And had not wit enough to say a word?

CLITON

Sir, when a woman keeps so quiet, she
210 Has qualities you won't find every day.
That is a creature made by heaven, most rare
And only fashioned by some miracle.
And violence is done to nature when
Heaven makes a girl inclined to silentness.
215 For me, never does love disturb my nights,
And, when I feel like it, I take potluck.
But natur'lly women who can hold their tongue
Impress me and appeal to me so much
That, even were she the dowdiest girl in town,
220 I would select her as a beauty queen.
I'll wager it is she who's called Lucrece.
Your lady love must have a different name.
That is not hers. The one who held her tongue –
She is the prettiest, or I'll be damned.

DORANTE

225 You needn't swear or lay it on so thick.
I'll take your word. Here come my dearest friends.
They seem astounded, judging by their looks.

Scene Five

DORANTE, ALCIPPE, PHILISTE, CLITON

PHILISTE
[*to* ALCIPPE]
On water? Music and collation too?

ALCIPPE
[*to* PHILISTE]
Yes, a collation, and with music too.

PHILISTE
[*to* ALCIPPE]
Yesterday night?   230

ALCIPPE
[*to* PHILISTE]
                        Yes.

PHILISTE
[*to Alcippe*]
Good?

ALCIPPE
[*to* PHILISTE]
                        Magnificent.

PHILISTE
[*to* ALCIPPE]
Offered by whom?

ALCIPPE
[*to* PHILISTE]
                That's what I'd like to know.

DORANTE
[*greeting them*]
How marvellous to see you here again!

ALCIPPE

And I am overjoyed to greet my friend.

DORANTE

Forgive my joy at seeing you again.
235 I interrupted you. Most rude of me.

PHILISTE

You may at all times, Sir, make free with me.

DORANTE

What were you talking of?

ALCIPPE
    A courtly deed.

DORANTE

Of love?

PHILISTE
  I think it was.

DORANTE
    Continue, pray.
This word excites my curiosity.
240 May I not share the news with you?

ALCIPPE
      It's said
That someone gave a concert for a girl.

DORANTE

On water?

ALCIPPE
  Yes.

DORANTE
Water can fire love's flame.

PHILISTE

Sometimes.

DORANTE

And this was all last night?

ALCIPPE

It was.

DORANTE

Fire shines more brightly in the shades of night.
The time was chosen well. She's beautiful?   245

ALCIPPE

In many people's eyes, she's rated so.

DORANTE

The music?

ALCIPPE

Not at all to be disdained.

DORANTE

Perhaps it was enhanced by a repast?

ALCIPPE

So people say.

DORANTE

Lavish?

ALCIPPE

A princely meal.

DORANTE

And don't you know the man who gave the fête?   250

ALCIPPE

You laugh?

DORANTE

I laugh to see you shattered by
An entertainment which was given by me.

ALCIPPE

You?

DORANTE

I myself.

ALCIPPE

What! You've already found
Someone to court?

DORANTE

Well, I can manage *that*,
255 For I've been back in Paris for a month.
It's true that I am rarely seen by day.
By night, incognito, I pay some calls.
And so . . .

CLITON
[*whispers to* DORANTE]
You don't know what you're saying, Sir.

DORANTE

Be quiet. If you warn me once again . . .

CLITON

260 Must I keep quiet at such shocking lies?

PHILISTE
[*to* ALCIPPE *sotto voce*]
What luck for you that you ran into him;
Your rival gives himself away to you.

DORANTE
[*coming back to them*]
As you're my dearest friend, I'll tell you all.
I'd hired five boats to make a better show;

In each of four of them I placed a band   265
Whose music would entrance the saddest heart.
Violins in the first; voices and lutes
Came next, then flutes, and oboes in the fourth,
From which in turn came waves of harmony
Lulling the ear with sweetness infinite.   270
The fifth was large, for the occasion lined
With interlacing, coolness-breathing boughs;
With fragrant bouquets at each end combined
Of jasmine, orangeflower and pomegranate.
I turned this boat into a banquet hall.   275
Thither I led the lady of my heart,
A beauty five fair followers enhanced,
And the repast was served immediately.
I won't describe it all in detail, or
The name and sumptuousness of every dish,   280
But say that, in this bower of delights,
They served six courses of twelve dishes each,
The while the waters, cliffs and vibrant air
Re-echoed to the strains of all four bands.
Thousands of fireworks, after we had dined,   285
Shooting up heavenwards, both straight and crossed,
Made night turn into day, and scores of them
Poured on the waters such a stream of flame,
It seemed that, to make fiercer war on them,
Fire's element had fallen from heaven to earth.   290
We danced, after this pastime, till the dawn
Which the sun in its jealousy advanced.
Had we advised him, his unwelcome rays
Would not so soon have marred my slight success,
But, being disinclined to heed our wish,   295
He broke it up and ended all the fun.

ALCIPPE

These marvels flow most smoothly from your tongue.
Paris is large, but such a fête is rare.

DORANTE

I had been taken unawares. My love
Had granted me only an hour or two.   300

147

PHILISTE

But it was lavish and superbly planned.

DORANTE

This slight affair was all I could arrange.
When time is short, one can't discriminate.

ALCIPPE
[*taking leave*]
At greater leisure we shall meet again.

DORANTE

305   A pleasure, Sir.

ALCIPPE

I'm green with jealousy.

PHILISTE
[*to* ALCIPPE]
But there's no reason to be so upset,
For his account does not agree with yours.

ALCIPPE
[*to* PHILISTE]
Place and time *do*. The hell with all the rest.

Scene Six

DORANTE, CLITON

CLITON

May I now speak without offending you?

DORANTE

310   It's up to you to speak or not to speak.
But, when there's someone, stop your insolence.

ACT ONE SCENE SIX

CLITON
Sir, when you're speaking, do you always dream?

DORANTE
When do you see me dream?

CLITON
                Well, dreaming is
What, were you not a master, would be called
Lying.   315

DORANTE
    Halfwit!

CLITON
             I lose the other half,
Hearing you speak of concerts and of war.
You see our battles unendangered, and
Give parties which don't cost a penny. Why
Pretend that you've been back for one whole year?

DORANTE
I show more passion thus in paying court.   320

CLITON
Why, does war show you in a better light?

DORANTE
What a fine way to charm a lady if
You say to her at once: 'I bring to you
A heart fresh from the university?
If you want laws and precedents, I'll give   325
Chapter and verse from the whole legal code,
The new Digest, the old – and all that stuff
What Baldus, Alciatus says of them.'
Won't such a line impress the women. How
Will this approach help me to conquer hearts?   330
A legal swot's not likely to get far.
You fare much better as a man of war.

The secret lies in putting on an air.
You lie adroitly, swear a few round oaths,
335 Show off with lots of words above their heads,
Mention the foe's defeated generals,
And bring in castles whose barbaric names
Carry more weight the more they wound the ear,
Or always harp on angles, trenches, lines,
340 Watchtowers, advance works, mines and counterscarps.
Reel them off anyhow. They make your mark.
You get yourself admired by acting up;
And some, because they have a nimble tongue,
Pass as important men, and so they're in.

CLITON

345 You may convince your audience with your tales,
But this girl won't take long to find you out.

DORANTE

By then I'll have obtained access to her,
And, far from dreading that I'll come to grief,
If ever bores should foist themselves on us,
350 This way we can communicate by code.
That, Cliton, is the strategy of love.

CLITON

To tell the truth, you take my breath away.
We know of wizards with their magic wand,
But never did they conjure up a feast
355 Like this. You go one better than their spells.
You'd be a genius writing novels, since
You juggle so with banquets and with wars,
Your heroes in a trice would span the earth,
And it would be no effort on your part
360 To pepper it with pomp and with suspense.
For flights of fancy you're a natural.

DORANTE

I love to dare those who retail the news.
As soon as one of them comes up who thinks

What he will tell us will be shattering,
At once I dish him up a dreamed-up tale   365
Which leaves him thunderstruck and speech-bereft.
If you could know the pleasure that it gives
To make them swallow their jejune reports . . .

CLITON

It must be grand, but after all, these ploys
Can get you into real trouble, Sir.   370

DORANTE

I'll wriggle out of them. But all this talk
Keeps me from seeking out the girl I love.
Let's try and find her. If you follow me,
I'll teach you soon a different way to live.

ACT TWO

Scene One

GERONTE, CLARICE, ISABELLE

CLARICE

375 I know he must be good since he's your son,
But to accept a husband sight unseen,
However glowingly you picture him,
Is overrating marriage. What is more,
To let him pay addresses, call on me,
Be the official suitor for my hand,
380 Unless your plans are fully realized,
Would set too many tongues a-wagging. Find
Some way to let me catch a glimpse of him
Without making me seem undutiful.

GERONTE

385 Yes, you are right, fair, virtuous Clarice.
What you command is equity itself,
And, as it's *we* who're subject to your laws,
I'll come back presently with my Dorante.
Beneath your window I'll delay the boy,
390 So that at leisure you can study him.
Examine his appearance, figure, face,
And see the kind of man I've picked for you.
He's fresh from lawschool, but no pedant he.
Although you needn't take a father's word,
395 Ex-student though he be, I'd say that now
Few courtiers cut a better dash than he.
But you will judge of him by his repute.
I want him wed, since he's my only son,
And above all I want him wed to *you.*

CLARICE

I'm greatly honoured by this flattering choice.   400
I shall await him with impatience, Sir,
And even now I love him on your word.

Scene Two

ISABELLE, CLARICE

ISABELLE

You'll see him, then, but not commit yourself.

CLARICE

What can I make of him from so far off?
I'll see the outside, the appearances,   405
But can I be assured of all the rest?
In these deceiving mirrors what's within
Is hid. And faces sweetly can deceive.
What inner blemishes they charm away.
Often fine semblances conceal base souls.   410
The eyes are crucial when we make this choice,
But to leave all to *them's* to hazard all.
To live unworried, do not flout them, but,
Ev'n unobeyed, they must be satisfied.
One should accept their No and not their Yes,   415
And let one's love mature on other grounds.
The marriage bond which lasts throughout our life,
Which ought to cause more terror than desire,
If one's not careful, fairly often binds
Like to unlike and living to the dead.   420
And, since these ties impose a master, I,
Before accepting him, must know him and
His character.

ISABELLE

Well, let him speak to you.

CLARICE

But, if he hears of it, Alcippe will be
425 Jealous.

ISABELLE

What matter if you have Dorante?

CLARICE

I still am not prepared to write him off,
And the agreement on our marriage, were
His father here, would still be carried out.
For full two years he has been promising
430 And then delaying. Now it's business, now
Illness, or roads unsafe, or days too short.
In brief, the worthy father won't leave Tours.
All these delays are just a pretext, and
I'm in no mood to die of constancy,
435 And every hour of waiting cuts our price.
Old maids become an object of contempt.
Maidenhead brings repute, but stales with time.
Its death is awkward if it's long delayed.
Time's not a god which it can disregard,
440 And honour's lost in keeping it too long.

ISABELLE

So you would leave Alcippe for someone else,
Because you feel he'd suit you better.

CLARICE

                                        Yes.
I'd leave Alcippe. Before I made the change,
I'd have to have another man in tow,
445 Know that he suited me and be prepared
To link his fate to mine by marriage. If
That weren't sure, I wouldn't take the plunge,
For after all Alcippe's a bird in hand.
His father *may* arrive, however late.

ISABELLE

'o see to that and rule out any risk,   450
ucrece, your friend, can do a lot for you.
he has no jealous suitor to placate.
et her write to Dorante suggesting that
Ie stand beneath her window late tonight.
s he's still young, he'll fall for it, and there,   455
Inder a bogus name, you'll talk to him
Vithout Alcippe discovering the ruse.
Dorante will think it's no one but Lucrece.

CLARICE

A bright idea that. Lucrece, I'm sure,
Vill write a billet doux for me at once.   460
t's really masterly to think of it.

ISABELLE

May I still say that, if I guess aright,
This unknown suitor made a hit with you?

CLARICE

Ah! if Dorante was half as fine as he,
He wouldn't find it hard to oust Alcippe.   465

ISABELLE

Don't speak of him. He's coming.

CLARICE
      What a bore,
Go to Lucrece's place and fill her in
As much as possible about my fix.

Scene Three

CLARICE, ALCIPPE

ALCIPPE

Ah! Clarice, Ah! Clarice, inconstant girl!

CLARICE
[*first line aside*]

470 Has he already guessed my marriage plans?
What's wrong, Alcippe? Why these distressing sighs?

ALCIPPE

What's wrong, you faithless girl? You know what's wrong
Just ask your conscience. It will tell you what.

CLARICE

Speak softer or my father may come down.

ALCIPPE

Your father may come down, you two-faced chit.
475 That father gambit only goes for *me*.
At night, upon the river . . .

CLARICE
Well, at night?

What is this all about?

ALCIPPE
Yes, the whole night.

CLARICE

Go on.

ALCIPPE
What, don't you blush?

CLARICE
Whatever for?

ALCIPPE

480 Come, you should die of shame to hear of it.

CLARICE

To hear of it? What's deadly about that?

ALCIPPE

What! you can hear and ask about the rest?
Would not you blush if I should tell you all?

CLARICE

All what?

ALCIPPE

Your fun and games from A to Z.

CLARICE

I just can't understand a word you say.   485

ALCIPPE

I try to speak. 'My father may come down.'
Then you remember. It's a splendid trick!
But with your gallant when you spend the night . . .

CLARICE

Alcippe, you're mad!

ALCIPPE

Now I've no grounds to be,[1]
Since you've come out in your true colours. Yes,   490
To spend the night in dance and banqueting,
Be with your gallant all the night till dawn
(That's yesterday). You had no father *then*.

CLARICE

Is this a joke? What is this mystery?

ALCIPPE

This mystery is new, but known to all.   495
Next time, select a gallant who's discreet.
He told me all himself.

CLARICE
Himself?

ALCIPPE
Dorante.

1. The implication is: mad with love.

CLARICE

Dorante?

ALCIPPE

Go on. Pretend you're ignorant.

CLARICE

If ever I have seen or known Dorante . . .

ALCIPPE

500 Have I not seen his father here with you?
Faithless, ungrateful, fickle one, you spend
Days with the father, evenings with the son!

CLARICE

His father has for long been friends with mine.

ALCIPPE

This friendship, then, was what you talked about?
505 I've pinned you down and yet you dare reply!
You need more details to discomfit you?

CLARICE

Alcippe, I don't know what the son is like . . .

ALCIPPE

Well, when you saw him, it was very dark.
Didn't he choose four bands to play for you,
510 And give you a magnificent repast?
Six sumptuous courses of twelve dishes each?
His conversation was unwelcome *then*?
When all his fireworks lit up both the banks
Had you no time to scrutinize his face?
515 Did you not dance with him till dawn? Did not
You study him on the way back at least?
Is that enough? Then blush and die for shame.

CLARICE

I certainly won't blush at such a tale.

ALCIPPE

So I'm a scoundrel, jealous, off my head?

CLARICE

Someone's had fun making a fool of you,   520
Alcippe, believe me.

ALCIPPE

Do not fob me off.
I know your devious ways and guess your tricks.
Farewell. Go, love and follow your Dorante;
Leave me in peace, and never think of me.

CLARICE

Listen to *me*.   525

ALCIPPE

Your father may come down.

CLARICE

No, he can't hear us, and he won't come down,
And I have all the time to put you straight.

ALCIPPE

No, I am deaf unless you'll marry me,
Unless, while we await our marriage day,
You, with two kisses, plight your troth to me.   530

CLARICE

To clear my name, what do you ask of me,
Alcippe?

ALCIPPE

Two kisses and your hand, your troth.

CLARICE

That's all?

ALCIPPE

Make up your mind, and do it quick.

CLARICE

I have no time. My father may come down.

Scene Four

ALCIPPE

535 Go, mock my grief, since you're no longer mine.
By these indignities you break my chains.
Help my rejected love to turn to ice;
Help me to turn it into anger. Now
I crave for justice, and will soon ensure
540 Full retribution on your gallant. If
He is a man, this very day our arms
Will soon decide whether you laugh or cry;
Rather than ever see him with my girl,
May all my blood be mingled with his own.
545 But here's this rival whom his father backs,
And ancient friendship yields to new-found hate.
The sight of him inflames my wounded heart.
But I'll not pick a quarrel with him here.

Scene Five

GERONTE, DORANTE, CLITON

GERONTE

Dorante, let's stop. This marathon of yours
550 Might put me out of breath and make me ill.
These buildings are superb and well laid out.

DORANTE

Paris to me seems like a fairy tale.
I saw this morning an enchanted isle
Deserted *then*; *now* it's inhabited.
555 Some new Amphion[1] without masons' help
Has changed these bushes into marble halls.

1. Wishing to gird ancient Thebes with a wall, Amphion saw the rampart rise of its own accord while he played on his lyre.

GERONTE

Paris each day changes before your eyes;
In the whole Pré aux Clercs[1] the scene's transformed,
And there is nothing in the whole wide world
Like the Palais Royal's superb façade.[2]   560
A whole town built in an imposing style
Seems conjured up out of an ancient moat,
And, by its splendid roofline, makes us feel
All its inhabitants are gods and kings.
To change the subject, you must know my love   565
For you.

DORANTE

An honour dearer than my life.

GERONTE

As you're my only child, and, as I see,
You enter on a perilous career,
In which ardour for glory drives you on
And forces you each day to risk your life,   570
Before misfortune carries you away
To make you act somewhat more cautiously,
I've found a wife for you.

DORANTE

[aside]
My dear Lucrece!

GERONTE

I chose myself the girl you are to wed –
Virtuous, fair and rich.   575

1. An area on the left bank of the Seine from the Rue Mazarine to the Rue de Bourgogne which was 'developed' around 1640.
2. This was originally built (1629–36) for Richelieu, and, after his death in 1642, became the Palais Royal or royal palace. Its gardens crossed the old Charles V moat. The district was expanding rapidly when *The Liar* was first performed (1644).

DORANTE

To choose her well,
Take all the time, dear father, in the world.

GERONTE

I know her well enough. Clarice is fair
And virtuous as any of her age.
Her father's always been my closest friend.
580 The matter's settled.

DORANTE

Ah! I shudder, Sir.
To burden me so young with such a load.

GERONTE

Do as I bid.

DORANTE
[*the first words aside*]
I must resort to guile.
What! now that I must in the wars acquire
A good repute, distinguishing my arm ...

GERONTE

585 Before another arm can strike you down,
I must have someone to make up for you.
I want a grandson who'll maintain your rank,
A prop of my old age, a scion of
My line. I wish it.

DORANTE
You're inflexible!

GERONTE

590 Do as I bid.

DORANTE
But it's impossible.

162

GERONTE

Impossible?

DORANTE

Allow me publicly
To beg your pardon as I clasp your knees.
I'm ...

GERONTE

What?

DORANTE

Sir, in Poitiers ...

GERONTE

Speak and get up.

DORANTE

I'm married, then, since I must tell you all.

GERONTE

Wed? Without my consent?   595

DORANTE

At gunpoint, Sir.
You'll have it quashed by your authority,
But both of us were forced into the match
By the most unexpected quirk of fate.
Ah! if you knew ...

GERONTE

The truth, the whole sad truth!

DORANTE

Her family is good. As to her wealth,   600
If it's not quite as great as you might wish ...

GERONTE

Let's have the facts, then, since the thing is done.
She's called?

DORANTE

Orphise. Her father's Armedon.

GERONTE

I've never heard of one or t'other name.
605 Go on.

DORANTE

I got a sight of her as soon
As I arrived. She'd melt a heart of stone.
She was so lovely, and so utterly
Did her bright eyes gently enthrall my soul.
I therefore found a way to contact her,
610 And persevered in my addresses so
Effectively with this enchanting girl,
She grew so fond of me as I of her.
She granted me small favours secretly,
And I pursued my conquest to the point
615 I slid into her chamber quietly
To chat with her a part of every night.
One evening when I had gone up to her –
The second of September, I recall –
Yes, it was on that day that I was caught.
620 That very night her father supped in town.
Returning home, he comes, knocks at the door.
She's paralysed, turns pale, hides me away,
Opens, and with a ready wit, at once
Entwines herself around the old man's neck,
625 Conceals, by kissing him, her disarray.
He takes a seat, tells her his marriage plans
For her and of a bid that has been made.
Judge how my heart beats painfully. But she
Parries so well by her adroit reply,
630 Without upsetting me, she humours him.
This agonizing talk at last is done.
The old man makes to go. My watch then chimes.
He, turning to his startled daughter, asks:
'Since when this watch, and who has given it you?'
635 'Acaste, my cousin, has just sent it me,'

She says, 'and wants to have it mended here,
Since there's no specialist in Argenteuil.
It's chimed already thrice in half an hour.'
'Give it to me,' he says, 'I'll see to it.'
Then she comes over to my hiding place. 640
I slip it to her, but my luck was out.
The chain gets tangled with my pistol, and
Presses the trigger. Then the shot goes off.
Judge of our shock at this catastrophe.
She falls to earth. I think her dead. 645
The father, scared, at once makes for the door.
He bawls out 'Murder' and appeals for help.
His son, two serving-men, cut off our route.
Furious at this debacle and fighting mad,
Through all these three I hew myself a way. 650
Another mishap ruins me again;
My sword breaks in three pieces in my hand.
I'm forced, disarmed, back to her room. Orphise,
Somewhat recovered from her first affright,
With splendid promptness and resourcefulness, 655
Makes fast the door, locks herself in with me.
We build a new defence by piling up
Benches, trunks, beds, tables and even stools.
We barricade ourselves; elated, think,
By buying time, to carry still the day. 660
But, as this rampart rises by our toil,
They pierce the wall from an adjoining room.
So I was caught, and had to come to terms.
  [*Here,* CLARICE *sees them from her window, and*
  LUCRECE, *with* ISABELLE, *sees them from there*
  too.]

GERONTE

It comes to this, you *had* to marry her.

DORANTE

I had been found at night alone with her, 665
So I was cornered. She's a lovely girl.
The scandal was immense, her honour lost.

If I refused I'd answer with my head.
Her fight for me, her peril and her tears,
670 To my enamoured heart were added charms.
Hence, to preserve her honour and my life
And to attain with her the height of bliss,
With but a single word, I calmed the storm,
And did what any lover would have done.
675 Choose now to see me perish or enjoy
A treasure of inestimable worth.

GERONTE

No, no. I'm not so churlish as you think,
And find your mishap so explainable,
My love excuses you, and I regret
680 Only that you have kept it dark so long.

DORANTE

Since she's not wealthy, I have held my tongue.

GERONTE

A father's not too worried about wealth.
She's fair, of decent stock, and virtuous.
You love each other. That's enough. Farewell.
685 I'll tell Clarice's father that it's off.

Scene Six

DORANTE, CLITON

DORANTE

How do you like my story and my dodge?
The old man fell for it. I came off well.
An idiot in my place would have got stuck;
He would have wasted time in moans and groans,
690 And, though in love, would just have toed the line.
What a good secret artful lying is!

CLITON

What! all you said was pure invention?

166

DORANTE
                              Yes.
What you've been listening to was just an act
To keep my heart and soul for fair Lucrece.

CLITON
What! Sir, the watch, the sword, the pistol too?   695

DORANTE
I thought them up.

CLITON
                    Do me the favour, Sir,
When you indulge in these great masterstrokes,
Give me a little sign to put me wise.
Though I've been often warned, I fall for them.

DORANTE
Don't be afraid to fall for them again.   700
You'll be the sole confidant of my heart,
The treasurer of all my secrets.

CLITON
                        Well,
With these credentials I would dare to hope
That I might guard against them – only just
But, talking above love, this girl of yours . . .   705

Scene Seven

DORANTE, CLITON, SABINE

SABINE
[*gives him a note*]
Read this, Sir.

DORANTE
Where's it from?

SABINE

It's from Lucrece.

DORANTE

Tell her I'll come.

[*Exit* SABINE, *and* DORANTE *continues.*]
                    Cliton, do you still doubt
To which of these two girls this name belongs?
Lucrece now shares the passion she inspires,
710 And from her window wants to talk to me.
You *still* think it's the other one. You're mad.
Why should *she* write? I never spoke to *her*.

CLITON

Sir, let's not quarrel just on that account.
You'll soon know, when you hear her, if it's she.

DORANTE

715 Find a way to get in, and then worm out
Details about her wealth, her family.

Scene Eight

DORANTE, LYCAS

[LYCAS *gives* DORANTE *a note.*]

DORANTE

Another note.

                    [*He goes on, after reading it.*]
                    I know not what offence
Has set Alcippe and me at loggerheads.
No matter. Tell him I will gladly come
720 Presently.

                    [*Exit* LYCAS, *and* DORANTE *goes on.*]
                    I arrived here from Poitiers
Last night, and only showed my face today.
Already I've a duel, marriage, love.

For a beginning, really, that's not bad.
Let's have a lawsuit just to round things off.
Let anyone who wants take on ev'n more   725
Tough propositions. I will eat my hat
If he can cope with them as well as I.
But let's see who it is dares challenge me.

ACT THREE

Scene One

DORANTE, ALCIPPE, PHILISTE

PHILISTE

Yes, both of you acted as gentlemen,
730 And both come out blameless from this affair.
Thank heaven by happening to find you here,
I made the two of you good friends again,
And thus, with honours even, send you home.
It was a happy, rare coincidence.

DORANTE

735 Ev'n more for me, since I have given him
Full satisfaction without knowing why –
But now, Alcippe, *do* put me out of pain.
What was the reason for your burst of hate?
Have I been slandered by some ill report?
740 Be frank, Sir, so that I can set you right.

ALCIPPE

You know why well enough.

DORANTE

                 The more I think,
The less I see how I've offended you.

ALCIPPE

Well, then, since I must tell you everything,
I've for two years been secretly in love.
745 It's all sewn up. The match is in the bag;
We feel we have to keep it secret, though.
And yet to my belovèd, who must be
Mine and mine only, or she's false to me,
You're off'ring music, dancing, a repast.

You cannot fail to see how piqued I am,   750
Because, to play me such a nasty trick,
You hid, deliberately, your return,
And have today come out of hiding just
To brag to me about your prowesses.
This conduct stuns me. It seems obvious   755
Your only object was to do me down.

DORANTE

I, were my courage still in doubt, would not
Cure you of either error or offence,
And we as rivals would cross swords again.
But, as you know my valour, both of you,   760
Let me in brief clear up the mystery.
The girl for whom the fête was held last night
Cannot have given you grounds for jealousy,
She was, a short time back, on business here,   765
And I am sure she can't be known to you.

ALCIPPE

My dear Dorante, I'm overjoyed to see
Our disagreement end so soon.

DORANTE
                              Alcippe,
Next time, please don't fly off the handle and
Follow your first impulsive jealousy.   770
Until you know the truth, restrain yourself
And do not start where rightly you should end.
Farewell. Your servant, Sir.

Scene Two

ALCIPPE, PHILISTE

PHILISTE
                    You're still upset?

ALCIPPE

Out of the frying pan into the fire!
775 Who could have given the repast to her?
Who is the culprit? What am I to think?

PHILISTE

Clarice's ardour fully equals yours.
This entertainment was for someone else.
Your page's error's at the back of it.
780 Himself deceived, he has deceived you too.
He and Lucrece's servants told me all.
He saw her go into Lucrece's house,
But missed Hippolyta and Daphne who
Had chanced that day to dine with her. He sees
785 Them leave, their faces shaded by their hats,
And keeping at a distance, follows them.
The colours[1] and the carriage took him in.
All was Lucrece's. It misled him, and,
Taking them for Clarice and for Lucrece,
790 He did a great disservice to your love.
Up to the water's edge he sees them drive,
And, from the carriage, climb into a boat.
He sees the courses carried in, and hears
Some music (very second-rate, I'm told).
795 But there's no cause for you to worry now,
For, after all, the carriage had been lent.
Your information's wrong. These other two
In perfect quiet spent the night at home.

ALCIPPE

My luck is out. Thus, without any grounds,
800 I have made all this fuss with my beloved.

PHILISTE

I'll patch it up. But there is something else.
The man Dorante, who is the secret cause
Of all this upset you have just described

1. The *colours* are those of the servants' livery.

This lavish banquet readied on the spot,
Who, hiding his arrival for a month,   805
Visits incognito a girl at night,
Arrived in town yesterday from Poitiers
And slept the whole night peacefully at home.

ALCIPPE

What! his repast ...

PHILISTE
                    Is just a whopping lie;
Or, when he gave it, that was in his dreams.   810

ALCIPPE

Dorante has shown in this unprogrammed fight
Such mettle as to rule out cowardice,
And valour's school does not teach trickery.
A man of courage always keeps his word.
He will not tolerate such abject tricks,   815
And flees from lying as from death itself.
That cannot be.

PHILISTE
                    Dorante is, I presume,
Valiant by nature, but from habit lies.
You must be somewhat less incredulous
And wonder at our joint naiveness. We   820
Are greenhorns to be taken in like this.
A banquet garnished with six services,
Four bands, courses galore and fireworks too,
And all got ready in an hour or two,
As if the fixtures needed for the meal   825
Came down from heav'n on stage machinery.
Whoever took his word like you and me
May have lacked sense, but not credulity.
For me, I saw that all this badinage
Did not agree with what the page had said.   830
What about you?

ALCIPPE

Jealousy blinds the heart,
Which, sight unseen, believes each word it hears.
Let's leave Dorante and all his barefaced lies.
Let's find Clarice, ask her to pardon me.
835 No wonder when I spoke, she did not blush.

PHILISTE

Wait till tomorrow. Let me take a hand.
I'll go and talk to her and pave the way,
Dispel her anger, cheer her up again.
Don't in your eagerness expose yourself
840 To her first burst of fury.

ALCIPPE

If the light
Of the departing day does not deceive,
I think I see her with her Isabelle.
I'll follow your advice and keep away
Till she can laugh about my jealousy.

Scene Three

CLARICE, ISABELLE

CLARICE

845 Isabelle, come, let's go and meet Lucrece.

ISABELLE

It's not yet late, and there's no need for haste.
She's ready to do anything for you.
I'd hardly spoken when she penned the note.

CLARICE

850 I would be just as quick to help her out.
But, from her window did you see Géronte?
And, fancy, this much vaunted son of his
Is just the man who flirted so with me.

ISABELLE

Yes, I identified him to Lucrece;
The moment that Géronte had disappeared,
Seeing him with his serving man alone,   855
Sabine, we saw her, handed him the note.
You'll talk to him.

CLARICE

How cunning, Isabelle!

ISABELLE

Well, this technique is not completely new,
Is he the only one to make his mark,
Turning himself from student into knight?   860
How many talk of Germany like him,
And swear they've fought in every big campaign,
Seize every chance, assume a knowing air,
Tell of the odd defeat and horses lost,
Who, picking up these terms from a gazette,   865
Leave Paris only for their villages,
And pose with us as first-hand witnesses
Of all these wars they read or dream about.
Doubtless he thinks, or I'm entirely wrong,
Spirited girls are fond of fighting men,   870
And, taking *you* for *me*, he promptly judged
You'd like a plumèd cap more than a quill[1]
In hand. And so, to please you, he appeared
Not as he is, but as he wants to be.
You would, he felt, be more approachable   875
In the new status he assumed for you.

CLARICE

In cheating he's a master. He excels.
First he duped *me*. Now, he has duped Alcippe.
This jealous wretch believes – it's on his brain –
Dorante gave you a river fête last night.   880
(Could anything be more improbable?)
Alcippe accuses me of fickleness,

1. A pun on the word 'plume', which means both feather and quill.

175

And rants away in what was Greek to me.
I let him[1] chat me up all night, he says.
885 He talks to me of music, ball and dance,
Of a superb and opulent repast –
So many courses and so many rounds.
My feelings and my brain are in a whirl.

ISABELLE

But that's a sign of Dorante's love for you,
890 And of his passion's great dexterity.
He must have known about Alcippe and you,
And so, to oust him, roused his jealousy.
He promptly carried out another move.
His father was put up to speak to yours.
895 What more can lightning suitors do than get
Their fathers' backing and their rival fixed?
Your father, and his too, favour the match;
He loves you. *You* like *him*. It's in the bag.

CLARICE

It is, as much as it will ever be.

ISABELLE

900 What! your heart's changed, and you won't follow it?

CLARICE

You've dropped your guard and have misprised your
reach.[2]
Try and explain his trickery again.
He's wed, but no one's ever heard he was.
His father's cancelled his request to mine,
905 Highly embarrassed, looking very glum.

ISABELLE

And I say, cunning fellow, in my turn.
He really loves and masters cheating if
He cheats and cheats just for the fun of it.

1. *Him* refers to Dorante.
2. The two metaphors in this line are taken from fencing.

The more I think of it, the less I see
What great advantage he expects from you. 910
But now what will you do? Why speak to him?
Is it to laugh at him or tell him off?

CLARICE

It would at least suit me to silence him.

ISABELLE

I would prefer to leave him in the cold.

CLARICE

I want to talk from curiosity. 915
I've caught a glimpse of someone in the dark.
If it was he, I might be recognized.
Let's go then to Lucrece's window, since
It's in her name I have to speak to him.
My jealous friend – I can fall back on him. 920
Knowing all that I do, that won't be hard.

Scene Four

DORANTE, CLITON

DORANTE

This is the time and place fixed by the note.

CLITON

I've got the picture from the servant. She's
The only child of a high magistrate. 925
I've told you of her wealth, age, family.
But it would give me, Sir, a real good laugh
If your Lucrece could lie as well as you.
It would be such a treat, Lord strike me down,
I'd like her for an hour to have the gift 930
So that she could outsmart you for a while.
You're Betty Martin and she's all my eye.
I'd hear the tallest tales from both of you.

DORANTE

Heaven bestows this grace on very few.
One needs alertness, wit and memory.
935 One mustn't get confused, and still less blush.
But someone's at the window. Let's move up.

Scene Five

CLARICE, LUCRECE, ISABELLE [*at the window*];
DORANTE, CLITON [*below*]

CLARICE [*to* ISABELLE]

While we are talking, keep a good look out.

ISABELLE

When your old man is ready to come out,
940 I shall be here to give a warning sign.
[ISABELLE *goes away from the window and is no longer visible.*]

LUCRECE [*to* CLARICE]

He's talking to my father about you.
Clarice, speak in my name, and I'll keep mum.

CLARICE

Is that you there, Dorante?

DORANTE

                    Yes, it is I
Who seeks to live and die for you alone.

LUCRECE [*to* CLARICE]

945 His gallant words are in the same old vein.

CLARICE [*to* LUCRECE]

He could have spared himself this vain constraint.
Has he already recognized my voice?

CLITON [*to* DORANTE]
It's she, and this time, Sir, I grant you're right.

DORANTE [*to* CLARICE]
Yet, it is I who gladly would efface
The days I've lived without adoring you.   950
Life without seeing you is misery.
It's not a life, or but a gloomy one.
It's one long death, and I must frankly own
That life's worthwhile if one's Lucrece's slave.

CLARICE [*to* LUCRECE]
My dear, he flirts with each of us in turn.   955

LUCRECE [*to* CLARICE]
He gives free rein to love and trickery.

DORANTE
My life is yours, dear lady, to command.
I would be happy were it lost for you.
Do with it what you will. Tell me which way
You have decided to make use of me.   960

CLARICE
Just now I'd something to propose to you,
But there's no longer any need for me,
For it's impossible.

DORANTE
                    Impossible?
For you I'd dare anything anywhere.

CLARICE
Even to marry me when you are wed?   965

DORANTE
I married? Someone has been hoaxing you.
Whoever told you so has played you up.

179

CLARICE [*to* LUCRECE]

He *is* a scoundrel!

LUCRECE [*to* CLARICE]

All he does is lie.

DORANTE

I've never married. If these calumnies
970 Are meant . . .

CLARICE

Do you still think your word's believed?

DORANTE

The forkèd lightning blast me if I lie!

CLARICE

A liar's always lavish with his oaths.

DORANTE

If you had any feeling left for me
Which can be damaged by this false report,
975 Then hesitate no longer or suspect
What I can easily disprove to you.

CLARICE [*to* LUCRECE]

It sounds like truth. For his effrontery
So naturally carries off a lie.

DORANTE

In order to dispel the slightest doubt,
980 Let me tomorrow offer you my hand.

CLARICE

You'd make a thousand offers in one day.

DORANTE

You'll send my credit up so much in town,
The place will be on fire with jealousy.

CLARICE

It's all that one like you deserves. A man
Who says that he's a thunderbolt of war,   985
And all he ever plied was pen or glass,
Who yesterday came from Poitiers and says
He's courted me in Paris for a year,
Who gives the whole night through parties and balls,
Although he's spent it silently in bed,   990
Who says he's married and at once recants,
That's a fine way to heighten one's prestige.
Tell me yourself the proper name for him.

CLITON [*to* DORANTE]

Get out of *that*, and you'll be really smart.

DORANTE [*to* CLITON]

Don't be alarmed, everything in good time.   995

[*To* CLARICE]

For each of these inventions there was cause.
One day I'll give you satisfaction for
Them all. But now, as for the most important one,
I feigned the marriage. Why should I deny
What will oblige you to commend my ruse?   1000
I feigned it, and expose myself to scorn.
But what if this were done for you alone?

CLARICE

Me?

DORANTE

You. Listen. As I could not consent . . .

CLITON [*to* DORANTE]

Please tell me if you are about to lie.

DORANTE [*sotto voce to* CLITON]

Wretch! Hold your tongue, or else I'll tear it out.   1005

[*To* CLARICE]
Well, since to serving you I link my fate,
My love would not allow me to accept
The girl my father wanted me to wed . . .

CLARICE [*sotto voce to* LUCRECE]
He's off again. Let's hear him.

DORANTE
                        This device
1010 Kept my enamoured heart for fair Lucrece,
And by this marriage dreamed up on the spot,
I slipped out of the one arranged for me.
Blame me for falling into grievous faults;
Call me a rogue and master of deceit!
1015 At least, though, praise me for my faithfulness
And to these strictures add a suitor's name.
This marriage gets me clear of all the rest.
I flee all other bonds to die in yours.
Thus, free to enter into marriage ties,
1020 I pass as wedded for all else but you.

CLARICE
Your newborn love is far too violent,
And always leaves me somewhat sceptical.
How come you find me so attractive when
You've hardly seen me, do not know me well?

DORANTE
1025 *I* do not know you? You are motherless.
Your father's name is Périandre. He's
A magistrate adroit and circumspect.
His yearly revenue's ten thousand crowns.
You lost a brother in th' Italian wars.
1030 You had a sister who was called Julie.
Do I not know you? Tell me if I don't.

CLARICE [*to* LUCRECE]
Cousin, he knows you, and is after you.

LUCRECE [*aside*]

I wish he were!

CLARICE [*to* LUCRECE]
Let's try to clear this up.

[*To* DORANTE]
I wished to talk to you about Clarice.
One of her friends asked me about her hand.   1035
Would you consider marrying the girl?

DORANTE

Do not by such a question try my love.
I have displayed the bottom of my heart,
And, from now on, you can't be ignorant.
I feigned this marriage to protect myself.   1040
My passion is for you alone, Lucrece,
And for Clarice I've nothing but contempt.

CLARICE

You are, I fear, a trifle hard to please.
Clarice is of good family and fair.
Lucrece may seem to you more beautiful,   1045
But better men would be content with her.

DORANTE

A great defect, though, tarnishes her charms.

CLARICE

What's that?

DORANTE
            Well, she does not appeal to me.
And, rather than be married off to her,
I would prefer to wed a Turkish girl.   1050

CLARICE

And yet, today, they say, in broad daylight,
You clasped her hand and talked to her of love.

DORANTE

Someone's been telling you a pack of lies.

CLARICE [*sotto voce to* LUCRECE]

Listen to him. I'll bet he'll swear to it.

DORANTE

1055 May heav'n . . .

CLARICE [*sotto voce to* LUCRECE]

What did I tell you?

DORANTE

Strike me down,

If I have talked to anyone but you!

CLARICE

I'll not put up with such crude impudence
After what I have seen myself today;
You're bluffing, yet you dare to take an oath
1060 As if I could endure or swallow it.
Farewell. Be off. Believe, I beg of you,
This is an entertainment I enjoy,
And often for the pleasure it can yield,
I've pulled the wool o'er many other eyes.

Scene Six

DORANTE, CLITON

CLITON

1065 Well, as you realize, murder will out.

DORANTE

Ah! Cliton, now it's touch and go for me.

CLITON

The outcome's doubtless better than appears,
And access to her should be easier.
But I am just that bore who's in the way,[1]
Forcing the two of you to speak in code.   1070

DORANTE

Perhaps. What do you think?

CLITON

                    That's some Perhaps!

DORANTE

You think that, after all, I shall give up,
And feel all's lost for some slight obstacle?

CLITON

If you should ever like to liquidate
And for your treasure ever get a bid,   1075
I would advise you, sell it off dirt cheap.

DORANTE

But why do you believe I'm not in love?

CLITON

At every turn you tell the blackest lies.

DORANTE

I told the truth.

CLITON

                    But, when a liar speaks,
Coming from him, it has a hollow ring.   1080

DORANTE

Then I must try through some less suspect mind
If I can make her less standoffish. Well,
Let's think of other means before I sleep

    1. A reference back to lines 347 ff.

To win the unbelieving darling round.
1085 Often their humour varies with the moon.
One deals out scorn who wishes to be wooed.
Whatever she decides, tomorrow is
Another day, and night brings counsel then.

ACT FOUR

Scene One

DORANTE, CLITON

CLITON

But will Lucrece be up already, Sir?
She's not a one for stirring early.   1090

DORANTE

                    Learn
One often finds much more than one expects.
This place is better for my dream of love.[1]
From here I see her window, and this sight
Will print her picture deeper in my heart.

CLITON

Sir, à propos of dreams,[1] haven't you found   1095
Some remedy to put things right again?

DORANTE

I've just recalled a secret you yourself
Gave me as being quite infallible:
A suitor is successful if he spends.[2]

CLITON

The secret's splendid, but is misapplied.   1100
It only works if used with a coquette.

DORANTE

I know Lucrece. She's virtuous and discreet.
I would get nowhere just by making gifts.

1. A use of the word 'dream' in different senses – reverie and dreams
(i.e. lies) – see lines 314–16.
2. See lines 85 ff.

She's above that; her servants, though, have hands,
1105 And, though she'll disavow them on the point,
That talisman will loosen all their tongues.
They'll talk, and often they're worth listening to.
Whate'er it costs, some of them must be bought.
If the girl comes who handed me the note,
1110 After what she has done, I'm sure she'd play.
I'll be unlucky if I cannot find
The way to pay for its delivery.

CLITON

That's more than certain, judging by myself.
I don't say No when folks look after me.
1115 And since, when they make presents, they do *that*,
I'm always in a most complaisant mood.

DORANTE

Plenty of people have the same approach.

CLITON

But while we're waiting for Sabine to come
And for your gifts to her to take effect,
1120 Alcippe has fought a duel, so they say.

DORANTE

With whom?

CLITON

Nobody knows. But this report
Suggests a man vaguely resembling you.
And, had I not been with you all day long,
I would suspect you of this latest ploy.

DORANTE

1125 Were you with me when at Lucrece's place?

CLITON

Ah! Sir, could you have played this trick on me?

DORANTE

We duelled yesterday, and I had sworn
Never to speak of that adventure, but
To you the sole confidant of my heart
And treasurer of all my secrets.[1] I   1130
Will keep naught from you, as I promised you.
For some six months we had been enemies.
While visiting Poitiers, he challenged me,
And, since they made us patch the quarrel up,
We swore in secret each upon his sword,   1135
At the first opening we would come to blows.
Last night we met. Our hate flares up again,
Turns our embrace into a challenge. Well,
I soon get rid of you, rush off to him.
We settle, without seconds, the affair,   ·   1140
And, with two thrusts transfixing him, ensure
He never will be able to be ill.
He falls covered in blood.

CLITON
And so he's dead?

DORANTE

It seemed to me he was.

CLITON
I pity him.
He was a gentleman. Rarely does heav'n ...   1145

Scene Two

DORANTE, ALCIPPE, CLITON

ALCIPPE

I wish, dear friend, to share my joy with you.
I'm happy, for my father ...

1. Dorante repeats the promise made in lines 701–2. The 'secrets'
revealed are, of course, fresh inventions of the hero's.

DORANTE
Yes?

ALCIPPE
. . . is here.

CLITON [*to* DORANTE]
This is a place for reverie all right.[1]

DORANTE
Your joy's unusual. Such a meeting is
1150 No special pleasure for a man like me.

ALCIPPE
A mind which overflows with joy assumes
Its slightest hint is quickly understood.
Know then the happy day is almost here
Which will unite Clarice and me. To wed,
1155 We waited only for my father's Yes.

DORANTE
That's what I was unable to divine.
I'm very glad. You're on your way to her?

ALCIPPE
Yes, I shall bear this happy news to her,
And wished, in passing, just to let you know.

DORANTE
1160 All the more reason for my gratitude.
And so your love fears no reverses now.

ALCIPPE
While at the house my father's resting up,
I wanted, duty bound, to call on her.

CLITON [*sotto voce to* DORANTE]
The men you kill appear in splendid form.

1. The same pun as in 1095.

ALCIPPE

have full confidence in both of them.   1165
Forgive love's eagerness. It cannot wait.
Farewell.

DORANTE

Heav'n grant you marriage without cares.

Scene Three

DORANTE, CLITON

CLITON

He's dead! What! Sir, you try to fool me too.
Fool *me*, the sole confidant of your heart,
The treasurer of all your secrets. With   1170
All these credentials I had grounds to hope
That I might guard against it, only just.

DORANTE

You think I've merely dreamed this duel up?

CLITON

I'll swallow anything if you insist.
But all the time you spin so many tales.   1175
With you, one needs good eyes and all one's wits.
Moor, Jew or Christian, nobody is spared.

DORANTE

Alcippe's recovery surprises you.
The state I put him in was dangerous,
But nowadays some cures work miracles.   1180
Has no one told you of a source of life
Called sympathetic powder[1] by our men?
One daily sees astounding cures by it.

1. *Sympathetic powder* was introduced into France just after 1640. It
was made of calcined vitriol, and was supposed (as its name indicates)
to cure wounds from a distance. It was sprinkled on the blood of the
casualty, and then acted by *sympathy* on the body from which it had
issued.

CLITON

Yet they are not *quite* so astonishing,
1185 And no one's ever said it was so good
That someone left upon the ground as dead,
Who by two forceful thrusts has been transfixed,
Is seen just one day later fighting fit.

DORANTE

The powder's just the common one, and not
1190 Highly esteemed. But I know one which brings
Men back so quickly from the gates of death,
That in a trice all thought of that's erased.
Whoever knows it is a lucky man.

CLITON

Tell me the secret and I'll serve you free.

DORANTE

1195 I'd give it you and make you happy, but
The secret is a Hebrew formula
Which is as good as unpronounceable.
It would be useless treasure in your hands.

CLITON

So you know Hebrew?

DORANTE

Hebrew? Perfectly.
1200 I master full ten languages, Cliton.

CLITON

You'd really need ten of the richest tongues
In which to tell in turn so many fibs.
You chop them fine down into mince meat, and
Your body, all of it's stuffed full with truths.
1205 Not one of them comes out!

DORANTE

Untutored mind!
But here's my father.

Scene Four

GERONTE, DORANTE, CLITON

GERONTE
I was seeking you.

DORANTE [*aside*]
I wasn't seeking *you*. How badly timed
Is his arrival for my peace of mind.
Ah! how a father cramps a young man's style!

GERONTE
Since you're united by the marriage bond,   1210
I feel I'm really not approving it
If I disjoin what heav'n itself has linked.
Reason forbids it; and I feel my heart
Filled by a keen desire to meet your wife.
I'll write then to her father. Do so too.   1215
I'll tell him that, from what I've heard from you,
I feel most happy that a splendid girl,
So virtuous, has joined my family.
I'll then go on to say I long to see
The only hope of my declining years.   1220
You go in person to convoy her here,
For it's essential – duty orders it:
To send a servant would imply contempt.

DORANTE
He'll be surprised at your civilities.
I'm ready, but it would be all in vain.   1225
He'll not allow her to be sent to you.
She's pregnant.

GERONTE
Pregnant!

DORANTE
                Over six months gone.

GERONTE

I'm overjoyed to hear the news.

DORANTE

              I'm sure
You'll not endanger, Sir, her pregnancy.

GERONTE

1230 No, no. I'll be as patient as I'm glad.
I shall not jeopardize my grandchild's life.
This time my prayer has been heard by heav'n.
I think on seeing him I'll die with joy.
Goodbye. I'll change the letter I shall send,
1235 Congratulate her father, begging him
To take good care of her delivery,
As all my happiness depends on it.

DORANTE [*to* CLITON]

So off he goes as happy as a king.

GERONTE
[*turning back*]

Write to him too.

DORANTE

          I'll do so without fail.
1240 How kind of him!

CLITON

Quiet! He's coming back.

GERONTE

I don't remember what her father's called.
What is his name?

DORANTE

          Don't worry about that
And go to all the needless trouble. When
I close the packet, I shall add the address.

GERONTE

All in one hand would be much more polite. 1245

DORANTE [*the first line aside*]

I'll get this bee out of his bonnet yet.
Your hand or mine, it hardly matters which.

GERONTE

They're somewhat touchy, these provincial squires.

DORANTE

Her father knows the form at court.

GERONTE

Be quick.
Tell me . . . 1250

DORANTE

What shall I say?

GERONTE

He's called?

DORANTE

Pyrandre.

GERONTE

A few hours back, it was a different name.
It was – I've got it – it was Armedon.

DORANTE

Yes, that's his name. The other's his estate.
He took the name when he was in the wars,
And uses either one indifferently – 1255
Sometimes Pyrandre, sometimes Armedon.

GERONTE

That's an abuse custom has authorized.
I did so too myself when I was young.
Goodbye. I'll go and write.

Scene Five

DORANTE, CLITON

DORANTE
    At last I'm free

CLITON
1260 Liars should have a first rate memory.

DORANTE
My readiness of wit makes up for it.

CLITON
But they'll get to the bottom of it soon.
After you lost your bearings in the fix,
The rest can not for long be hid. They know
1265 The truth now at Lucrece's, and Clarice,
Piqued at your scorn, knows it as well. Annoyed
By your behaviour, she will take the chance
To drown you in embarrassment and shame.

DORANTE
Your fear's well founded, and time presses. Hence,
1270 We must at once persuade Lucrece to side
With us. But here's the one we're waiting for.

Scene Six

DORANTE, CLITON, SABINE

DORANTE
Dear friend, last night I was beside myself,
And so transported I was in no state
To think of you when I had read the note.
1275 But you won't lose by it; here's for your pains.

SABINE

I couldn't . . .

DORANTE
Do accept.

SABINE
You mustn't think
That I'm the kind . . .

DORANTE
Here.

SABINE
No.

DORANTE
Take it, I say.
I'm not ungrateful for a real good turn.
Be quick. Hold out your hand.

CLITON
Heav'ns! what a fuss!
Poor thing. She just needs to be taught the form.   1280
Between ourselves, this shilly-shallying
At times like this, my dear, is out of place.
If *one* hand's not enough, then hold out *both*.
You can't be bashful in the trade you ply.
Don't put on airs. All you need do is take.   1285
A bird in hand's better than in the bush.
This rain is gentle. When it falls on me,
I'd open ev'n my heart to catch the drops.
Take all you can get hold of nowadays.
And spurning gold is not a great man's vice.   1290
Get that into your head. Among us friends,
If you don't mind, I could go halves with you.

SABINE
That's asking a bit much.

DORANTE

You see, I mean
Later to do a great deal more for you.
1295 But, as I got this letter from your hand,
Would you deliver the reply for me?

SABINE

Certainly, Sir, but that does not imply
My mistress will accept or study it.
I'll do my best.

CLITON

My goodness, she becomes
1300 More gentle than a wife and suppler than
A glove.

DORANTE

It's clicked.[1] Hand it her, anyhow.
She hasn't such a strong dislike for me.
I'll be back presently to see what's what.

SABINE

Then I'll report on everything I've done.

Scene Seven

CLITON, SABINE

CLITON

1305 You see how deeds cut out the need for words,
This is a man who's dripping with the stuff.
As I can help you to be in with him . . .

SABINE

Let the rain fall, and leave the rest to me.

1. *It's clicked*, i.e. the trick of oiling the servant's palm (see lines 1099–1112).

CLITON

You've got the hang of it.

SABINE

     I may seem slow,
But I'm not such a nitwit as you think.   1310
I know my job, and my naive approach
Gets there as quickly as your grasping hands.

CLITON

Then if you know your job, tell me what hopes
My master has of pressing home his case.
Does she not care? Or will we make it?   1315

SABINE

         Well,
Since he's so open-handed, I'll be frank.
To put you right, Lucrece is not at all
Indiff'rent to your master's love for her.
She didn't sleep a wink the whole night long,
And I suspect she's half in love with him.   1320

CLITON

But on what privilege does she rely
To be so harsh when she is half in love?
Last night he'd nothing but contempt from her.
My dear, my master's, after all, a catch.
These half-way feelings are a strange affair.   1325
Were he to follow me, he'd leave Lucrece.

SABINE

He shouldn't be too quick. She loves him, sure.

CLITON

But if she does, she's being rather tough.
I never saw such manners.

SABINE
                    Well, she is
1330 Between the devil and the deep blue sea.
Her heart is conquered, but unwillingly,
Because his usual practice is to lie.
Last night, she saw him in the Tuileries,
Where all his story was a pack of lies.
1335 He's done the same already twice or thrice.

CLITON

The greatest liars sometimes speak the truth.

SABINE

She's grounds for doubting and distrusting him.

CLITON

She should have confidence in him. All night
He only turned and twisted in his bed.

SABINE

1340 Perhaps you lie just the same way as he.

CLITON

I'm just straightforward, and you do me wrong.

SABINE

But are you sure he doesn't love Clarice?

CLITON

He never loved her.

SABINE
        Certain?

CLITON
                I am sure.

SABINE

Then let him fear no more to pine in vain.
1345 Lucrece, on recognizing him, at once

Requested me on purpose to come out
To see if he would not approach us. So,
If he's sincere, the rest is in the bag.
Be off. You needn't tell me what to do.
I'll tell her everything I ought to tell.   1350

CLITON

Farewell. If you for your part do your stuff
Believe that, as for me, I'll make it rain.

Scene Eight

LUCRECE, SABINE

SABINE

How pleased a certain girl will be with me!
But here she is already, all aflame!
What eagle eyes she has. She's seen the note.   1355

LUCRECE

What did the master and the servant say?

SABINE

The two of them are singing the same tune.
The master's yours, and here's a note from him.

LUCRECE
[after reading it]

Dorante puts on an act. He's passionate.
But he's too often tried to take me in,   1360
And I am not the girl to trust his words.

SABINE

Neither do I, but I believe his gold.

LUCRECE

He offered gold?

SABINE

Look.

LUCRECE

You accepted it?

SABINE

To get you out of your uncertainty
1365 And show the virtues of his love for you,
I've taken the best witnesses of all,
And leave it to the whole world to decide
If gifts to servants mean no love for you
And if this act denotes a common soul.

LUCRECE

1370 I'm not opposed to your good fortune, but,
Since you are incorrect accepting it,
Don't mention it to me another time.

SABINE

What shall I tell this open-handed man?

LUCRECE

Tell him I tore his letter up unread.

SABINE

1375 O my good fortune, you've deserted me!

LUCRECE

Stir in two or three gentle words of yours,
Adroitly stressing women's nature. Thus,
Tell him that, given time, they may relent.
And mention above all the time and place
1380 Where he's most likely to run into me.
He's such a trickster. I need guarantees.

SABINE

Ah! if you knew the sufferings he endures,
You would no longer doubt his stricken heart.
All the long night, he sighs, groans and complains.

LUCRECE

To soothe the ills caused by this sad complaint,   1385
Administer some hope with lots of fear,
And keep him balancing between the two.
But don't commit *me* or make *him* despair.

Scene Nine

CLARICE, LUCRECE, SABINE

CLARICE

He's out to get you, and I'm rid of him.
But that's a loss I'll suffer easily.   1390
Alcippe makes up for it. His father's here.

LUCRECE

So that's a serious worry off your mind.

CLARICE

I'll soon be free of it. *You* are all set
To profit by a curious conquest. You
Know what he told me.   1395

LUCRECE

                        He was lying then.
But now he speaks the truth, I'll vouch for it.

CLARICE

Perhaps he does, but it's a big Perhaps.

LUCRECE

Dorante's a trickster, and he's shown he is.
But, if he still went on to pay me court,
Perhaps in time he'd make me doubt he was.   1400

CLARICE

But, if you love him, you've been warned at least.
So mind you watch your step and act your part.

LUCRECE

You go too far. For all you can assume
Is I'm inclined to trust, but not to love.

CLARICE

1405 To trust him isn't far from loving him.
Believe his love and you'll believe him too.
And one follows the other closely. Hence,
Whoever thinks she's loved, herself soon loves.

LUCRECE

Often th' effect of curiosity
1410 Is just the same as that of passion.

CLARICE

I,
Just to oblige, will take your word for that.

SABINE

The two of you will make me see bright red.
What is the point of all this chit and chat.
Don't be so coy, and stop this simpering,
1415 Or, strike me down, you won't get anywhere.

LUCRECE

She's crazy, but forget her. Tell me now
When all we three met in the Tuileries,
And he at once went overboard for you,
He had a good reception. Am I wrong?
1420 Was it love then, or curiosity?

CLARICE

Sheer curiosity. That was for laughs
And the sweet nothings he might say to me.

LUCRECE

I in my turn handle this note the same.
I took it, read it, but was uninvolved.
1425 Sheer curiosity. That was for laughs
At the sweet nothings he might write to me.

CLARICE

Reading and listening are two different things.
One's a great favour, one's civility;
But I'll be glad if things work out for you.
As things are now, I'm quite disinterested.   1430

LUCRECE

Sabine will tell him I have torn it up.

CLARICE

So you derive no benefit from it.
You're just inquisitive.

LUCRECE

Just as *you* were.

CLARICE

All right, but now it's time to go to church.

LUCRECE
[*to* CLARICE]

Let's go.   1435

[*To* SABINE]
Act, if you see him, as I said.

SABINE

Well, this is not my trial run. I know
Exactly what is biting both of you.
If I can't cure you, I'll be much surprised.
But he's a man to catch when in the mood.

LUCRECE

I'm sure he is.   1440

SABINE

Let's put this rain away.

ACT FIVE

Scene One

GERONTE, PHILISTE

GERONTE

This is a piece of luck to meet him. Now
I'll satisfy my curiosity.
You studied at Poitiers, so I recall,
And, like my son, you know the people there.
1445 So you are just the man to tell me of
The family and standing of Pyrandre.

PHILISTE

Pyrandre! Who?

GERONTE

One of its citizens,
Noble, they tell me, but not too well off.

PHILISTE

In all Poitiers, there is no nobleman,
1450 Or, to my knowledge, bourgeois of that name.

GERONTE

Perhaps you know him by his other name;
Pyrandre's also known as Armedon.

PHILISTE

Means nothing to me.

GERONTE

Father of Orphise,
The beauty who's the toast of all the town.
1455 You know the name of that enchanting girl
Who of these regions is the ornament.

PHILISTE

I swear Orphise, Pyrandre, Armedon
Have never ev'n been heard of in Poitiers.
If you need someone else to vouch for this . . .

GERONTE

To help Dorante, you're feigning ignorance.   1460
But I know all too well he loves Orphise,
And that, after a happy courtship, he
Was found alone up in her room with her.
His pistol there went off, betraying him.
So on the spot he had to marry her.   1465
I know the story, but my father's heart
Has given its consent. So there's no need
For you to be discreet about it all.

PHILISTE

What! so Dorante got married secretly?

GERONTE

As I'm indulgent, I forgive his youth.   1470

PHILISTE

Who told you so?

GERONTE

He did.

PHILISTE

Well, in that case
He'll give a true account of all the rest.
He knows the facts much better. Nor indeed
Should you be tempted to distrust him. But
He has a brilliant gift of fantasy,   1475
And that of guessing never was my line.

GERONTE

You mean to say his story's suspect.

PHILISTE

No.

He is reliable. Believe his words.
But, then, he dished us up a fine repast
1480 Last night, which showed a great inventiveness.
And, if this marriage tale is similar,
The fraud's complete and in the latest style.

GERONTE

Do you take pleasure in provoking me?

PHILISTE

My goodness, you were taken in like that.
1485 Come, let me be completely frank.
If that's the one daughter-in-law you have,
Your near relations can have quiet dreams.[1]
You get the point. Farewell. I've had my say.

Scene Two

GERONTE

O credulous old age, impudent youth!
1490 O all too obvious shame of my grey hair!
Is there a father wretched as I am?
Is there a worse affront for noble hearts?
Dorante's a trickster. This ungrateful boy
Tricks me, and then makes me a trickster too,
1495 For I'm the herald and accomplice of
His cock-and-bull, lying, impostor's tale,
As if I were resigned for all my days
To have to blush at my son's infamy.
The villain laughs at my forgivingness,
1500 And makes me still blush at my credulity.

1. The near relations can sleep untroubled as the non-existent daughter-in-law will never produce an heir to inherit Géronte's fortune.

Scene Three

GERONTE, DORANTE, CLITON

GERONTE

Are you a gentleman?

DORANTE [*first line aside*]
                    Oh what a bore!
Since I'm your son, there's little doubt of that.

GERONTE

Is it enough, then, just to be my son?

DORANTE

I am convinced of it, like all of France.

GERONTE

But do you also know, like all of France,   1505
This honourable title's origin?
Virtue alone has placed in this high rank
Those who have handed down their blood to me.

DORANTE

Then I'd not know what everybody knows –
Virtue acquired and blood transmits the rank.   1510

GERONTE

If virtue gives it, where the blood has failed,
Vice cancels it where blood has given it.
What's born by one means, by its contrary
Is killed. What one has done, the other can
Undo.[1] And, with this present vice of yours,   1515
You are no gentleman though born of me.

---

1. The sense of the somewhat involved passage from lines 1511 to
1516 is that virtue can give rank to those of lowly birth, and vice
versa strip of their rank those who are guilty of vice. What's born of
virtue is killed by vice.

DORANTE

I?

GERONTE

Let me tell you your impostures soil
So shamefully this gift of nature – speech.
Who calls himself a gentleman and lies
1520 Lies when he says so, and was never one.
Is there a baser vice, a darker stain,
More damning for a man destined for arms,
Can there be any weakness, any act,
From which a noble heart is more averse,
1525 Since, if it is belied but once, the shame
Can be effaced only if he will fight
And expiate in blood the grave affront
Which such an outrage stamps upon his brow.

DORANTE

What tells you that I lie?

GERONTE

What tells me so?
1530 Say if you can, say what your wife is called
The tale which yesterday you made me spread . . .

CLITON [*sotto voce to* DORANTE]

Tell him that sleep has made it slip your mind.

GERONTE

Add, add to this, with your effrontery,
Your father-in-law's name and his estate.
1535 Think up some subterfuge to hoodwink me.

CLITON [*to* DORANTE]

Summon your memory or wit to help.[1]

1. This refers back to line 935 and lines 1260–61.

GERONTE

With what embarrassment must I confess
That your effront'ry took me unawares,
That one so old should readily believe
What one so young reels off impudently.   1540
You make me, then, into a laughing stock,
Pass as weak-minded and a dotard. When
Have I held up a dagger at your throat?
Did I appear angry or violent?
If you had felt aversion to Clarice,   1545
What was the need for such a stratagem?
And could you ever doubt my father's heart
Would grant you all you wished for your content,
Since my indulgence, carried to extremes,
Approved your wedding to an unknown girl?   1550
This great excess of love I showed for you
Has neither touched nor won your heart. You have
Repaid me with an impudent pretence,
And shown for me no love, respect or fear.
Go. I disown you.   1555

DORANTE
Father, listen.

GERONTE
                 Ah!
To what? To tales invented on the spot?

DORANTE
No, the pure truth.

GERONTE
          Which your lips never speak.

CLITON [to DORANTE]
That's a real hit at all your cleverness.

DORANTE

I've fallen for a girl almost at sight,
1560 So beautiful, she's captivated me.
Lucrece she's called. You can find out about . . .

GERONTE

Tell me the truth. I know her family
And her. Her father is my friend.

DORANTE

                              My heart
Was by her dazzling glances so enthralled
1565 That, when you chose Clarice I was appalled
The moment that you let me know of it.
But, as I knew not if Lucrece's rank
And fortune were acceptable to you,
I did not dare reveal to you the love
1570 Her beauty had implanted in my heart,
And I was unaware until today
Mental adroitness was in love a crime.
But, if I dared to ask a favour, Sir,
Now that I know her family and wealth,
1575 I would entreat you by the dearest ties,
Blood and affection which unite us both,
To help me in my passion for this girl.
You win a father's Yes, and I'll win *hers*.

GERONTE

You're still deceiving me.

DORANTE

                              You don't trust *me*.
1580 Then trust at least Cliton who's standing here.
He knows my secret.

GERONTE

                       Don't you die of shame
At seeing me take more account of him,
And, though your father, doubting your good faith,

Giving more credit to your man than you.
Listen. Despite my fury I'll relent.   1585
I'll once again display a father's heart.
I'll once again risk my good name for you.
I know Lucrece and will request her hand.
But, if you raise the slightest obstacle . . .

DORANTE

To reassure you, let me come with you.   1590

GERONTE

Stay here. Stay here, and do not follow me.
I don't believe you, and I'm taking risks.
But be assured that if, for your Lucrece,
You show the slightest trickery or guile,
I never want to hear from you again.   1595
Otherwise, bear in mind this oath of mine:
I take to witness the bright sun above
That you will perish by a father's hand,
And your unworthy blood, shed at my feet,
Will do prompt justice to my honour's loss.   1600

Scene Four

DORANTE, CLITON

DORANTE

I'm not at all afraid of such a threat.

CLITON

You yield unwillingly and far too soon,
And this sharp wit which has deceived him twice
Ought in all fairness to go up to three.
Every third time, they say, is good or bad.   1605

DORANTE

Stop being funny, or you'll pay for it,
For something new is weighing on my mind.

213

CLITON

Is it remorse at having told the truth?
Unless it's some new devilry. For now
1610 I doubt whether you really love Lucrece.
And you're so fertile in such tricks that I
Take all you say to mean the opposite.

DORANTE

I really love her. There at least you're wrong.
The risk's too high, and that's what tortures me.
1615 If both the fathers do not come to terms,
All links are severed, and it is the end.
Besides, even if *they* reach a settlement,
Can I be sure the girl is keen on it?
I caught a glance of her not long ago.
1620 Her friend, though, is a most attractive thing.
Now that I've had a better look at her,
My first love really leaves me wondering.
My heart now hesitates between the two,
And, were it not already pledged, it would
1625 Be hers.

CLITON

Why then make all this show of love
And force her father to request her hand?

DORANTE

He wouldn't have believed me otherwise.

CLITON

What, even when speaking truth you really lied.

DORANTE

It was the only way to calm him down.
1630 Be damned he who unsealed my father's eyes.
With this fake wedding, I'd have had the time
To scrutinize my heart and choose in peace.

CLITON

But her companion after all's Clarice.

DORANTE

Then I have done myself a first-rate turn.
Lucky Alcippe, but much perplexed Dorante!   1635
Alcippe has only, though, what I refused.
Let's think no more of it. The place is filled.

CLITON

You're rid of her as well as of Orphise.

DORANTE

Let's take my wavering heart back to Lucrece
Which th' other almost stole beneath her eyes.[1]   1640
But here's Sabine.

Scene Five

DORANTE, SABINE, CLITON

DORANTE

How did my letter fare?
Did you deliver it to her fair hands?

SABINE

Yes, but ...

DORANTE

But what?

SABINE

She tore the letter up.

DORANTE

Unread?

SABINE

Unread.

1. Dorante, as always, confuses the two girls. He still thinks Lucrece
is Clarice and that it is the former who is going to marry Alcippe.

DORANTE

And you did not protest?

SABINE

1645 Ah! had you seen, Sir, how she scolded me.
I'll be dismissed. It's all as good as done.

DORANTE

Oh! she'll calm down, but here's a small douceur.
Hold out your hand.

SABINE

Sir!

DORANTE

Speak to her again.
I won't give up all hope immediately.

CLITON

1650 The hypocrite with all her curtseys! Look
How quickly her misfortunes are consoled.
She'll tell you more ev'n than you want to hear.

DORANTE

And so she tore the letter up unread.

SABINE

That's what she ordered me to tell you, Sir.
1655 But, to be frank ...

CLITON

How well she knows her stuff!

SABINE

She didn't tear it up. She read it all.
I can't mislead so generous a man.

CLITON

If there's a smarter minx, I'll eat my hat.

DORANTE

So, at that rate, she does not hate me.

SABINE
No.

DORANTE

She loves me? 1660

SABINE
Not that either.

DORANTE
Really?

SABINE
Yes.

DORANTE

There's someone else?

SABINE
Still less.

DORANTE
What are my hopes?

SABINE

I just don't know.

DORANTE
But tell me.

SABINE
Tell you what?

DORANTE

The truth.

SABINE

I'm telling it.

DORANTE

She'll love me though?

SABINE

Perhaps.

DORANTE

And when?

SABINE

When she believes your word.

DORANTE

1665 When she believes me. Ah! I'm mad with joy.

SABINE

When she believes you, then she is in love.

DORANTE

Then I will say it now and boast of it,
Since she can not doubt my sincerity:
My father ...

SABINE

Here he's coming with Clarice.

Scene Six

CLARICE, LUCRECE, DORANTE, SABINE, CLITON

CLARICE [*to* LUCRECE]

1670 Maybe he tells you true. That's rare with him.
You know his faults, so don't rush into things.

DORANTE

O you who can alone decide my fate ...

218

CLARICE [*to* LUCRECE]
It seems he's after *me*. He looks at *me*.

LUCRECE [*to* CLARICE]
Some glances by mistake have fallen on you.   1675
Let's see how he goes on.

DORANTE [*to* CLARICE]
                         How far from you,
Each minute costs my heart such agony,
And how I see by my experience
An hour's long absence tortures lovers' hearts!

CLARICE [*to* LUCRECE]
He just won't stop.

LUCRECE [*to* CLARICE]
            See what he's written me.

CLARICE [*to* LUCRECE]
Listen.   1680

LUCRECE [*to* CLARICE]
        You take for *you* what's meant for *me*.

CLARICE [*to* LUCRECE]
Let's clear the matter up.

[*Aloud to* DORANTE]
            You love me, then?

DORANTE [*to* CLARICE]
Alas! how little can love mean to you!
Since your fair eyes have subjugated me . . .

CLARICE [*to* LUCRECE]
You think this speech is still addressed to you?

LUCRECE [*to* CLARICE]

1685 I'm quite bewildered.

CLARICE [*to* LUCRECE]
Hear the hoaxer out.

LUCRECE [*to* CLARICE]
In view of what we know, it's somewhat crude.

CLARICE [*to* LUCRECE]
This is the way that he divides his heart –
It's you by day, and me by night he courts.

DORANTE [*to* CLARICE]
You are conferring. Ah! whate'er she says,
1690 Decide my fate on better counsels. She
Would badly prejudice my case with you.
She has some ground for being ill-disposed.[1]

LUCRECE [*to herself*]
Ah! that's too much. If I can't be revenged . . .

CLARICE [*to* DORANTE]
What she has told me's really very strange.

DORANTE
1695 It's just the product of her jealous mind.

CLARICE
I think it is. But do you recognize
Me now?

DORANTE
Of course. Let's stop this bantering.
It's you I talked to in the Tuileries,
Whom I at once regarded as my queen.

1. Dorante thinks he is speaking about Clarice whom he has refused
to marry.

CLARICE

f I, however, were to take her word,   1700
Your heart has fluttered for another ...

DORANTE
                                    For
Another I would have abandoned you?
Ah! rather, torn to pieces, let my heart ...

CLARICE

ndeed, if I believe her, you are wed.

DORANTE

You're making fun of me; just for a laugh,   1705
You take delight in hearing me repeat
That, to begin and end my life with you,
I say I'm married to all other girls.

CLARICE

Before you're linked in marriage with me, though,
You would be married to a Turkish girl.[1]   1710

DORANTE

Before I can be bound to someone else,
I'll, if you wish, be married in Algiers.

CLARICE

You've nothing but contempt, then, for Clarice?

DORANTE

You know the reason for my stratagem.
I'll stop at nothing if I can be yours.   1715

CLARICE

Myself, I'm going round in circles. Why,
Lucrece, just listen.

DORANTE [*sotto voce to* CLITON]
                What was that? Lucrece?

1. Echoes line 1050.

CLITON [*to* DORANTE]
Why, you've been had. The prettiest of the pair's
Lucrece. But which was she? I guessed aright,
1720 And, had we wagered, you'd have lost your bet.

DORANTE [*to* CLITON]
Last night I thought I recognized her voice.

CLITON [*to* DORANTE]
Clarice spoke at the window in her name.
Sabine assured me so in confidence.

DORANTE
Though I've been had, the other's just as good.
1725 And, since just now I thought her exquisite,
My heart's come into line with my mistake.
Don't breathe a word, and, in the new affair,
You'll see me play a different game, Cliton.
I'll not discard my line, but change my aim.

LUCRECE [*to* CLARICE]
1730 Let's see the height of his effrontery;
When you have told him all, he'll be surprised.

CLARICE [*to* DORANTE]
As she's my friend, she's told me everything.
Last night you courted *her* and slighted *me*.
Which of the two of us did you mislead?
1735 You spoke to her in fairly glowing words.

DORANTE
Since my return, I've spoken but to you.

CLARICE
Last night you didn't speak, then, to Lucrece?

DORANTE
Did you not wish to play a trick on me?
Didn't I recognize you by your voice?

222

CLARICE

Can he, for the first time, be speaking truth?   1740

DORANTE

To take my vengeance I was smart enough
To let you revel in your clumsy ruse,
And, taking you for her you wished to be,
  managed to outsmart you. Please don't think
That you can bluff me. I embarrassed you.   1745
Next time be careful whom you choose to dupe.
You thought you'd fool me. It was *I* fooled *you*,
But by a sham contempt which I belied.
For in a word, I love you, and I hate
Each day I've lived without my being yours.   1750

CLARICE

Why, if you love me, feign a marriage when
A father comes and asks my hand for you?
What was the point of this absurd deceit?

LUCRECE [*to* DORANTE]

Why write this note to *me* if you loved *her*?

DORANTE [*to* LUCRECE]

I have the feeling which these storms betray.   1755
You must have liked me, since you're so enraged.
But I've myself manoeuvred quite enough.
I must speak true. I love Lucrece alone.

CLARICE

Don't listen. He's the greatest rascal out.

DORANTE [*to* LUCRECE]

When you have heard me, you'll be sure I do,   1760
For, at the window, in your name, Lucrece,
Clarice was hoaxing me. I spotted her.
As you upset me, joining in this game,
I put you out and have avenged myself.

LUCRECE

1765 But last night, in the Tuileries, you said ...

DORANTE

It was Clarice that I was flirting with ...

CLARICE [*to* LUCRECE]

Don't listen any longer to this rogue.

DORANTE [*to* LUCRECE]

She had my flattery, but *you* my heart,
In which your eyes kindled a love I hid
1770 Till I induced my father to consent.
As all my words were so much fiction, I
Concealed my rank and my return.

CLARICE [*to* LUCRECE]

              He still
Accumulates one trick upon the next.
All he does is indulge in jugglery.

DORANTE [*to* LUCRECE]

1775 You are the only girl my heart adores.

LUCRECE [*to* DORANTE]

That's hardly what the facts bear out so far.

DORANTE

If now my father for your hand asks *yours*,
After that evidence, do you need more?

LUCRECE

After that evidence, I'll have to see
1780 If we have still some grounds for doubting you.

DORANTE [*to* LUCRECE]

Now that we've cleared things up, be undeceived.

[*To* CLARICE]
And you, Clarice, must always love Alcippe.
But for my marriage at Poitiers, he would
Be wifeless. I won't strike *that* jarring note,
But between me and you, you know it's true.   1785
Well, there he is, and there's my father too.

Scene Seven

GERONTE, DORANTE, ALCIPPE, CLARICE, LUCRECE,
ISABELLE, SABINE, CLITON

ALCIPPE
[*coming out of* CLARICE's *house and
speaking to her*]
Our parents are agreed, and you are mine.

GERONTE
[*coming out of* LUCRECE's *house and
speaking to her*]
Your father has fianced you with Dorante.

ALCIPPE
[*to* CLARICE]
A word from you will settle everything.   1790

GERONTE [*to* LUCRECE]
A word from you, and you'll be man and wife.

DORANTE [*to* LUCRECE]
Do not refuse to help me gain my end.

ALCIPPE
Have both of you been struck quite dumb today?

CLARICE
My father has complete authority.

LUCRECE

A daughter's duty is obeying him.

GERONTE [*to* LUCRECE]

1795 Come and receive this gentle sweet command.

ALCIPPE [*to* CLARICE]

Come then and add this gentle sweet consent.
[ALCIPPE *goes into* CLARICE's *house with her and*
ISABELLE, *and the others go into* LUCRECE's *house.*]

SABINE [*to* DORANTE *as he exits*]

If you are married, that's the end of rain.

DORANTE

I'll change this rain into a flood for you.

SABINE

You'll not have time even to think of it.
1800 My trade's worth nothing when the need is gone.

CLITON [*alone*]

Oh what a tangled web a liar weaves!
Few men could wriggle out of it like him.
And you who doubted if he'd ever win,
Learn how to lie from such rare mastery.

END

NICOMEDES

PREFACE

NICOMEDES (1651) is the one play of Corneille's written
after his main creative period (1637–43) to qualify for in-
clusion in his selected works. It was a favourite work of the
dramatist, and it has rightly been said that he expresses
himself more spontaneously in it than in any other. It has
verve, panache, a tight dramatic construction, rising suspense, a clash of political attitudes symbolized in the per-
sons of the main characters, but also the romanesque concept of ethics typical of the age (the hero returns from the
army to defend his lady who is being oppressed) and even a
few of the outward trappings of that approach, such as the
provision of hostages, the planned escape by a secret door,
and the issue of ultimata. It mingles, effortlessly and
effectively, soul-stirring tirades by the hero and his betrothed, Laodice, with the outright comedy of the doting
(but by no means unshrewd) Prusias and his actively in-
triguing queen (in scenes lifted almost bodily by Molière in
his *Hypochondriac*). And high politics alternates, as in real
life, with backstairs skulduggery, double agents and popular
risings. Little wonder that Victor Hugo regarded *Nicomedes* as one of the ancestors of the Romantics' new brand of
drama in which the genres were freely mixed.

Corneille, as he himself admits, took only the broadest
canvas from history, adjusting the character of Flaminius
(though partly misled by his modern sources on that score),
the role and end of Hannibal and other details to suit his
artistic purposes, and transforming a bloodthirsty tale of
oriental barbarism into a struggle between the still independent kingdoms of the Near East and the expanding
Roman Republic. As one critic has put it, this clash could
be regarded as a forerunner of a situation in which a
proud young sheikh seeks to throw off colonial domina-
tion.

Corneille had always, in his Roman plays, shown the

state at grips with an enemy or new concept (such as Christianity in *Polyeuctus*), but in *Nicomedes* it was particularly difficult to maintain a balance between the two forces, especially since the two most inspiring characters represent the desire of the independent kingdoms to restrain Roman expansion. To some extent, the position is retrieved by making a somewhat unconvincing distinction between Flaminius (acting from personal spite) and the Republic (which is guided by higher but none the less very interested motives). But the young hero always comes off best in his encounters with the envoy, who presents a somewhat risible picture when he crawls back after the failure of his attempt at flight (his return being in part explained in terms of the curious view that all the main characters should be reunited on the stage at the end).

If the historical background of ancient times contributes certain (modified) colours to Corneille's palette, contemporary events loom even larger in his vivid picture of the hero's battle for his cause. France at the time was deep in the civil war between the Queen Regent (in alliance with Mazarin) and the princes of the blood such as Condé, the victor of Rocroi (1643) over the Spaniards. Corneille had written a *Don Sancho* in 1650 which was widely regarded as an apology for Mazarin. Condé certainly disapproved of it. The present work, on the contrary, must be read in the light of the strong support accorded to Condé and the Fronde by Paris at the time. Soon after the play was first performed (in February 1653), Condé and the other rebel leaders were released from prison, and the obvious analogies with events in the drama greatly enhanced its success.

But the question goes much deeper than mere parallels. As Adam has pointed out (*Histoire de la Littérature Française au XVII Siècle*, Vol. II, p. 378), the political discussions in this play 'are no longer cold and eloquent, as in *Cinna* and *Pompey*. This besieged palace, the shouts of the riotous mob, the bloodshed, the troops overpowered, the approaching danger, the two women who finally reveal their hatred, what playwright would ever have devised such scenes before the civil disturbances in Paris [of the Fronde]?'

Many scenes can be seen in a new light if viewed against the background of the events of the time.

The play ends on a note of reconciliation. It suggests that Condé/Nicomedes (both of whom have served their country too well not to arouse jealousy) are no rebels but are merely demanding their rights. In the dénouement, they are no longer exposed to the wiles of (the unpopular) Mazarin or the unscrupulous Arsinoë. By implication, the settlement envisaged in the play is at the expense of the throne, but for Condé's partisans this point, if realized, was doubtless taken for granted.

It is significant, still in a historical context, that Corneille's attitude to the people, which was usually a highly disdainful one (as with most writers of the time) undergoes a sea change in *Nicomedes*, presumably because the lesser orders in Paris were solidly behind Condé and against the Queen Regent and Mazarin.

The characters are painted with a sure touch, especially the disreputable Prusias and Arsinoë, as well as the rapidly evolving Attalus. But both Nicomedes and Laodice are somewhat too consistently magnanimous for Anglo-Saxon tastes, quite apart from the obsessive insistence on regal rank and the faded elegance of some of the gallant repartees. It has also been rightly pointed out that the couple speak with one voice to the point of being often practically indistinguishable. Moreover, since there is never the slightest hint of a rift between them, and because they never stoop to intrigue, the initiative always lies with their enemies. The result is that their weapon is unfailingly and exclusively a lofty irony, which palls after a time. And everything conspires to bring the couple to safety by a combination of circumstances usually met with only in comedies or fairy tales.

Despite these blemishes, the play is a remarkable tour de force, and forms both an essential part of Corneille's opus and, through its realism (or, some would say, comic and down-to-earth aspects), a useful complement in the French seventeenth-century scene to Racine's more rarefied, if profoundly tragic masterpieces.

NICOMEDES: SUMMARY

ACT ONE

THE scene is Nicomedia, the modern Ismir, which is on the north-west sea coast of Asia Minor, roughly opposite what is now Istanbul. At the time of the action (about 180 B.C.), the town is the capital of the kingdom of Bithynia, ruled by the ageing Prusias who is completely in the hands of his second wife, Arsinoë. Nicomedes, the son by the first marriage, is a disciple of Hannibal and a consistently victorious general who has greatly enlarged his father's realm. He has left his army brusquely and returned to court to denounce a plot against him engineered by the queen through two assassins who have confessed their guilt.

Arsinoë seeks to procure his downfall, since she is jealous of his military glory and wishes to find a throne for her son, Attalus. The latter has just returned from Rome, where he has been held (and educated) as a hostage to the Romans for his father's conduct. Arsinoë is aided in her intrigues by Flaminius, the Roman ambassador, the son of the general defeated and killed by Hannibal (in Corneille's version of history) at Lake Trasimene (217 B.C.), and the artificer of Hannibal's betrayal and consequent suicide after the Carthaginian general had been given refuge at Nicomedia.

Nicomedes is betrothed to Laodice, queen of Armenia, who is detained at Prusias' court, her late father having entrusted her to that king and destined her hand to Nicomedes. The prince reports to her on the plot against him in the army and on his intention of securing justice against the queen of Bithynia, his stepmother, for her part in these machinations. Laodice swears to support him in his struggle.

The couple is joined by Attalus who makes a declaration of love (not the first one) to Laodice. The young queen brushes him off ironically. Attalus has never seen Nicomedes, who takes advantage of the situation to provoke his rival. Arsinoë comes on the scene, and she and her stepson exchange icy insults. Arsinoë, left alone with her confidante, explains that she has no intention of murdering Nicomedes, but merely wishes to provoke him into returning to court where the two assassins (in Arsinoë's pay) will withdraw their accusations and charge Nicomedes with using them to discredit the queen. The result will be to have the king disown his elder son and leave the throne open for Attalus.

ACT TWO

PRUSIAS complains of his son's unbidden return to court. He is irked by his debt of gratitude to his constantly victorious son. Nicomedes accepts the king's proposal that he should reply to Flaminius on the king's behalf. The Roman envoy ask Bithynia to give Attalus, as a Roman protégé, a crown. Nicomedes resents this attempt by the Romans to dictate to Bithynia, and turns down the request. Flaminius explains that the proposal need not affect Nicomedes' rights. Attalus can gain a crown by marrying Laodice. The prince replies that it is for her to choose her husband. He then leaves on an angry note of challenge.

ACT THREE

PRUSIAS attempts to railroad Laodice into marrying Attalus. When he has gone, Flaminius vaunts the advantages of such a step as involving an alliance with Rome, but his approach is also unsuccessful. Nicomedes joins the two, and taunts the envoy. After the latter's departure, he tells Laodice that he has denounced Arsinoë's plot against him to Prusias. Laodice foresees trouble. Seeing Attalus in the offing, she withdraws. Nicomedes reproaches his stepbrother with having disregarded a promise to fight for Laodice without outside support. Attalus defends himself ingeniously. Nicomedes is summoned to the king's presence. Meantime Arsinoë explains to Attalus her strategy against Nicomedes. Attalus is shaken at her double-dealing, and expresses doubt as to Nicomedes' guilt.

ACT FOUR

ARSINOË puts up a superb act in front of her doting husband, presenting herself as the outraged benefactress of the prince. Nicomedes refutes her posturing, and protests his innocence. He insists, to Arsinoë's embarrassment, that the plotters be put to death for their false accusations. She withdraws, swearing that she will never outlive her husband. Prusias summons his son to choose between succession to the throne and Laodice. Nicomedes plumps for his betrothed. Flaminius enters. Prusias decides to proclaim Attalus heir, and has Nicomedes arrested, with the intention of sending him to Rome as a hostage. Attalus is left alone with Flaminius, who reveals that Rome opposes his marriage with Laodice, since thereby he would become too powerful. Attalus now sees through Roman policy (divide and rule), and his admiration for Rome cools. He decides inwardly to back his stepbrother and to try and rescue him.

ACT FIVE

ON learning of Nicomedes' arrest, the people revolt, led by Laodice's retainers. Arsinoë's two hirelings from the army are lynched. Nicomedes is proclaimed the people's leader. Prusias' right-hand man reports that he can no longer vouch for Nicomedes' safety. Arsinoë suggests that Nicomedes be smuggled out of the palace on to a galley and taken off to Rome by sea. Meanwhile, the king must keep the mob in play. Attalus rushes off, making some enigmatic remarks.

Laodice, when informed of these developments, swears she will march at the head of the Bithynian and her Armenian troops to Rome and liberate her beloved. Attalus arrives, and reports that the prince has escaped. Prusias and Flaminius are in flight. They reappear, having decided to give themselves up. Laodice promises forgiveness, and Nicomedes, on entering, after having calmed the rising, promises a general pardon. It turns out that it was Attalus who freed his brother. The play ends on a note of general reconciliation, with Prusias still submissive to Rome, but no longer hostile to his elder son or to that son's marriage with Laodice. Attalus is promised a consolation prize of a new kingdom to be conquered by Nicomedes.

TO THE READER

THIS is a play of a rather unusual kind. For indeed it is the twenty-first which I have had performed on the stage; and, after having had some forty thousand lines recited, it is very difficult to find something new without straying somewhat from the high road and risk losing one's way. Love and passion, which should be the soul of tragedy, play no part in this one. Nobility of soul reigns alone in it, and regards its misfortunes with such a disdainful eye that they cannot wrest from it a groan. It is combated by intrigues, and opposes their machinations with only a lofty prudence which walks unmasked, which perceives peril unmoved and wishes for no other support than virtue and the love which it imprints on the hearts of every people. The historical account, which has so admirably lent me the material to illustrate this quality, is taken from Justin; and here is how he relates it at the end of his thirty-fourth chapter:

At the same time, Prusias, King of Bithynia, decided to murder his son, Nicomedes, in order to advance his other sons which he had had from another wife and whom he had sent to Rome to be brought up; but this plan was revealed to the young prince by the very people who had undertaken to execute it; they did more. They exhorted him to return tit for tat to so cruel a father and to set for him the snares which the villain had prepared for him, and they had no difficulty in convincing him. Thus, as soon as he had entered his father's kingdom, to which that father had summoned him, he was proclaimed king; and Prusias, driven from the throne, and abandoned even by his retainers, however hard he tried to hide, was killed in the end by his son, and lost his life by a crime as great as that which he had committed by giving orders to assassinate that son.

I have suppressed from the stage the horror of so barbarous a catastrophe and have not portrayed either the father or the son as having any plan to kill his relative. I have shown the son as being in love with Laodice, so that the union with a neighbouring crown could give the Romans more umbrage and form a greater inducement to make them oppose it. I have combined this story with that of the death of Hannibal which took place somewhat earlier at the court of that king, and his name forms no slight ornament to my work. I have made Nicomedes a disciple of his, so as to confer on him more valour and fierceness against the Romans, and I have taken advantage of the embassy on which Flaminius was sent by them to the king, their ally, to demand that the old enemy of their greatness should be delivered up to them, and have had him given secret instructions to foil this marriage which was bound to arouse their jealousy. I arranged, in order to win over the queen who, as is customary with second wives, has a complete hold on her old husband, that he brings home one of her sons, who (according to my source) was brought up in Rome. That has two consequences. For on the one hand he obtains the downfall of Hannibal, and on the other he opposes Nicomedes with a rival wholeheartedly backed by the Romans, and jealous of his glory and his budding greatness.

The assassins who revealed to the prince the bloodthirsty plans of his father have given me the idea of other intrigues to make him fall into the snares which his stepmother had set for him. And, as to the end, I have arranged it in such a way that all the characters in it act nobly, the ones rendering to virtue what they ought to render, and the others remaining within the firm bounds of their duty, thus leaving a rather illustrious example and providing a very pleasant conclusion.

The play, when performed, had a good reception, and, as they are not the worst lines which have come from my pen, I have reason to hope that, when read, the play will not lose any of the reputation which it has so far acquired, and will not be regarded as unworthy of its predecessors. My main aim has been to depict the policy of the Romans abroad and how imperiously they dealt with their allied kings, their maxims aimed at preventing them (the kings) from expanding and the care taken to curb their greatness when it began to become suspect to them through its increase and its greater prestige as a result of new conquests. This is the character I have conferred on the Republic in the person of its ambassador, Flaminius, who is faced by an intrepid prince who sees his fate sealed, unmoved, and defies Rome's haughty massive power, even when he is overwhelmed by it. This hero fashioned by me deviates somewhat from the rules of tragedy, since he does not seek to arouse pity by the excess of his misfortunes; but the outcome has shown that the firmness of great hearts which excites only admiration in the soul of the spectator is sometimes as pleasant as the compassion which our art bids us beg for their sufferings. It is good to take some slight risk and not always subscribe slavishly to its precepts, were it only to practise that of Horace:

Et mihi res, non me rebus, submittere conor,[1]

but the outcome must justify this daring; and, in taking a liberty of this nature, one remains guilty unless one is extremely lucky.

1. And I strive to subject things to myself, and not myself to things.

CAST

PRUSIAS, *King of Bithynia*
FLAMINIUS, *Ambassador of Rome*
ARSINOE, *Prusias' second wife*
LAODICE, *Queen of Armenia*
NICOMEDES, *eldest son of Prusias by his first wife*
ATTALUS, *son of Prusias and Arsinoë*
ARASPES, *captain of the guards of Prusias*
CLEONE, *confidante of Arsinoë*

The scene is in Nicomedia.[1]

1. The capital of Bithynia, a kingdom in the north-west of Asia Minor.

NICOMEDES

ACT ONE
Scene One

NICOMEDES, LAODICE

LAODICE

After so many martial feats, what bliss   1
To see you reign over my heart again,
To see, beneath the laurels on your brow,
Such a great conqueror my conquest, and
Lay all the glory gained by his exploits   5
As an illustrious homage at my feet.
And yet, despite the favours heaven accords,
My terror-stricken heart is closed to joy;
To see you saddens me; my loving heart
Regards the court as fraught with danger. There   10
Your stepmother holds sway. Your royal sire
Sees through her eyes, reveres her views alone,
And takes her wishes as his sovereign law.
Judge then, my lord, how safe you are. The hate
Which she so naturally feels for you   15
Has been rekindled now because of me.
Her son, your brother, who has just returned ...

NICOMEDES

Princess, I know he's here and pays you court;
I know that Rome, which kept him hostage, has
At last dispatched him home for worthier ends.   20
This present to his mother was the price
Roman Flaminius paid for Hannibal.
The king would have obeyed Rome's orders, but
That hero, by a poisoned cup, forestalled

25 A Roman triumph's last indignity
To which his dreaded name had destined him.
After my last campaign, I had annexed
All Cappadocia to Bithynia when,
Learning the news and furious at the loss
30 Of Hannibal and at the threat to you,
I left my army to Theagenes
To fly to Nicomedia to your aid.
You needed me, lady. I see you do,
Since the king's harassed by Flaminius still.
35 If he came here for Hannibal who's dead,
His stay, prolonged, must have another cause;
This can be you alone. He lingers on
To help my brother to importune you.

LAODICE

His Roman virtues will no doubt embrace
40 The interest of the queen most ardently.
Giving up Hannibal to him, she's gained
His backing – which makes me distrust him. But,
Sir, I have still no reason for complaint.
Whatever he may do, what need you fear?
45 Glory and love have little hold on me
If to sustain my troth I need you here.
If I can be so mad as to prefer
Attalus to all Asia's conqueror –
Attalus as a hostage reared by Rome,
50 Or rather fashioned as a slave by them
With nothing in his heart but servile fear,
Who trembles at an eagle and respects
An aedile!

NICOMEDES

Rather let me die before
I stoop to thoughts so base and jealous. Not
55 Your weakness but their violence I fear;
And, if once Rome comes out against us . . .

LAODICE

No.

I am a queen. Rome thunders but in vain.
I take no orders from it or your king.
If he's my guardian, that is only so
In execution of my father's wish;   60
He pledged my hand to you. No one but I
Can alter *that*, and choose a king for me.
By his and my decree, Armenia's queen
Is plighted to Bithynia's royal heir,
And never will demean herself so far   65
As to accept a throneless subject. Sir,
Be reassured.

NICOMEDES

Ah! *that* I cannot be
When you're in danger from a fury who,
Being all-powerful, will stop at naught
To win the throne's succession for her son.   70
There's nothing sacred she'll not violate.
She who surrendered Hannibal could well
Force you to yield, and be as true to you
As to the rights of hospitality.

LAODICE

But nature's rights, have they the privilege   75
To shield you from her, given this sacrilege?
Sir, your return, far from frustrating them,
Exposes you, and after that myself.
Unauthorized, it will be deemed a crime.
And you are cast as the first victim whom   80
Mother and son, seeing I do not flinch,
Will immolate, to rob me of support.
If I need *you*, should they use force on *me*,
The king must fear you – and the queen herself.
Go back, back to the army. Show them there   85
Ten thousand arms all poised for my revenge.
Speak, strength in hand, and from beyond their reach.
If they detain you here, they've naught to fear.

Do not rely upon your courage or
90 The lustre of a hundred victories;
However great your valour, *here* you have
Only two arms to fight with, like the rest.
And, were you the world's terror and delight,
Whoe'er comes here, offers the king his head.
95 I say again, go back, Sir, to your men;
Show to the court nothing but your renown;
Secure your life that mine may be secured;
If people fear you, I'll have naught to fear.

NICOMEDES

Back to the army? Ah! know that the queen
100 Has honeycombed it with assassins bought
By her. Two are unmasked. I've brought them here
To prove her guilt and undeceive the king.
Though he's her husband, he's my father still,
And, even if he can silence nature's voice,
105 Three sceptres added to his throne by me
Will speak instead of it and plead my case.
And, if our destiny, bent on my fall,
Plots it at court as well as in the field,
With danger everywhere, would you begrudge
110 The honour to expire before your eyes?

LAODICE

No. I no longer say I tremble. No.
If I must die, I'll die along with you.
Let us take courage and we'll make those blench
Who plan, with craven tricks, to crush us. You
115 The people love, and hate these sordid hearts.
Great power flows from such a following.
But hither comes your brother Attalus.

NICOMEDES

He's never met me. Don't reveal my name.

Scene Two

LAODICE, NICOMEDES, ATTALUS

ATTALUS

What! Always this inexorable mien?
Can I not catch a favourable glance?   120
A glance devoid of your severity,
And such, in short, as when it wins all hearts?

LAODICE

My mien may not be right for winning hearts,
But, if I wished to, I could soon unbend.

ATTALUS

No need to conquer mine, since it is yours.   125

LAODICE

I shall not then assume a smiling air.

ATTALUS

Since you've assumed it, please continue it.

LAODICE

Your heart's not mine. I'd rather give it back.

ATTALUS

You don't esteem it or you'd keep it.

LAODICE

I
Esteem you too much to dissemble. Sir,   130
Your rank and mine exclude unfrank debates;
I have no place in which to put your heart.
This fort is occupied. I've told you so
Repeatedly. Speak then no more of it.
At first one bears it; afterwards it jars.   135

ATTALUS

How fortunate the holder of the fort!
How happy, too, the man who could contest
Possession and outgeneral its lord.

NICOMEDES

To win the fort would cost full many a head,
140 Sir, for this conqueror keeps his conquests well.
His enemies have still to learn the art
To storm a fort once he has taken it.

ATTALUS

The fort can be attacked in such a way
That, valiant as he is, he'll be dislodged.

NICOMEDES

145 You might be wrong.

ATTALUS

        And if the king so wills?

LAODICE

The king, prudent and just, wills only what
He can.

ATTALUS

    What cannot sovereign grandeur do?

LAODICE

Speak not so boldly. If he's king, I'm queen;
And all the weight of his authority
150 Can only act by prayer and courtesy.

ATTALUS

No, but such action often can strike home
To queens like you living in his domains;
And, if a king's requests will not suffice,
Rome which has brought me up will speak for me.

NICOMEDES

Rome, Sir?   155

ATTALUS

Yes, Rome. Do you then doubt it will?

NICOMEDES

I hope no Roman's listening to you now.
If Rome but knew with whom you were in love,
Far from according you its full support,
It would be angry at its protégé
Thus tarnishing the lustre of its name,   160
And would perhaps degrade you there and then
From the proud rank of Roman citizen.
Did Rome give you that name to earn its hate,
Soiling it by your passion for a queen,
And know you not that Rome disdains to place   165
A king above its humblest citizen?
Though you have lived with these high-hearted men,
You've soon unlearned the maxims which they taught.
Call back a pride worthy of Rome and you;
Merit a name of which we live in dread,   170
And do not sink to ignominy such
As worshipping in vain Armenia's queen.
Think that, to touch your heart, you need at least
A tribune's daughter or a magistrate's;
That Rome allows you to aspire so high   175
Despite your birth which should have barred the way,
Since, honouring you by adopting you,
Rome let you hope for such a lofty match.
Force, break, destroy such shameful chains, and leave
Queens to the monarchs who are scorned by it.   180
In short, conceive of more ambitious plans,
The better to deserve your rightful claims.

ATTALUS

If this man's one of yours, then silence him.
Lady, seek to restrain such insolence.
To see how far it was disposed to go,   185

247

I've curbed my anger and have let him speak;
But now I fear it will explode and that,
If he goes on, farewell to my restraint.

NICOMEDES

Sir, if I'm right, what matter who I am?
190 Is right the less through borrowing my voice?
But, leaving love aside, yourself be judge.
The name of Roman is so precious and
Both queen and king have bought it dear enough
Not to be pleased to see it thrown away,
195 Since to obtain it they deprived themselves
Of the delight of guiding your first steps.
They sent you off when you were barely four;
Was that only to see this rank disdained,
And you renounce, by marrying a queen,
200 Their share in all the majesty of Rome?
Of such a treasure both were jealous, and ...

ATTALUS

Yet once again, is this man one of yours?
And do you feel for your diversion that
You cannot bid him to be silent?

LAODICE
Since
205 Calling you Roman he has roused your ire,
I'll call you, if you like, a sovereign's son.
As such you readily must recognize
An elder prince must be your master and
His anger feared. You know that ties of blood
210 Do not prevent your having different ranks.
You should respect him as his birth demands
And, far from seeking in his absence what ...

ATTALUS

He has the honour now of being yours,
But, if you say a word, it will be mine;
215 And if my lesser age affects my rank,

You will correct my fate's injustice. But
If I, as a king's son, must yield to him,
Let me, for once, speak as a Roman. Know
That none is born whom heaven has not ordained
To live unmastered and hold sway o'er kings.   220
Know that my love's great aim is to avoid
The shame not to be destined to a throne.
Know ...

LAODICE

     I suspected that my diadem
Charmed you at least as much as I myself;
Such as I am, though, both the crown and I,   225
All is your elder's who will be your king;
And, were he here, standing before you now,
You might think twice before offending him.

ATTALUS

I wish he were. My love and valiancy ...

NICOMEDES

Sir, make some wish which is less dangerous.   230
For, if he heard it, he might well himself
Ask satisfaction for this love of yours.

ATTALUS

What insolence! Where's your respect for me?

NICOMEDES

I do not know which of us lacks respect.

ATTALUS

You know my rank and dare speak thus to me?   235

NICOMEDES

Sir, my advantage is I know to whom
I speak. Since you do *not*, you cannot say
If I owe *you* or you owe *me* respect.

ATTALUS

Ah! lady, suffer my unbounded wrath . . .

LAODICE

240 Consult the queen, my mother, on this point.
She comes this way.

Scene Three

NICOMEDES, ARSINOE, LAODICE, ATTALUS,
CLEONE

NICOMEDES

Inform the prince, your son,
I beg you, who I am. Knowing me not,
He flies into a passion, is distraught,
Which ill befits such a fine character.
245 I'm sorry for him.

ARSINOE

You are here, my lord?

NICOMEDES

Yes, I am here, and Metrobates too.

ARSINOE

The villain!

NICOMEDES

But he has said nothing yet
Which might create uneasiness in you.

ARSINOE

But what's the cause of this surprise return?
250 What of your army?

NICOMEDES

It is in good hands,
And I have no great call to hurry back.

Here I had left master[1] and mistress. You
Have robbed me of the one, both Rome and you.
I've come to save the other from them and
From you.   255

ARSINOE
That's why you're here?

NICOMEDES
                              Yes, and I hope
You'll help me with my father on this point.

ARSINOE
I shall assist you as you hope I shall.

NICOMEDES
We are assured of having your good will.

ARSINOE
Only the king decides whether I act.

NICOMEDES
This favour you will do to both of us?   260

ARSINOE
Ah! rest assured I'll leave no stone unturned.

NICOMEDES
I know your heart. Have no doubts as to mine.

ATTALUS
But this is Nicomedes.

NICOMEDES
                              Yes, it's I
Who've come to see if I must yield to you.

ATTALUS
Forgive me if, knowing you not at all . . .   265

1. Hannibal.

NICOMEDES

Show yourself, prince, a worthier rival. If
You planned to occupy this fortress[1] here,
Then do not swerve from such a daring move.
But since I fight my battles all alone,
270 Threaten me not with Rome and with the king.
I shall defend it single-handed. You,
Do so attacking. I shall set aside
The prestige of the crown, an elder's rank,
Which destines me to be your master. Thus
We can decide what makes a better man –
275 Hannibal's lessons or the laws of Rome?
Farewell. I leave you to reflect on this.

Scene Four

ARSINOE, ATTALUS, CLEONE

ARSINOE

What! you apologized to one who dared
Defy you?

ATTALUS

I was taken by surprise.
280 This prompt return dumbfounds me, foils your plans.

ARSINOE

You do not see. It plays into my hand.
Fetch the ambassador of Rome for me;
To my apartment without retinue
Bring him, and let me guide your destiny.

ATTALUS

285 But if we must . . .

1. The usual conceit of the age for the woman being courted – in this case, Laodice.

ARSINOE
　　Be off and have no fear,
And expedite this talk and our designs.

Scene Five

ARSINOE, CLEONE

CLEONE
You keep from him a plan involving him!

ARSINOE
I fear he may take fright on learning it;
I fear the virtue he's imbibed in Rome
May rob me of the fruit of my intrigues;　　　　　290
He may not think that trickery and crime –
All becomes lawful if it wins a throne.

CLEONE
I would have thought Rome more unscrupulous.
Hannibal's death has tarnished its repute.

ARSINOE
Do not impute such unjust deeds to them.　　　　　295
A single Roman did it, and by my
Contrivance. No. Rome would have let him live,
Nor breached the laws of hospitality.
Rome to its cost knows his ability.
It could not bear its foes to welcome him;　　　　　300
But though, prudently mindful of the past,
I had him banished from the Syrian court,
Rome would have let him, unconcernedly,
Spend with an ally his remaining days.
Flaminius,[1] he alone, stung by the shame　　　　　305

　1. *Flaminius.* Corneille has here, following the sixteenth-century historian, Amyot, confused Flaminius, a consul who died (but not, as far as is known, at Hannibal's hand) at the battle of Trasimene in 217 B.C. when the Carthaginian general inflicted a crushing defeat on the Romans, and Flaminius, who was ambassador to Prusias in 183 B.C., but who was not related to the consul in question.

Inflicted on him by his sire's defeat.
For, when the Roman eagle, as you know,
Beheld at Trasimene its legions fall,
Flaminius' father was their general,
310 And there he died, transpierced by Hannibal.
This son, urged on by thirst of vengeance, then,
Was ready to collaborate with me.
The hope of laying hands on Hannibal
Thus paved the way for my dear son's return.
315 Through him I roused Rome's keenest jealousy
Of Nicomedes' Asian[1] conquests, and
Fear, lest Laodice, by marrying
The prince, could join his father's states with hers.
The Senate was alarmed there might arise
A grandiose empire under grandiose rule.
320 Flaminius thus induced the Senate to
Appoint himself as Rome's ambassador,
To foil this marriage and to check his[2] fame.
That is the only aim Rome has in mind.

CLEONE

And so Attalus woos Laodice!
325 But why did not Rome act before the prince
Returned from camp and reinforced her love?

ARSINOE

To thwart a conqueror backed by all his men
Ready to follow where his anger leads
Was far too great a risk. I thought it best
330 To lure him hither from his lair. And this
My Metrobates did. He cunningly
Feigned to reveal in panic my commands,
Saying he was suborned to murder him.
He has, thank heaven, adroitly brought him back.
335 The prince will ask the king for justice and
Complain. And this will lead him to the verge
Of ruin. I'll not justify myself.

1. *Asia*, here and *passim*, means Asia Minor.
2. Refers to Nicomedes.

I'll use his charge to strengthen my prestige.
I simulated fear on seeing him;
I blenched and let a cry escape from me.   340
He thought, but wrongly, he had caught me out;
Even his return was engineered by me.

CLEONE

Whate'er Rome does or Attalus may plan,
How can you think Laodice will yield?

ARSINOE

But I'm involving Attalus with her   345
Only to trick the king, Rome and the court.
I do not seek to win Armenia's throne,
But to Bithynia's sceptre I aspire.
And once this diadem is in our hands,
Let the queen choose a husband for herself.   350
I'll pressure her only to rouse her and
To make her lover and herself react.
The king, hard pressed by the ambassador,
Will act for fear of giving Rome offence,
And Nicomedes, stung by righteous wrath,   355
Will certainly flare up and brave the king.
His father's hasty-tempered, just like him,
And I shall fan his anger into flame.
If the prince to my move at all reacts,
My venture's certain and his downfall sure.   360
You know my inmost heart and all it plans.
But in my room Flaminius waits for me.
Let's go. Guard well the secret of the queen.

CLEONE

You know me much too well to be concerned . . .

ACT TWO

Scene One

PRUSIAS

Without my orders, he is back at court?

ARASPES

365 My lord, you would be wrong to be disturbed,
And Nicomedes' great nobility
Is a strong physic against fear of him.
In other men so sudden a return
Ought to be deemed suspicious, for it smacks
370 Of disrespect, and justifies distrust
Of hidden reasons for such hastiness.

PRUSIAS

I see them all too well. His rash return
Directly questions my authority
375 Which he rejects. After his victories,
There are no crowns above his mighty arm.
He is a law unto himself. As such,
He cannot be a hero and obey.

ARASPES

Men of his stamp are ever thus. They feel
380 That following duty tarnishes their fame,
And these great hearts, swoll'n by their exploits' fame,
Lording it in the army, they become
Accustomed to the heady drafts of power,
And find obedience is stiff medicine.

PRUSIAS

385 Speak out, Araspes. Say a subject's name
Abases all their glory to the dust;

That, though they're destined to the throne by birth,
If the succession tarries, they revolt.
A father keeps too long what's due to them,
Which is devalued if delayed too long;   390
Thence springs a host of underhand intrigues
Among the people and his entourage;
And, if one does not venture quite to end
His odious reign and his distressing life,
An insolent and sham obedience leaves   395
An empty title and usurps his power.

ARASPES

This might be feared from anyone but him.
For any other, you would call a halt;
But no such warning's needed for you now.
You're a good father. *He's* a noble prince.   400

PRUSIAS

If I were not, he would be criminal.
He owes his innocence to me alone.
A father's love justifies him, or else
That love alone deceives and ruins me.
For it is to be feared that in the end   405
He's fought in vain against ambition, and
Silenced the voice of nature in his heart.
Who wearies of a king can weary of
A father. And a thousand parricides
Show naught is stronger than the urge to reign.   410
And, once that starts to lie in wait for us,
Nature is blind and honesty is mute.
Shall I be frank? He's served me all too well.
He's stripped me of my power, increasing it.
He does me homage only if he will,   415
And I am ruled by him who makes me reign.
For me to see him here he's risen too high.
One shrinks from those whom one's indebted to,
And his exploits speak loud with his approach.
His very presence is a mute reproach;   420

It tells me he has made me thrice a king.[1]
From him I hold more than he has from me,
And, if one day I leave the crown to him,
My head bears three his valour's won for *me*.
425 I blush within, and my embarrassment,
Which is revived and grows at every turn,
Ceaselessly conjures up this gnawing thought
That, giving three, he may take one from me.
He need but dare and can do all he wills.
430 Judge my sad plight should he will what he can.

ARASPES

For any other man than he I know
What statesmanship and reason would dictate.
A subject who's become too powerful,
Though without crime, cannot be innocent.
435 One does not wait for him to launch a coup.
It's treason to be able to betray,
And a wise ruler will make certain none
Can merit just and greater punishment,
And by a salutary move forestall
440 Ills which they have or might well have prepared.
But, Sir, the prince is far above such crimes,
As I have said.

PRUSIAS

And will you answer for
His loyalty, his ventures to ensure
His brother's fall, revenge for Hannibal?
445 And think you he will be indiff'rent to
His brother's love[2] and Hannibal's decease?
Have no illusions. Vengeance is his aim.
He has the pretext and the power for it;
He is the rising star my states adore.

1. See line 105 above. The three kingdoms conquered by Nicomedes
were Cappadocia (lines 28 and 467), Pontus (lines 468 and 699) and
Galatia (700). Bithynia was the kingdom which Prusias inherited. The
total area thus under that king's rule covered roughly the whole of the
northern half of Asia Minor.
2. For Laodice.

He is the people's and the soldiers' god.   450
Sure of his men, he's come to rouse the mass
And with his power swoop on what's left of ours.
But what remains, though unsubstantial still,
Is not perhaps entirely powerless.
However, I'll be diplomatic, use   455
An iron hand, but in a velvet glove,
To drive him out with glory, mingling thus
My anger with reward for his deserts;
But, if he won't obey or dares complain,
Whate'er his valour or my fear for him,   460
Were the whole state endangered by my move . . .

ARASPES

He's here.

Scene Two

PRUSIAS, NICOMEDES

PRUSIAS

Well, Sir, whoever sent for you?

NICOMEDES

Only the wish in person to depose
Here at your feet, my lord, another crown,
To have the honour of your fond embrace   465
And be the witness of your happiness.
With Cappadocia fortunately linked
To Pontus and to great Bithynia's realm,
I come to thank my father and my king
For having deigned to use my services,   470
Chosen my arm for so much glory and
Given me the honour of his victory.

PRUSIAS

You should have done without my greetings and
Sent me your thanks in your dispatches. You

475 Should never have detracted by a crime
From your bright victory-enhanced prestige.
To leave my camp's a capital offence,
Heinous in all, worst in a general.
Despite this conquest, anyone but you
480 Had forfeited his head for such a deed.

NICOMEDES

I know I've erred, and my imprudent heart
Yielded too easily to my desire.
My love for you committed this offence;
It alone led my duty far astray.
485 If joy at seeing you again were less,
I would be blameless, but so far from you
That I'd prefer to lose some slight prestige
And let such bliss cost me a minor crime.
I'll never fear even the harshest law,
490 If your love judges what my love has done.

PRUSIAS

Threadbare excuses sway a father's heart,
And in a son all errors are forgiven.
I'll look on you only as my support.
Receive the meed of honour due to you.
495 Rome's envoy asks an audience of me;
He'll see the confidence I have in you;
You'll listen to him and reply for me.
For after all you are the real king;
I'm but a shadow. Age has left to me
500 But empty homage paid to my grey hairs.
Perhaps I'll only keep it for a day.
Let the state's interest be your sole concern.
Accept today its highest dignity;
But, all the same, forget not your offence;
505 And, as it undermines my sovereign power,
Go back tomorrow to make full amends.
Restore its lustre to my boundless power;
Wait to receive what I inherited,
Inviolable, whole. Do not allow

Wickeder men than you to cheapen it.   510
The people and the court who're watching you
Would disobey you since you'd disobeyed.
Set them a new example. Show them all
That our first subjects are the first t' obey.

NICOMEDES

I shall obey, and sooner than one thinks;   515
But give me my obedience's reward.
Armenia's queen is due in her domains;
Our vict'ries have unbarred the road to them.
It's time that star shone in her native sky;
Grant me the honour to escort her home.   520

PRUSIAS

That behoves you alone. This glorious task
Calls for a king himself or royal heir.
But, to dispatch her to Armenia
Some ceremony is, you know, required.
While I make ready her departure, go   525
Back to the army and await her there.

NICOMEDES

She needs no preparation to depart.

PRUSIAS

I should be loath thus to insult her rank.
But here's the envoy. We must hear his words.
Then we shall see what steps this plan demands.   530

Scene Three

PRUSIAS, NICOMEDES, FLAMINIUS, ARASPES

FLAMINIUS

I am about to leave. Rome orders me
To make one more request on its behalf.
Rome has for twenty years brought up your son,

And you may judge our lavish care for him
535 By the high virtues, the illustrious marks,
Which blazon forth in him your royal blood.
Above all, he is trained in governing.
It is for you to testify to it
If you think highly of his schooling. Rome
540 Implores you to arrange for him to rule.
And you would slight its great esteem for him
If you allowed this prince to live and die
A subject. Act, then, that I may report
To Rome which kingdom you assign to him.

PRUSIAS

545 The people's and the Senate's care for him
Will never find in me an ingrate, Sir.
I think he has the qualities to reign.
I cannot doubt it after what you say.
But here you see the prince, my elder son,
550 Whose never-tiring arm has crowned me thrice.
He comes straight from another victory.
For such great feats I owe him some renown;
Grant him the honour to reply for me.

NICOMEDES

You alone can make Attalus a king.

PRUSIAS

555 Only your interest is affected here.

NICOMEDES

But speaking, I shall think of yours alone.
Rome should not meddle or the Senate take,
While you still live, the right to rule your state.
Live, my lord, reign until your burial;
560 Let, after that, nature and Rome decide.

PRUSIAS

For friends like these we must constrain ourselves.

NICOMEDES

Dividing your estate, they will your death,
And friends like Rome, in any well run state ...

PRUSIAS

Ah! set me not at loggerheads with Rome.
Be more respectful, to such allies, Sir.   565

NICOMEDES

I cannot bear to see kings snubbed by them;
And whosoe'er this son Rome's sending back,
I would return this present joyfully.
If he is so well trained how to command,
He's a rare treasure Rome should not let go;   570
Rome should retain its protégés to wield
The consulate or the dictatorship.

FLAMINIUS

Sir, in these words which grate upon our ears,
You see the poison spread by Hannibal;
He, Roman grandeur's treach'rous enemy,   575
Has in this heart placed but contempt and hate.

NICOMEDES

No, but he left me firm on this one point,
Not to fear Rome and hold it in esteem.
I'm his disciple and I'm proud of it;
And, when Flaminius tarnishes his name,   580
One day I'll call him to account, for he
Reduced my master to the poisoned cup.
This hero, he should not forget, began
His triumphs over Rome at Trasimene.[1]

FLAMINIUS

This is an outrage.   585

1. At Trasimene, according to Corneille, Hannibal defeated and killed
Flaminius' father. The suggestion that this was Hannibal's first victory
over the Romans is inaccurate. Hannibal had already defeated the
Romans in 218 B.C. at Trebbia.

NICOMEDES
Outrage not the dead.

PRUSIAS
And you, do not attempt to sow discord.
Speak to the point on his proposal.

NICOMEDES
                                    Well,
If as an answer more is still required,
Rome has decreed that Attalus shall reign;
590 Since everywhere its power is absolute,
It is for kings to yield when Rome commands.
Attalus' heart, spirit and soul are great
And all great qualities of a great king.
But can we take a Roman's word for it?
595 By some great exploit let him prove his worth;
If he has this outstanding valour, Sir,
Give him your troops. Let's see his great exploits.
Let him do with these troops what I have done
For you, and reign over his conquered lands,
600 Crowning his brow with laurels of his own.
My arm is at his service. From now on,
If he accepts, I'll be his deputy.
The Romans' own example points the way.
The famous Scipio was his brother's aide,
605 And, when they both unthroned Antiochus,
The elder brother as lieutenant fought.[1]
The Hellespont and the Aegean sea,
What's left of Asia on our frontiers ranged,
Offer wide scope for his ambition.

FLAMINIUS
                                    Rome
610 Takes under its protection all the rest,

    1. Scipio the Asian, with the famous Scipio the African (his elder
brother) as his lieutenant, defeated Antiochus at the battle of Sipylus
in 190 B.C.

And you can make no further conquests there
Without your running into fearful storms.

NICOMEDES

I know not the king's wishes on this point;
Perhaps one day I'll be the ruler, and
Then we can gauge the weight of all these threats.   615
You may, however, fortify these posts,
And raise new obstacles to my new plans,
Arrange for seasonable Roman aid;
And, if Flaminius is their general,
We'll find a new Lake Trasimene for him.   620

PRUSIAS

Prince, you abuse my kindness. Some respect
Is due the rank of an ambassador.
The honour delegated to you here . . .

NICOMEDES

Either you let me speak or silence me.
I cannot frame a different answer for   625
A king who on his throne's dictated to.

PRUSIAS

You outrage me myself by talking thus,
And you should lay a check upon your tongue.

NICOMEDES

What! I'm to listen while they bound your states
And stop my conquering arm in mid-career.   630
They even dare to threaten you. And I
Must not return them threat for brutal threat?
I am to thank the man who tells me straight
I may not win, unpunished, victories.

PRUSIAS
[*To* FLAMINIUS]

Sir, you must pardon his impetuous youth.   635
Reason and time may temper his excess.

NICOMEDES

Reason and time have opened wide my eyes,
And age will open them but wider still.
If, like my brother, I had lived till now
640 Showing imaginary valiancy
(For this I call it if not backed by deeds,
And admiration for so many knights
Whose merit he has seen shine forth in Rome
Is nothing if he does not copy it);
645 If I had lived then in the same repose
As he, beside his heroes, lived in Rome,
Rome would have left me all Bithynia
Handed by father down to eldest son,
Rome would be far less keen to see him reign
650 If under me your arms had won no lands.
But, since Rome sees three conquered sceptres, linked
To your Bithynia, concentrate such power,
That must be split, and, under this fine plan,
Attalus cannot be my subject! And,
655 Since he can serve Rome in debasing me,
He outshines Alexander. I must yield
To him, raising him to my royal rank,
My father's realm or what my blood has won.
Thanks to the gods, my past achievements and
660 My future greatness have offended Rome.
That can be cured, Sir, by you speedily.
But do not ask a son for his consent.
The master who in life first guided me
Never instructed me in felony.

FLAMINIUS

665 If I interpret you aright, you've fought
From interest rather than from valiancy.
The rarest exploits you have carried out
Have given your father crowns in trust for you.
He's but the guardian of their grand reward,
670 And for yourself alone you've conquered them,
Since all this grandeur, flowing from the throne,
Cannot be shed on anyone but you.

I thought you somewhat more disinterested.
The Romans act not for themselves alone.
Scipio, whose courage you so praised just now,   675
Had no desire to reign over the walls
Of Carthage. Everything he did for Rome
Brought him but fame – the title African.
Only in Rome is such a spirit found.
The rest of men is made of other stuff.   680
As to the politics which make you think
We fear in you too many crowns combined,
If you would follow sensible advice,
You would soon drop such high-faluting thoughts.
In deference to the king I'll say no more.   685
Take leisure to reflect on this affair.
Allow your martial fires to belch less smoke,
And you'll perhaps see things in focus.

NICOMEDES
                              Time
May give a verdict which will let us see
Whether the thought is sound or but a dream.   690
Meanwhile . . .

FLAMINIUS
                 Meanwhile, if you're enchanted by
The prospects of new conquests by your arms,
We'll set no bounds to them, but, since one's free
Against whoe'er it be to serve one's friends,
If you don't know, I shall inform you, Sir,   695
And give you notice to avoid a shock.
And, for the rest, be sure you will possess
All you already covet in your heart.
Pontus and Cappadocia will be yours,
And, with Galatia, the Bithynian crown.   700
Your father's realms, these trophies of your blood,
Will not raise Attalus to your high rank.
Since sharing them is torture for you, Rome
Has never planned to be unjust to you.
That prince will reign, but not at your expense.   705

NICOMEDES

[*To* PRUSIAS]

Armenia's queen requires a husband, Sire.
There could be no more favourable chance.
She's in your hands. You can dispose of her.

NICOMEDES

So that's how Attalus is to be king!
710 As you have said, without depriving me.
A subtle plot, and those who've worked it out
By devious paths have compassed worthy ends.
I'll make but this disinterested reply.
Sir, treat the princess as the queen she is.
715 Touch not in her the crown's prerogatives,
Or to maintain them I shall die myself.
Of this I warn you, and would add that kings,
Though in our realm, are never ruled by us,
And *here* she is sole mistress of herself.

PRUSIAS

720 Have you no other point to make to him?

NICOMEDES

None, Sir, but this. Knowing my power, the queen
Is driving me to harsh extremities.

PRUSIAS

What can your insolence do against her at
My court?

NICOMEDES

Naught but be silent or speak out.
725 Yet once again, be sure Laodice
Is treated as the queen she is. It's I
Who beg you to.

Scene Four

PRUSIAS, FLAMINIUS, ARASPES

FLAMINIUS
How now! He thwarts us still!

PRUSIAS
A lover thinks it no great miracle.
This overweening spirit would deny
Us access to Laodice's proud heart;   730
But everyone must walk his destined path.
In royal marriages love holds no place;
Reasons of state, far stronger than its bonds,
Can find a way to put its ardour out.

FLAMINIUS
If she's in love, she'll want to have her way.   735

PRUSIAS
No, Sir, I'll answer for Laodice.
But don't forget she is a queen. Her rank
Would seem to force us to observe the forms.
I've after all complete control of her,
But will make orders pass as a request.   740
Let's call on her. You, as ambassador,
Yourself propose this marriage to her. I
Shall introduce you and shall stand by Rome.
She's in our hands. Love cannot hamper us.
Let's see what she replies to our démarche,   745
Then take this chance to table our demands.

ACT THREE

Scene One

PRUSIAS, FLAMINIUS, LAODICE

PRUSIAS

Queen, since this title so entrances you,
Its loss would doubtless cause you some alarm.
Who always kings it never reigns for long.

LAODICE

750 I shall, my lord, follow your sage advice;
And, if I reign, you'll see that I observe
This statesmanlike and noble policy.

PRUSIAS

The road you've chosen is completely wrong.

LAODICE

If I should lose my way, you'll put me right.

PRUSIAS

755 You scorn Rome overmuch, and should respect
A king who is a father to you.

LAODICE

Sir,
You would agree I give them both their due,
If you'd but see what 'tis to be a king.
If I as queen receive an embassy,
760 That would be acting as a sovereign power,
Encroaching on your rights, and in your realm
Belittling your authority. Hence, Sir,
I'll not receive it; I'll deny myself
The honour due me in my land alone.
765 There in full splendour on my throne I can

270

Honour both Rome and its ambassador,
Answer him as a queen and as befits
Both the petition and petitioner.
Here I am not quite master of this craft,
For I am naught beyond Armenia's bounds.   770
All that this lordly name of queen allows
Is not to bow to any other throne,
To live untrammelled, and as sovereigns take
Myself, pure reason and the gods alone.

PRUSIAS

These gods, your sovereigns, and the king, your sire,   775
Gave me their power over you in trust,
And at some later date you still may learn
What royal reason is in every land.
To put it to the test, I'll send you back
With a stout escort to Armenia. Come,   780
Let us set out. Tomorrow, since you wish,
Prepare to see your native land laid waste.
Prepare to see it, to its furthest bounds,
Visited by the horrors of grim war,
To see mountains of dead and streams of blood.   785

LAODICE

Then I shall lose my realm and keep my rank,
And these vast ills my pride brings down on me
Will make me, not your subject but your slave.
My life is yours, but not my dignity.

PRUSIAS

We'll soon make this ungoverned heart submit,   790
And, when your eyes, stricken with all this woe,
See Attalus upon your fathers' throne,
Then, then, perhaps you'll beg him, but in vain,
To put you back on it by wedding you.

LAODICE

If e'er your war should bring me to that pass,   795
I would be sorely changed in soul and heart.

But, Sir, perhaps you will not go so far.
The gods will take some interest in my lot;
They will inspire you or will find a man
800 To fight so many heroes lent by Rome.

PRUSIAS

In a presumptuous youth you place your trust.
His doom is sealed. He'll drag you down with him.
Think well and face the facts. And choose between
Being Laodice and being queen.
805 If you would reign, make Attalus your king.
Farewell.

Scene Two

FLAMINIUS, LAODICE

FLAMINIUS
Perfect nobility of soul . . .

LAODICE
Follow the king. Your embassy is done.
And, I repeat, do not delude yourself.
810 I should not and will *not* lend you an ear.

FLAMINIUS
That's why I speak, since you're in danger, less
As an ambassador than as a friend
Who, moved to pity by your self-willed fate,
Tries to avert the ills you hasten to.
815 I dare to tell you, then, in confidence,
Highheartedness has to be tempered with
Prudence, and in its interest take account
Of both the time and place in which one lives.
Such spiritedness, ev'n in kingly souls,
820 Without this virtue is a random force.
It's blind, and honour ill interpreted
Disjoins it so from real happiness,

Itself it yields to what it ought to fear,
Reaps admiration – only at the price
Of being pitied, sighing that 'I had   825
The right to reign, but it availed me naught.'
You thwart a king whose many-legioned force
Obeys him and is schooled to Victory.
You are, here in his court, within his power.

LAODICE

I do not know if honour can mislead,   830
My lord, but I shall answer as a friend.
My prudence is not yet quite lulled asleep,
And, without asking by what quirk of fate
Highheartedness now rates so low with you,
I shall explain to you why my resolve   835
Is not as random as you feel. I shall
Avail myself of my full right to reign
And outmanoeuvre any counterclaim.
I see a powerful army at the front
Which, as you say, is used to victory.   840
But led by whom, under what general?
The king, if he relies on it, may err,
And, if he should invade Armenia, I
Would counsel him to raise another force.
But I am in his realm, live in his court,   845
And have scant reason not to fear him. Sir,
Even in his court beyond Armenia's bounds,
Nobility can find support against
Tyranny. All can see the wrong that's done
By crooked maxims to the public weal.   850
Both Nicomedes and his stepmother
Are known, as is her deep abiding hate,
The bondage of the king, and (all the more)
Which of his friends are dangerous. For me,
Whom you believe on the abyss's edge,   855
My scorn for Attalus is no caprice,
And greater scorn would be his portion if
He were to reign simply by wedding me.
I would regard him like the common herd,

860 As one deserving of a different fate,
　　More of a subject than a husband. And
　　Marriage would make no difference to his rank.
　　My people would disdain him, following me.
　　A heart of mettle would not bear this slight.
865 Thus, by refusing him, despite his suit,
　　I spare his pride eternal, deep despair.

FLAMINIUS

　　If what you say is true, then here you're queen.
　　You're sovereign of the army and the court.
　　The king is but a figurehead, and has
870 Only the power you deign relinquish him.
　　What! you go even so far as sparing him!
　　You must excuse my daring after that.
　　Let Rome at last speak to you with my voice.
　　You still may hear an envoy, or, if this
875 Grates on your ear outside Armenia,
　　As Roman citizen, I'll dare to say:
　　To be Rome's ally and be backed by Rome
　　Is nowadays the only way to reign.
　　That is the way to keep one's neighbours back,
880 One's people quiet and one's foes in fear.
　　A prince cannot be parted from his throne
　　If honoured with the title of Rome's friend.
　　Attalus is more absolute with that
　　Than all whose forehead bears the regal crown.
885 And, to conclude . . .

LAODICE

　　　　　　　Enough. You're clear. All kings
　　Are kings only as far as you allow.
　　But if Rome's whim disposes of their realms,
　　Rome has done little for its Attalus.
　　And, holding such abundance in its gift,
890 Should not persist in begging thrones for him.
　　For such a cherished prince what diffidence!
　　Should Rome not offer him me with a crown,
　　Not pester me t'accept a subject's hand,

I, who would even reject a monarch's suit
Were he Rome's nominee, and if his links   895
With Rome tarnished the sovereign power in him?
These are my feelings undissembled. I
Will have no kings who stoop to servitude,
And, since I thus reveal my inmost thoughts,
My lord, lose no more time in threats or prayers.   900

FLAMINIUS

How in your blindness I must pity you.
Yet once again I urge you, ponder well.
Remember what Rome is, what it can do,
And, if you love yourself, displease it not.
Carthage destroyed, Antiochus undone,   905
Naught we can do can alter Rome's resolve.
All bows to Rome on sea, trembles on land,
And Rome today is mistress of the world.

LAODICE

The mistress of the world. You'd frighten me
Were it not for Armenia and my heart,   910
Had not great Hannibal disciples, did
He not in Nicomedes live again,
And had not left in such distinguished hands
Th' unfailing secret of defeating Rome.
So brave a follower will certainly   915
Apply these lessons to the very end.
Asia is witness where three sceptres won
Show at what school he learned so much so well.
These are but trial blows, but they suggest
The capital should fear a masterstroke.   920
And he one day ...

FLAMINIUS
                    That day is still far off,
Lady, and, if need be, you can be told
What gods smite from on high profaning hands
And that her shade, even after Trebbia and

275

925 Cannae, still terrified your Hannibal.[1]
But here it is, this Rome-destroying arm.

Scene Three

NICOMEDES, LAODICE, FLAMINIUS

NICOMEDES

Either Rome's minions have great latitude,
Or you are slow in seeing to your task.

FLAMINIUS

I know my orders. If I stay or leave,
930 I'll give account to others, not to you.

NICOMEDES

Then go ahead, I beg you, and let me
Now in my turn have converse with the queen.
You've made such rapid progress in her heart,
Your conversation has enthralled her so,
935 That, straining every nerve, I'll not efface
What you've endeavoured to instil in it.

FLAMINIUS

The ills in which your friendship plunges her
Lead me to pity and to counsel her.

NICOMEDES

To give her charitable counsel thus
940 Smacks of a queer soft-hearted envoyship.

[*To* LAODICE]
What craven actions has he put to you?

---

1. Trebbia (218 B.C.) and Cannae (216 B.C.) were two victories of
Hannibal over the Romans. Flaminius naturally does not mention
Trasimene in which, according to Corneille's version, the father of
Flaminius was defeated and killed by Hannibal.

FLAMINIUS

This is too much, Sir. You forget yourself.

NICOMEDES

Forget myself?

FLAMINIUS

Know that in every land
An envoy's sacred dignity must be . . .

NICOMEDES

Vaunt not so much its splendour and its rank.   945
The envoy ends where starts the counsellor;
He goes beyond his mandate, derogates.
But, Lady, has he given you his reply?

LAODICE

Yes.

NICOMEDES

Know then, I regard you only as
Attalus' agent, as Flaminius, and,   950
If you should goad me, I should add perhaps
As Hannibal, my master's poisoner.
That's all the honours you shall have from me.
If they suffice not, go and tell the king.

FLAMINIUS

Though a good father, he will right my wrongs,   955
Or, if he won't, Rome will have justice done.

NICOMEDES

Go, clasp the knees of Prusias and of Rome.

FLAMINIUS

Deeds will reply for me. Look to yourself.

Scene Four

NICOMEDES, LAODICE

NICOMEDES

That counsel should be given to the queen.
960 My generous instincts now give way to hate;
I spared her in that I did not disclose
The infamous assassins' baleful plans,
But she has forced my hand. Her crime will out.
The king has heard the two conspirators.
965 Since their reports may well astound him, he
Himself will undertake their questioning.

LAODICE

I know not what the consequence will be;
But I don't follow all this strategy,
Or how the queen provokes this open clash;
970 The more she ought to fear, the less she does;
The more you can traduce her with her crimes,
The more she treats you as her mortal foe.

NICOMEDES

She's stolen a march on me and seeks to show
That my complaint's inspired by spite alone;
975 And this deceptive mask of brazenness
Covers her weakness and conceals her fear.

LAODICE

Court mysteries are often so well hid
That even the shrewdest can make naught of them.
When you were not at court to champion me,
980 I had no war to fight with Attalus.
Rome did not interfere between us two.
Nay more, you're suffered here but for a day.
And in that day Rome in your presence has
Warmly campaigned to make me marry him.
985 But I see nothing in this reasoning

Which cannot wait until you leave the court.
And always some storm-darkened cloud is there
Which wounds my view and rouses my distrust.
The king adores his wife, fears Rome, and is
A trifle jealous of your great exploits.   990
At least he's much too good a husband, Sir,
To be the father that he ought to be.
But how untimely Attalus arrives!
What brings him hither? What concern or plan?
I cannot see what we should make of it.   995
But I will foil him if it's in my power.
I'll leave you.

Scene Five

NICOMEDES, ATTALUS, LAODICE

ATTALUS
Lady, such a pleasant talk
Displeases you when I take part in it.

LAODICE
Your importunity is, I must say,
Boundless. But with an alter ego you can talk.   1000
He knows my heart and will reply for me
Just as he answered to Flaminius for
The king.

Scene Six

NICOMEDES, ATTALUS

ATTALUS
I've driven her out. I shall withdraw.

NICOMEDES
No, I have something I would say to you.
I had renounced the rank of eldest son,   1005

279

All the advantages of being heir,
And, wishing solely to defend my love,
I asked you to attack too on these lines,
And above all not to fall back upon
1010 Either the monarch's or the Romans' help.
But either this has slipped your memory,
Or you forget whatever you are bid.

ATTALUS

My lord, you make me disremember when
You fail to equalize our handicaps.
1015 You give up some superiority.
True, but do you give up Laodice?
The virtues which ensure her love for you,
The soaring all-enchanting qualities –
Three sceptres and six battles won, assaults
1020 With glorious exploits on a hundred walls –
With all these trumps, the issue's not in doubt.
Then make her take an equal view of us.
Show her no more this stream of glory which
Vict'ry has shed so lavishly on you,
1025 Allow her to forget, just for this once,
Both your rare merits and your famous deeds,
Or let Rome and the king weigh in the scale
Against her love, against your gallantry.
The little ground I've gained makes clear enough
1030 That I can never counterbalance you.

NICOMEDES

You surely did not idle when in Rome,
Since you make such an elegant defence.
You may lack spirit, but you don't lack wit.

Scene Seven

ARSINOE, NICOMEDES, ATTALUS, ARASPES

ARASPES

ir, the king sends for you . . .

NICOMEDES
                    He sends for me?

ARASPES

es.   1035

ARSINOE
  Calumny is easy to disprove.

NICOMEDES
 know not why you come to tell me so,
ince I have never harboured doubts on this,
ady.

ARSINOE
    If ever you had doubts on it,
ou'd not have brought, with your misguided hopes,
eno and Metrobates all this way.   1040

NICOMEDES
 was determined on concealing all,
But you have forced my hand. I've made them speak.

ARSINOE
Truth forces them, more than your bounty does.
These common men keep not their promises;
Both have said more than they had planned to say.   1045

NICOMEDES
 grieve for you, but you have willed it so.

ARSINOE

And do so still, but I am only vexed
At having seen your honour badly smirched,
And adding to your titles to renown
1050 A poor suborner's noble epithet.

NICOMEDES

What, I suborned them against *you*, you say?

ARSINOE

I have the sorrow. You will have the shame.

NICOMEDES

And thus you think you will discredit them?

ARSINOE

No, sir. I but rely on what they've said.

NICOMEDES

1055 What did they say you so wish to believe?

ARSINOE

Two words of truth redounding to your fame.

NICOMEDES

May I not know of you these vital words?

ARASPES

The king's impatient. You are much delayed.

ARSINOE

You'll gather them from him. He's stayed for you.

NICOMEDES

1060 I have begun to grasp your drift at last.
His love for you, driving out his for me,
Will make you innocent, me criminal.
But . . .

ARSINOE

Sir, go on. This 'but', what does it mean?

NICOMEDES

'wo words of truth which make me breathe again.

ARSINOE

1ay I be told what are these crucial words?   1065

NICOMEDES

'ou'll hear them from the king. I'm late for him.

Scene Eight

ARSINOE, ATTALUS

ARSINOE

Ve triumph, and great Nicomedes now
ees all his machinations come to naught.
'he two accusers he himself produced
Vhom I'm supposed to have egged on to kill,   1070
uborned by him himself to slander me,
'ould not act out so foul a stratagem.
Both have accused me. Both, too, have confessed
The shameful trick the prince has played on me.
How truth will out when kings in judgement sit!   1075
And find a way to issue from men's hearts!
How lies are easily exposed by it!
Vishing to ruin *me*, they've ruined *him*.

ATTALUS

am delighted such imposture has
eft your renown even greater and more pure.   1080
But, if you take a closer look at it,
f you were less inclined to plot his fall,
You could not, without some slight scruple, be
o credulous about these evil men.
'his treacherous couple now admits they were   1085

Suborned by you, suborned by him as well.
Against such virtues and such victories,
Can we place any faith in such base slaves?
One cannot credit villains self-confessed.

ARSINOE

1090 You are too noble-hearted. And I see
Even your rival's honour's dear to you.

ATTALUS

If I'm his rival, I'm his brother too.
We're but one blood, and in my heart this blood
Is loath to label him a slanderer.

ARSINOE

1095 Less loath to stamp me as a murderess –
I, whose eclipse is sure unless he fails.

ATTALUS

If I could not believe them against *him*,
When they accused *you*, I believe them less.
Your virtue is above all thought of crime.
1100 Let me then still feel some esteem for him.
His great prestige at court breeds jealousy.
Hence, this is but a cowardly attempt
To ruin him. It is an envious move
Which seeks to blacken his unsullied fame.
1105 For me, judging of others by myself,
I credit him with what I feel myself.
With such a rival nothing's underhand.
I'll not contrive his downfall by intrigue.
I'll borrow aid, but honourably, and
1110 I'm sure his acts are no less chivalrous;
He strives for naught where glory does not lead,
And, fighting me, counts on himself alone.

ARSINOE

You're guileless of the world and of the court.

ATTALUS

Should one treat love except with princely heart?

ARSINOE

My son, you treat it like a callow youth.   1115

ATTALUS

I have seen naught but virtues when in Rome.

ARSINOE

By new experience time will make you see
The qualities for a king's retinue.
If Nicomedes is your brother still,
Remember that I am your mother too.   1120
Despite all the suspicions you've conceived,
Come, let us hear what the king thinks of this.

ACT FOUR

Scene One

PRUSIAS, ARSINOE, ARASPES

PRUSIAS

Show the prince in, Araspes.

[*Exit* ARASPES.]
                  You, my queen,
Restrain your sighs which pierce me to the heart.
1125 Why plunge me into grief with your laments,
When you command it without aid from tears?
What need for tears to act in your defence?
Do I then doubt his crime, your innocence?
And do you feel that everything he's said
1130 Has so impressed me as to shake my faith?

ARSINOE

Ah! Sire, naught can make good the harm that's wrought
By even a slight deceit on innocence?
How can a falsehood be defused too soon
To give back lustre to a noble heart?
1135 Some shameful memory will cling to it
Which stains ev'n the most glorious repute.
How many slanderers are there in your court?
How many blind supporters of the prince,
Who, once they know that I have been traduced,
1140 Will think your love alone has cleared my name?
And, if the slightest trace of guilt remains,
If even the humblest still suspect me, am
I worthy of you; are not such alarms
So serious as to deserve my tears?

PRUSIAS

1145 Ah! you are over-nice, and you misjudge
A husband who adores you as he ought.

Honour is stronger after calumny,
And shines the brighter when it is besmirched.
But here is Nicomedes, and I mean . . .

Scene Two

PRUSIAS, ARSINOE, NICOMEDES, ARASPES,
GUARDS

ARSINOE

Spare him, Sire, spare the pillar of our state!   1150
Spare all these fertile laurels in his hand!
Spare this great conqueror of cities! Spare . . .

NICOMEDES

Spare me for what? Is it because I've won
Three sceptres which my fall would give your son,
Because in Asia I have borne your arms   1155
So far that even Rome is jealous, or
Sustained too well the royal majesty,
Filled with the roar of my exploits your court,
Applied too well Hannibal's strategy?
If I need mercy, choose among my crimes.   1160
There they all are; and, if to these you add
Having believed bad men by others bribed,
Having an undissimulating soul
Which has been hoodwinked by their artifice,
That is a credit, not a crime in one   1165
Who lives amidst the army far from court,
Whose one ally is honesty, and who,
With no remorse, suspects no stratagem.

ARSINOE

I take it back, Sire. He's no criminal.
If he has sought to brand me endlessly,   1170
He but obeys a stepson's inborn hate
Aroused by the mere name of stepmother.
His heart by this aversion prejudiced

287

Ascribes to me the blows that rain on him.
1175 If his great master, Hannibal, despite
Official guarantees was panic-struck,
If he entrusted freedom and repute
More to despair than hospitality,
These insane terrors are contrived by me.
1180 However much he loves Laodice,
If Attalus like him has eyes for her,
It's I who force Rome to support that prince.
I am the source of Nicomedes' ills,
And, to avenge his master and to save
1185 His mistress,[1] if he tries to sever us,
All in a jealous lover[2] is excused.
This vain weak effort does not move my soul.
I know my only crime's to be your wife.
This name alone drives him to harass me.
1190 Apart from that, what can he charge me with?
Have I, in the ten years of his command,
Ever refused to magnify his fame?
And, when effective aid was needed and
The least delay would have been fatal, who
1195 Better than I urged the dispatch of help?
Who got him out of his debacles? Who
Had more at heart to plead his case with you?
To speed the flow of soldiers and supplies?
You know it's true, my lord, and, as my thanks,
1200 After supporting him with heart and soul,
He has, I see, tried to discredit me.
But in a jealous lover all's excused,
As I have said.

PRUSIAS
What can you say to this?

NICOMEDES
The queen's good offices leave me amazed.
1205 I will not say that this substantial aid,

1. In the seventeenth-century sense of 'beloved'.
2. Similarly 'lover' is used in the sense of 'admirer'.

By which she's saved my honour and my life,
Of which she trumpets out the list to you,
Was all for Attalus' aggrandisement,
Which she was building up for him through me,
And even then preparing for today.   1210
Whatever motives may have urged her on,
Let heaven be judge which reads her inmost thoughts;
It knows how she has prayed for my success;
It will be fair to her, perhaps to both
Of us. However, in this touching scene,   1215
She's spoken for me. I shall speak for her,
And must remind you in her interest that
You leave unpunished two most wicked men.
Send Metrobates, Zeno to the rack.
Her honour bids you make this sacrifice.   1220
Both have accused her, both retracted, though,
Exonerating her and blaming me.
They've not improved their case, and merit death.
They have made game of an august princess.
Offence once offered to a rank like ours   1225
Is not made good except by streams of blood.
No one goes free because he will recant.
This knav'ry must expire upon the rack,
Or all your royal blood will be exposed
To the mere whim of a disloyal mind.   1230
This dangerous example puts our lives
At hazard if it goes unpunished.

ARSINOE
                    What?
Punish these men for their sincerity,
Which of a sudden made them speak the truth,
Which has revealed his plot to ruin me,   1235
Which gives you back your wife, wrests me from death,
Which has deterred you from condemning her
And cloak all that under my interest? *That*
Is being much too clever, too adroit.

289

PRUSIAS

1240 Let Metrobates answer for himself.
Clear yourself of a base and shameful crime.

NICOMEDES

Clear myself, Sire? You can't believe I'll try.
You know too well that somebody like me,
When guilty, aims at loftier designs;
1245 It needs a grander crime to tempt my soul
Where power's shadow covers honour's crimes.
To rouse your people and to make your troops
Redress the wrongs inflicted on a queen,
To rescue her from you by force of arms,
1250 Sweeping both Rome and Attalus aside,
Invade your realm against their tyranny
With all your soldiers and Armenia's, *that*
Is something which a man like me might do,
Could he resolve to violate his troth.
1255 Trickery is for petty souls alone,
And that is really women's apanage.
Then punish both these perjurers, my lord,
And mete out justice to the queen and me.
As death approaches, conscience' voice is heard;
1260 Concern for god curtails respect for man,
And fickle spirits, as they near their end,
Might well recant a second time ...

ARSINOE

My lord ...

NICOMEDES

Speak, lady, and explain the reason why
These executions are so much delayed,
1265 Or we shall think that, at the doors of death,
Remorse would seize them, to your great distress.

ARSINOE

His hate for me, you see how great it is.
I vindicate him. He accuses me.

But doubtless my mere presence angers him,
And, if I leave, his fury will abate.   1270
Calm will return to his high mettled soul,
And will no doubt save him from other crimes.
I do not ask you on compassion's grounds
To give me a protecting sceptre or
To offer Attalus some standing, Sire,   1275
By sharing royal power between them. If
Your Roman friends took certain steps, it was
Without my knowledge. Nay, I need them not.
I love you too much not to follow you
As soon as in my arms you cease to live;   1280
And on your tombstone my first pangs of grief
Will shed my blood together with my tears.

PRUSIAS

My dear!

ARSINOE

Ah! yes, Sire, that ill-omened hour
With your last sighs will close my destiny,
And thus, since never will he be my king,
What need I fear? What can he do to me?   1285
All that I ask you for this son of yours[1]
Who's given him[2] already such offence
Is that he should return to end his days
In that same Rome where you have had him reared   1290
To eat his heart out, risk and gloryless,
Full of your unavailing love for me.
This great prince serves you, and will serve still more
When what offends his eyes has left the scene.
And fear not Rome or Roman vengeance, for   1295
Over its power his valiance will prevail.
He knows the secrets of great Hannibal
Who vanquished Rome with such decisive blows
That Africa and Asia both admire
The benefits from it to Carthage and   1300

1. Attalus.
2. Nicomedes.

Antiochus.[1] I shall withdraw; and you
Can give full scope to your paternal love.
I cannot bear to see before your throne
A prince I honour slight me shamelessly,
1305 Or be obliged to rouse your ire against
A son so worthy of you and so brave.

Scene Three

PRUSIAS, NICOMEDES, ARASPES

PRUSIAS

Sir, to be brief, this scene distresses me.
Whate'er you're charged with, you're no recreant.
But Rome's complaining. Let us yield a point,
1310 And reassure the queen who fears you. I
Am fond of you and deep in love with her.
This hatred must not last eternally,
And sentiments which should endure for aye
Should not obsess my heart to harrow it.
1315 I'd like to harmonize nature and love,
Be a good husband and a father too.

NICOMEDES

My lord, would you accept your son's advice?
Be neither.

PRUSIAS
Then what should I be?

NICOMEDES
Be king.

Don once again this noble character.
1320 Real kings are not husbands or fathers, Sire.

1. After the defeat of Zama, Carthage was forced to accept extremely harsh peace conditions (201 B.C.). Antiochus of Syria, who gave Hannibal asylum thereafter and made war on the Romans, was also defeated at Magnesia, and paid a heavy price for the support granted to the Carthaginian leader.

Consider but the throne; forget all else.
Reign. Rome will fear you more than you fear Rome.
Despite this power, so grandiose, so vast,
You can already note her fear of me
And how Rome hopes to profit by my fall,   1325
Since Rome foresees how firmly I shall reign.

PRUSIAS

I'll reign, then, ingrate, since you bid me to.
Choose my four crowns or choose Laodice.
Your king decides 'twixt Attalus and you.
Obey me, not as father, but as king.   1330

NICOMEDES

If you were king, too, of Laodice,
And had some right to offer her to me,
I would beg leisure to reflect on it.
To please you, though, and not to anger her,
I, without vain rejoinders, shall obey   1335
What you intend and not what you have said,
Transferring to this cherished brother all
My rights; Laodice must choose herself.
This is my choice.

PRUSIAS
                   What pettiness of soul,
What madness blinds you for a woman so?   1340
Why! you prefer her to those glorious spoils
Added by you to your ancestral realms!
After such vileness are you fit to live?

NICOMEDES

I find your own example splendid, Sire,
For you prefer a woman to the son,   1345
Thanks to whose arm these states were joined to yours.

PRUSIAS

Do I renounce a diadem for her?

NICOMEDES

Do I myself renounce them for my love?
What do I yield my brother with your realms?
1350 Can I lay claim to them before you die?
Forgive these words. The point is delicate,
But kings like any other men expire;
Your peoples then would need a king and have
To choose between prince Attalus and me.
1355 We are not so alike that piercing eyes
Are needed to perceive the difference.
And such is primogeniture, it can
Recall an exile to ascend the throne.
And, if their sentiments accord with yours,
1360 I have brought others under your control;
And, were the Romans to resent my deed,
I for myself would do what I have done
For you.

PRUSIAS

I shall take care you don't.

NICOMEDES

           Yes, if their tricks
Contrive to make you sacrifice your son;
1365 If not, your realms, ceded to Attalus,
Will be his only to the day you die.
This is no secret. I shall tell him so;
In order that he can prepare himself.
But here he is. He's heard.

PRUSIAS

           Go ingrate, go.
1370 I'll see he's king without my shedding blood.
Tomorrow . . .

Scene Four

PRUSIAS, NICOMEDES, ATTALUS, FLAMINIUS,
ARASPES, GUARDS

FLAMINIUS
If you're wroth on my account,
My lord, I have received but slight offence.
The Senate might, it's true, be angry. Still
I have some friends in it who'll win it round.

PRUSIAS
I'll see it's satisfied. And Attalus   1375
Tomorrow will receive a crown from me.
I'll make him king of Pontus, my sole heir;
And, as to this unruly spirit, Rome
Will judge of the offence between you both.
He'll replace Attalus as hostage, and,   1380
For more dispatch, I shall deliver him
As soon as he has seen his brother crowned.

NICOMEDES
Send me to Rome?

PRUSIAS
There you'll get your deserts.
Go, ask Rome for your dear Laodice.

NICOMEDES
I'll go, I'll go, Sire, since you wish it so.   1385
There I'll be more a king than you are here.

FLAMINIUS
Rome knows your exploits, and bows down to them.

NICOMEDES
Softly, Flaminius. I am not there yet.
The road, all things considered, is not safe,
And those escorting me might lose their way.   1390

PRUSIAS

Araspes, lead him off. Double his guard.

[*To* ATTALUS]

Give thanks to Rome, and always bear in mind
That, as its power is the source of yours,
By losing its support you forfeit all.

[*To* FLAMINIUS]

1395 You, Sir, excuse me if in my distress
Over the sore afflictions of the queen,
I shall console her, leaving you with him.

[*To* ATTALUS]

Once again, thank your backers, Attalus.

Scene Five

FLAMINIUS, ATTALUS

ATTALUS

What shall I say, after so many boons
1400 Which are too great even for the greatest hearts?
There are no bounds to your affection which
Exceeds your promises and my desire.
However, I admit my father's throne
Is not the zenith of my happiness.
1405 What moves my heart and charms my senses is
The chance to conquer fair Laodice.
The rank of king which equals me with her . . .

FLAMINIUS

Won't make her heart less hostile to your love.

ATTALUS

Sir, opportunities can change a heart.
1410 Besides, it was her dying father's wish;

And even Armenia's queen herself admits
She's pledged to wed Bithynia's royal heir.

FLAMINIUS

That does not bind her, and, queen as she is,
She will obey as far as pleases her.
Think you she'll love in you a crown you gain   1415
From a great-hearted prince she dearly loves?
You who deprive her of protection, Prince,
You of his downfall sole artificer?

ATTALUS

Once he is gone from her, what will she do?
Who'll back her cause against the court and Rome?   1420
For I still count upon your help.

FLAMINIUS

                    Sometimes
Events can take an unexpected course;
Not to mislead you, I can give no pledge.

ATTALUS

That would be my undoing. I would be
An object of contempt and not a king   1425
If the crown robbed me of your friendship. But
My fear's unfounded. Rome's more constant. Have
You no instructions?

FLAMINIUS

                    Yes, for Attalus,
A prince reared from the cradle in Rome's midst;
But, for the king of Pontus, I have none.   1430

ATTALUS

What! You need new instructions. Can it be
That Rome rejects its handwork and that
My dawning glory causes jealousy?

FLAMINIUS

Prince, what temerity! What words are these?

ATTALUS

1435 You yourself tell me how I must explain
Your great republic's inconsistency.

FLAMINIUS

I shall explain it and shall cure you of
An error into which you seem to fall.
Rome backed you with Laodice, and would
1440 Even wrongfully have given you her throne.
Friendship for you made this imperative,
But Rome has made you king by other means,
And Rome could not without dishonour now
On your behalf indulge in such constraint.
1445 Then leave this queen completely free to wed.
Bear your addresses to some other heart.
Rome will itself see to your marriage.

ATTALUS

                                        But
What if Laodice returns my love?

FLAMINIUS

This might again make it appear that Rome
1450 Was exercising subterfuge or force.
This match would cast a shadow on its name.
If you believe me, think no more of it,
Or, if you like not my advice, at least
Think not of it without the Senate's Yes.

ATTALUS

1455 When coolness follows so much ardour, Rome
Merely hates Nicomedes, loves me not,
And when Rome feigned to smile on my desires,
It merely sought his fall, not my ascent.

FLAMINIUS

Not to reply to you in wounding terms
1460 On this impressive first ingratitude,
Follow your penchant and insult your friends.

ou are a king. All is permitted you;
ut since today should have brought home to you
hat Rome has made you what you are to be,
hat, losing Rome's support, you're nothing, then   1465
hat the king told you so, remember well.

Scene Six

ATTALUS

Attalus, was it thus your forebears reigned?
A king, and have so many overlords?
Ah! at this price the crown already palls.
f we need masters, one is ample. He   1470
s far too noble, too magnanimous,
Ever to be a sacrifice to Rome.
Let's show them boldly we have eyes to see,
And from so harsh a yoke set free our land.
Since in all things their interest guides them, we   1475
Must drop their hollow friendship and adopt
Their policy. Be jealous of their power
And, copying them, act for ourselves alone.

ACT FIVE
Scene One

ARSINOE, ATTALUS

ARSINOE

This rising I foresaw. There's naught to fear.
1480 It blazes up and in a moment dies,
And, if the darkness lets this uproar swell,
Day will disperse the phantasies of night.
I'm less upset by the mob's mutiny
Than by your heart's persistence in its love.
1485 Inflamed by this infatuation, you
Do not return her scorn for you by scorn.
Take your revenge and leave the heartless girl,
Now destiny has placed you over her.
You should have loved her throne and not her eyes.
1490 You'll reign without her. Why pursue her then?
Offer your heart to kinder beauties. Since
You now are king, Asia has other queens
Who, far from forcing you to pine, would soon
Spare you the need for offering yourself.

ATTALUS

1495 But . . .

ARSINOE

Well, all right. Let us suppose she yields.
Do you foresee the future ills I fear?
When she has crowned you as Armenia's king,
She will involve you in her hate for me.
But will that be the end of her revenge?
1500 Can you with tranquil mind sleep in her bed?
And will she scruple to avoid the sword
Or poison to avenge her lover's loss?
How far will not an outraged woman stoop?

ATTALUS

These are but pretexts to conceal the truth!
Rome which dislikes to see a king with power,   1505
Fears Nicomedes and would fear me too.
I must no longer seek to wed a queen,
Or else I would displease Rome's sovereign might;
And, since thereby I would betray myself,
For Rome to stomach me, I must obey.   1510
I know how by profound diplomacy,
She'll soon achieve dominion of the world.
As soon as any state expands its realm,
Its fall alone can cure Rome's umbrage, for,
To make a conquest gives offence. Even more   1515
To place too many arms beneath one head;
And Romans say they're right when they make war
To crush such treason which contests their sway.
They who're the first of men to dominate
Would keep us as we are beneath their heel,   1520
And over kings wish such ascendancy
That they alone are independent. For
I know them, and I've seen their jealousy
Demolish Carthage, smash Antiochus.
To shun such ruin, I'll abase myself   1525
And yield to reasons which I cannot change.
All the more so since Nicomedes is
Delivered up to them as prisoner.
This valiant foe ensures my troth. He is
A lion poised ready to pounce on me.   1530

ARSINOE

That's what I wished to say in confidence;
But I'm delighted at your shrewdness. Times
May change. Be careful then to reassure
These jealous Romans whose support you need.

Scene Two

FLAMINIUS, ARSINOE, ATTALUS

ARSINOE

1535 My lord, this is a glorious victory
To make a man in love[1] believe me. I
Have brought him back to follow duty's path,
And reason has resumed its sway o'er him.

FLAMINIUS

Try, Lady, now whether you'll find a way
1540 To make the rioters see reason too.
The evil grows; it's time for you to act,
Or, if you wish to, you will wish too late.
Do not imagine you will foil their rage
By giving them their head remissively.
1545 Rome is familiar with these mutinies,
But never chose the path which you propose.
When called upon to calm the populace,
The Senate spared no compromise, no threat,
And thus it lured its host of mutineers
1550 Back from the Quirinal and Aventine
Whence they'd have made a horrible descent
Had Rome for long written their fury off
And merely left them to disintegrate,
As you on this occasion seem to do.

ARSINOE

1555 With such a great example, we should not
Deliberate. Do what the Senate did;
And the king . . . Here he is.

1. Attalus.

Scene Three

PRUSIAS, ARSINOE, FLAMINIUS, ATTALUS

PRUSIAS
There is no doubt
As to the cause of all this rioting.
The rebel leaders are Laodice's
Followers.   1560

FLAMINIUS
I suspected it was she.

ATTALUS
Thus are your love and care for her repaid!

FLAMINIUS
Act now; and, if you'll be advised by me ...

Scene Four

PRUSIAS, ARSINOE, FLAMINIUS, ATTALUS,
CLEONE

CLEONE
Everything's lost, failing swift countermoves.
The mob clamours for Nicomedes, and
Begins to take the law into its hands.   1565
It's lynched Zeno and Metrobates.

ARSINOE
Well,
It is no longer therefore to be feared.
Its fury will be sated by their blood.
It will exult in these illustrious deeds,
And feel that Nicomedes is avenged.   1570

FLAMINIUS

Were this a leaderless, unplanned revolt,
I would, as you do, fear its outcome less.
The people by their death might be appeased.
But a coherent plan does not collapse.
1575 It will pursue its aim till victory;
Once it has tasted blood, it knows no bounds.
That lures it on, excites it, dulls the sense
Of horror, leaves it dead to pity and
Fear.

Scene Five

PRUSIAS, FLAMINIUS, ARSINOE, ATTALUS,
CLEONE, ARASPES

ARASPES

From all sides, the people throng this way.
1580 Each minute sees your guards disperse, and it
Is bruited in this very palace that
The prince will not for long be in my hands.
I cannot answer for him . . .

PRUSIAS

Let us go.
Let's give them back this idol of all hearts.
1585 Let us obey this base, disloyal mob,
Which, tired of me, wishes to make him king,
And, from a balcony, to calm the storm,
On his new subjects hurl his severed head.

ATTALUS

Ah! Sir.

PRUSIAS

Thus, he will be restored to them.
1590 If thus they ask, thus they shall have him.

ATTALUS

                              Ah!
That would mar all by handing to their rage
All that lies closest to your dignity.
And, I make bold to add, your majesty
Will be hard put to find a refuge.

PRUSIAS

                    So,
We must then be resolved to do its will –   1595
Surrender Nicomedes with my crown.
I have no doubt that, carrying the day,
He will demand either my crown or death.

FLAMINIUS

Even if there is some justice in this plan,
Is it for you to order that he die?   1600
What pow'r over his life do you retain?
He is Rome's hostage, and no more your son.
His father may forget it. I do not.
Disposing of his life, you challenge Rome;
I'm answerable to the Senate and can not   1605
Consent. My galley's ready in the port.
The palace has a secret door to it.
If you still wish his death, let me withdraw.
Let my departure manifest to all
That Rome has counsels juster and more mild.   1610
Do not expose me to the shameful sight –
Its hostage killed before its envoy's eyes.

ARSINOE

Will you allow me, Sire, to intervene?

PRUSIAS

Ah! nothing you could say would be amiss.

ARSINOE

Heaven has inspired me with a plan I hope   1615
Will leave Rome satisfied and you appeased.

If he[1] is ready now, he can at once
Carry away his hostage easily.
This secret door favours our enterprise.
1620 But, to make matters simpler, Sire, appear
Before this mob with soft and soothing words.
At least engage it in an argument,
Playing for time while, tranquil, undisturbed,
The galley bears away the people's hope.
1625 If it should storm the palace, he'll be gone;
You'll feign to be, like it, puzzled, surprised;
You'll lay the blame on Rome, vow vengeance on
All who are shown to be in league with it;
You'll send out ships in hot pursuit at dawn,
1630 And dangle hopes to them he'll soon be back,
While obstacles you will yourself create
Will on all sides help on the stratagem.
However wildly it may rage today,
It will not stir while it still fears for him,
1635 As long as it presumes its efforts vain.
It seems too easy here to set him free,
And, if he is, we both of us must flee.
For once he's at their head, they'll make him king.
You too believe so.

PRUSIAS
Ah! I must confess

[*To* FLAMINIUS]
1640 Heaven has inspired you with this counsel. Sir,
Could anything more clever be devised?

FLAMINIUS
It guards your life, honour and liberty;
Besides, Laodice's your hostage. But,
Losing our time means losing all our trumps.

PRUSIAS
1645 Then we must waste no more. Action forthwith.

1. Flaminius.

ARSINOE

Take with you but Araspes and three men;
A larger group would harbour traitors. I
Will go and apprehend Laodice.

[*To* ATTALUS]
Where are you bound for, Attalus?

ATTALUS
                        I'm off
To keep this bold rebellious mob in play,   1650
And cap your stratagem by one of mine.

ARSINOE

Remember that your fate and mine are one.
If I'm in danger, it's because of *you*.

ATTALUS

I'll die in the attempt or rescue you.

ARSINOE

Be off. But hither comes Armenia's queen.   1655

Scene Six

ARSINOE, LAODICE, CLEONE

ARSINOE

The cause of all our ills, must she remain
Unpunished?

LAODICE
        No. Although she thinks she will,
Even now I guarantee she'll pay for them.

ARSINOE

You know her crime. Prescribe the penalty.

LAODICE

1660 A slight rebuff suffices for a queen,
Who, as things are, has seen her plans misfire.

ARSINOE

To make her pay for her temerity,
The diadem should from her brow be torn.

LAODICE

That is no policy for noble hearts.
1665 They soon forget when they have won the day.
They merely wish their foes discomfited.

ARSINOE

Who reasons thus seeks only slight amends.

LAODICE

I was not born to joy in violence.

ARSINOE

To cause revolt 'mongst subjects of their king,
1670 To arm them all with fire and sword, incite
Their insolence to storm the palace gates,
For you is but the mildest violence.

LAODICE

We're talking past each other. Lady. What
I say of you, you have applied to me.
1675 I have no problem as regards myself.
I've come to take you into custody,
So that your royal rank is not exposed
To a wild disrespectful throng's caprice.
Send for the king, recall your Attalus,
1680 And let me guard their kingly dignity.
This raging mob may not acknowledge them.

ARSINOE

Was ever haughtiness the like of yours?
You who alone have roused disorder here,

Who in my palace are my captive, you
Who'll answer with your life for all   1685
The slight done to my rank by such a crime,
You still talk with the same proud hardihood
As if I had to beg your mercy!

LAODICE
                    You
Persist in talking to me in this tone,
And you refuse to see I'm in command,   1690
That, when I please, you'll be my victim. And
Blame me not for this grandiose revolt.
Your people's guilty, and in all of them
All these seditious cries are criminal.
But as for me who am a queen and who   1695
Have roused these rebels here to conquer you,
It's always been allowed by right of war
To fire revolt among one's enemies.
Who carries off my husband is my foe.

ARSINOE
I am your foe then, and whate'er transpires,   1700
If once this mob invades the palace, then
Your life is forfeit. That I promise you.

LAODICE
You'll never keep your word, or on my tomb
All your kings' blood will form a hecatomb.
But have you still amongst your retinue   1705
Another Metrobates? Fear you not
All your retainers have already been
Won over by my devious practices?
Are they so ready to destroy themselves,
So tired of life as to obey your call?   1710
I do not covet your Bithynia's crown,
Only free access to Armenia, and,
If at one stroke you wish to end your woes,
Give me back him whom you withhold from me.

ARSINOE

1715 You'll find him trav'lling on the road to Rome,
Whither Flaminius takes him. Ask him back,
But haste, I beg you. Drive your oarsmen hard;
By now his galley sails the open seas.

LAODICE

Ah! If I thought so . . .

ARSINOE
Lady, doubt it not.

LAODICE

1720 Then flee the furies which possess my soul.
After the blow of this indignity,
Respect, nobility of heart, are fled.
No, rather stay to be my hostage till
I free him from your shackles with my hand.
1725 I'll even go to Rome to break his bonds
With all your subjects and with all my own,
Hannibal rightly termed it mad to hope
To beat Rome elsewhere than in Italy.
Rome will behold me deep in its domains
1730 Sustain my fury with a million arms,
And, drowning tryanny in my despair . . .

ARSINOE

So after all you want Bithynia's crown.
And, with this fury which sweeps over you,
Could the king let you reign on his behalf?

LAODICE

1735 I'll reign there, Lady, without wronging him,
Since the king's but a shadow of a king.
What matters it to him who's in command
And who reigns, Rome or I, for him. But look
A second hostage falls into our hands.

Scene Seven

ARSINOE, LAODICE, ATTALUS, CLEONE

ARSINOE [*to* ATTALUS]
Have you discovered how they got away?   1740

ATTALUS
Ah! lady.

ARSINOE
   Speak, Sir.

ATTALUS
       All the gods enraged
Have plunged us into ills unspeakable.
The prince . . . He has escaped.

LAODICE
          Have no more fear.
I am again my old great-hearted self.

ARSINOE [*to* ATTALUS]
Do not take pleasure in alarming me.   1745

ATTALUS
Do not delude yourself to that extent.
Araspes with his feeble escort had
Already to the false door taken him.
Rome's envoy had already issued, too,
When in Araspes' heart a dagger plunged   1750
Threw him at Nicomedes' feet. His men,
Fearing to meet his fate, at once took flight.

ARSINOE
Who could have stabbed him at the secret door?

ATTALUS
Some dozen soldiers, who were guarding him
And the prince . . .   1755

311

ARSINOE
Ah! what traitors everywhere!
And how few subjects faithful to their lords!
Who did you learn this great disaster from?

ATTALUS
Araspes' comrades and Araspes too.
But hear still more what drives me to despair.
1760 I ran to make a stand beside the king.
It was too late. Astounded by events,
He had, abandoning himself to fear,
Taken a skiff to join Flaminius who
Was, I suspect, equally panic-struck.

Scene Eight

PRUSIAS, FLAMINIUS, ARSINOE, LAODICE, ATTALUS,
CLEONE

PRUSIAS
1765 No. We've come back in order to defend
Our honour or to die before your eyes.

ARSINOE [*to* PRUSIAS]
Let's die. Let's die, and put our lives beyond
The power unbridled of our enemies.
Let's not await their orders, jealous of
1770 The honour they would have to seal our fate.

LAODICE
Your deep despair wrongs such a valiant man
More than you did by sending him to Rome.
You ought to know him better. We're betrothed.
You should assume him worthy of my hand.
1775 I'd disavow him if it were not so,
If he did not live up to my esteem,
And did not show nobility of soul.
But here he is. Is he not as I've said?

Scene Nine

PRUSIAS, NICOMEDES, ARSINOE, LAODICE,
FLAMINIUS, ATTALUS, CLEONE

NICOMEDES

All's calm, my lord. I'd but to show myself
To quell immediately the mob's revolt.   1780

PRUSIAS

What! you defy me in my palaces,
You rebel.

NICOMEDES
                        That's a name I'll never bear.
I do not come before you to display
My joy at having shattered hated bonds.
I come, a loyal subject, to restore   1785
The peace which other interests had disturbed.
Not that I would impute some crime to Rome.
It follows the great art of policy;
Its envoy merely does what duty bids,
Seeking to wreak division in our power.   1790
But do not let Rome force us to that pass.
For Rome to fear you, give me back your love.
Forgive the people the impetuousness
Which, pitying my misfortunes, it displayed.
Forgive a crime it thought essential and   1795
Which will have but beneficent effects.

[*To* ARSINOE]
Pardon it, too, and suffer me to be
Mindful of your indulgence to the grave.
I know the cause of your hostility.
You would prefer to see my brother reign –   1800
Your son. And I will second your design,
If you can let him by my hand be king.

313

Yes, Asia offers me new conquests still,
And I shall gladly crown him with my hands.
1805 Yours to command where these new realms shall be,
And you shall see me offer him the crown.

ARSINOE

Must you so far carry your victory?
Holding my life and honour in your hands,
You seek new triumphs even in my heart.
1810 Against such greatness I have no defence.
My heart's indeed impatient to submit.
Add but this conquest to three sceptres, and
I'll feel I've won in you a second son.

PRUSIAS

1815 I too surrender, then, and can accept
My glorious son as my most glorious prize.
But, of the blessings which at last descend,
Tell us to whom we owe your safe return.

NICOMEDES

The hero of this exploit hid his face,
1820 But asked me for a diamond as a pledge,
And vowed tomorrow he would give it back.

ATTALUS

Will you, my lord, receive it from my hand?

NICOMEDES

Ah! let me always by this worthy gage
In my blood brother see a real king's blood.
1825 You're not the scheming slave of Rome. You are
The liberator of our precious line.
Brother, you break my bonds, but others' too –
Those of the king, the queen, hers [1] and your own.
But why so secret when you saved the state?

1. Laodice's.

ATTALUS

To see your virtues shine the brighter, Sir;   1830
To see them act alone against our wrongs,
Unfettered by these feeble services;
And be revenged on you and on myself,
If I'd misjudged events and characters.
But now ...   1835

ARSINOE
                    Enough. That was the stratagem
You promised me for me against myself.

[*To* NICOMEDES]
And I, my lord, am all the more content
That my own kin undoes the harm I've done.

NICOMEDES [*to* FLAMINIUS]
Sir, to be frank, every aspiring soul
Should deem itself pleased to become your friend.   1840
But we will have no more of these harsh laws. ―
We want to be your friends, and not your slaves.
If not, we'd rather be your enemies.

FLAMINIUS [*to* NICOMEDES]
That's for the Senate to decide upon.   1845
Meanwhile, I dare to state, on its behalf,
That, failing friendship, you'll have its esteem
As great as such a noble heart deserves.
It will in you have an illustrious foe,
If it can't make of you a loyal friend.   1850

PRUSIAS
The rest of us meeting auspiciously,
Tomorrow let us offer sacrifice,
And ask the gods who rule us to accord
Rome's friendship as our crowning happiness.

END

More About Penguins
And Pelicans

For further information about books available from Penguins please write to Dept EP, Penguin Books Ltd, Harmondsworth, Middlesex UB7 0DA.

In the U.S.A.: For a complete list of books available from Penguins in the United States write to Dept CS, Penguin Books, 625 Madison Avenue, New York, New York 10022.

In Canada: For a complete list of books available from Penguins in Canada write to Penguin Books Canada Ltd, 2801 John Street, Markham, Ontario L3R 1B4.

In Australia: For a complete list of books available from Penguins in Australia write to the Marketing Department, Penguin Books Australia Ltd, P.O. Box 257, Ringwood, Victoria 3134.

CORNEILLE

The Cid/Cinna/The Theatrical Illusion
Translated by John Cairncross

Le Cid was Corneille's first masterpiece and also the first major
work of the classical theatre. It radiates a youthful exuberance,
a sureness of touch and an all-pervading sensuality which made
it an overwhelming success. And Corneille's *Cinna*, his best-
known political drama, is characterized by a similar pulsating
tension.

John Cairncross's new, blank-verse translation ably conveys
the power and nobility of these two plays as well as the whim-
sicality and freshness of *The Theatrical Illusion* – a bizarre
comedy where the Spanish influence first becomes dominant
in his work.

RACINE

Iphigenia/Phaedra/Athaliah
Translated by John Cairncross

Phaedra, which Voltaire called 'the masterpiece of the human
mind', is the greatest of the plays of Jean Racine (1639–99).
In this sombre tragedy of the guilty passion of Theseus's
queen for her stepson, Hippolytus, Racine again chose a pagan
plot to express that amoral ruthlessness which shocked French
conservatives. (*Iphigenia* had similarly been based on Agamem-
non's terrible conflict over his daughter's sacrifice.) But he
was already swinging back to religion, and *Athaliah*, his final
play, was built on an Old Testament story.

Also published:
Andromache/Britannicus/Berenice

MOLIÈRE

The Misanthrope and Other Plays
Translated by John Wood

Molière himself said of *The Misanthrope* 'I cannot improve on it and assuredly never shall' – a verdict which time has confirmed. It is his acknowledged masterpiece, one of the supreme achievements of the European theatre, a play which renews its fascination for each generation. With it in this volume are two works of almost equal reputation – *Tartuffe*, a play with a stirring history which has long enjoyed success in the box office, and *The Imaginary Invalid*, the great comedy of doctors and patients in which Molière turned his own hypochondria and sufferings to comic account. For good measure there are also included *A Doctor in Spite of Himself*, one of the best known of the farces, and a charming comedy-ballet *The Sicilian*.

Also published:
The Miser/The Would-Be Gentleman/That Scoundrel
Scapin/Love's the Best Doctor/Don Juan

BEAUMARCHAIS

The Barber of Seville and The Marriage of Figaro
Translated by John Wood

Beaumarchais (1732–99) was a man of immense wit and feeling and it is our loss that his two great plays are only known to us through Rossini and Mozart. It was Beaumarchais who brought fun back into the theatre and broke the convention of formality which had grown up since Molière. His dialogue was colloquial and his people real in eighteenth-century Paris. The humour, liveliness, and vigour depend on an interplay of character which was quite new to his audiences.